Tai Chi and Chai Tea

Also by this Author

Mystery/Suspense:

Auntie Clem's Bakery
Gluten-Free Murder
Dairy-Free Death
Allergen-Free Assignation
Witch-Free Halloween (Halloween Short)
Dog-Free Dinner (Christmas Short)
Stirring Up Murder
Brewing Death
Coup de Glace
Sour Cherry Turnover
Apple-achian Treasure
Vegan Baked Alaska
Muffins Masks Murder
Tai Chi and Chai Tea
Santa Shortbread

Reg Rawlins, Psychic Detective
What the Cat Knew
A Psychic with Catitude
A Catastrophic Theft
Night of Nine Tails
Telepathy of Gardens
Delusions of the Past
Fairy Blade Unmade (Coming soon)
Web of Nightmares (Coming soon)
A Whisker's Breadth (Coming soon)

And more at pdworkman.com

Tai Chi and Chai Tea

Auntie Clem's Bakery #11

P.D. Workman

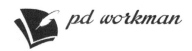

pd workman

ISBN: 9781989415634

For those bending over backward for others.

Chapter One

THIS TIME, IT WAS Terry who woke Erin up, rather than the other way around. He was gasping hard like he was running or maybe even having a heart attack. She reached for him beside her and found his body rigid as he fought for breath.

"Terry. Terry!" She shook him, trying to rouse him, her mind jumping to all kinds of possibilities. Maybe he was having a heart attack. Maybe he had suffered some sort of damage in Theresa's attack on him that the doctors hadn't discovered. He had thrown a clot, and it had gone into his lungs or heart. Or something had happened in his brain and it was a seizure.

He'd been hit on the head as well as choked out, and either one could have caused neurological damage. Maybe damage that the doctors hadn't seen or predicted. They had warned that his road to recovery might not be smooth.

"Terry!"

He gasped one last time and sat bolt upright in bed, shoving her away. Erin was hurt even though she knew that he wasn't conscious of what he had done. He was always gentle with her, and being pushed away like that sent her sense of danger into hyperdrive. She was sure, as ridiculous as it was, that she was going to be attacked.

Terry looked around. There was just enough light in the room to see his shape, not the expression on his face.

"Erin? Where are you? Are you okay?"

Erin breathed deeply, trying to slow her racing heart.

"It's okay," she soothed. "You just had a dream. Lie down, and come here."

It took a minute before he reacted, still looking around him as if there might be some danger lurking. He drew in a long breath and let it out slowly.

"It was just a dream?"

"Yes. Come on." She wrapped her arms around him and molded her body against his. She could still feel his rapidly-beating heart as well as her own. "Do you want to talk about it?"

She needed to get up early, so both of them were usually careful to avoid conversation late at night, but she wanted him to know that if he needed a listening ear, she was right there. If it would help him to calm down, then it would help both of them get back to sleep sooner.

"No." He let out a few more quick puffs of breath. "I don't even remember what it was. Not really. I wasn't dreaming something was happening. Just... a feeling."

"Mmm-hm." She cuddled close against him. She'd had plenty of night terrors herself. There wasn't always any narrative to go with the feeling, just that crushing anxiety, that sense of danger. "Do you need anything? A drink? A back rub?"

"No. I'll just go back to sleep."

She knew that he worried about her getting enough to sleep with her early-morning baker's hours. His first instinct would be to protect her rather than to deal with his own needs. She rubbed his shoulders in spite of his answer.

"Are you sure? I can get you something. Milk or tea...?"

"No," he assured her again. "It was just a dream. I'll be able to go back to sleep."

"Okay." She was still again, cuddled up against him, eyes closed, soaking in the warmth of his body and his musky smell. Despite being woken out of a sound sleep, she felt safe and comfortable with him there, the two of them intertwined. It helped to soothe her own nighttime fears.

"Should I get up and check the burglar alarm?" Terry asked, rousing Erin. "Are you sure that it's armed?"

Usually, he didn't worry about the burglar alarm when he stayed over with her. He was more concerned if she was by herself. If he, an experienced police officer, was there, he didn't think anyone would be stupid enough to break in.

But his squad car wasn't parked in front of the house anymore. Since he had been taken off of active duty, it had been parked in the police department's parking lot. And since Stayner had been contracted to cover Terry's duties, he was the one who had been driving it. He wasn't a full-time hire, so he didn't get to drive it home at the end of his shift as Terry had, but Erin knew that Terry still didn't like the idea of someone else driving 'his' car when he wasn't there.

"I set the alarm," she assured him. "You don't need to check. Besides, if there were a burglar, Orange Blossom would be letting us know. And probably K9 too."

Hearing his name, Orange Blossom gave a soft meow and jumped up on the bed next to Erin. He sniffed her ear, investigating why she wanted him. Erin giggled. K9 was in his crate, but she was sure he would be making noise if he had heard or sensed an intruder in the house. And Orange Blossom, her little attack cat, was very territorial and had raised the alarm in the past when someone had managed to bypass her burglar alarm.

"Blossom, lay down," Erin ordered. She turned away from Terry to deal with him. She scratched his ears and kissed him on top of the head, then pushed him down to lie beside her. It took a few times before he was content to curl up against her, purring loudly in contentment.

"Do you think you could get him to turn the engine down a bit?" Terry asked dryly, putting his arms around Erin from behind her and holding her close again, so that she was sandwiched between the two of them, cozy and warm.

"It doesn't work. The more you ask him to be quiet, the louder he gets."

Terry knew how loud Orange Blossom could be, so he accepted this. They both just lay there, listening to his rumbling purr. It was a comforting sound, and Erin soon found herself drifting off again.

Chapter Two

ORNING CAME TOO SOON. It seemed like she had only been asleep for another five minutes when her alarm sounded. Erin reached over to shut it off. She pushed Orange Blossom out of her way and slid her feet out of the bed. She knew better than to hit snooze. If she fell back asleep for even just five more minutes, she would be even more groggy, and she wouldn't have the time she needed to get her engine running before work. She'd be draggy and grumpy all morning.

She would never have considered herself a morning person before starting the bakery. But once she managed to wake herself up, she found the extremely early hours of the morning exhilarating. She loved getting the gluten-free baking into the ovens every morning, working side-by-side with Vic or one of her other employees. The smell of the baking bread and muffins and the quiet of the early morning made her feel calm and peaceful at the beginning of the day, something that she desperately needed with everything that had happened since she had first arrived in Bald Eagle Falls to open Auntie Clem's Bakery.

She used the commode, splashed cold water on her face, and started the kettle heating in the kitchen. Looking across the yard to Vic's loft apartment over the garage, she could see it was still dark. Vic hadn't managed to pry herself out of bed yet. But she would. Despite her youth, Vic was very responsible, and Erin had never had to harass her to get her out of bed in the morning. She loved having Vic just across the back yard from her and hoped that Vic wouldn't move away any time in the near future. The two of them worked well together and were good friends, and it was convenient living so close together. They each had their separate spaces, but even when off work, could often be found in the kitchen together.

It wasn't long before she saw the light go on across the yard. Erin was at the kitchen table drawing up her list of tasks for the day when Vic made her way in the back door, yawning and pulling her long, blond hair into a ponytail behind her head.

"Morning, sunshine," she greeted around the yawn.

Erin laughed. "Good morning. You slept a little late."

"No," Vic yawned again, covering her mouth with the back of her hand. "I think you're mistaken. This is what the rest of the world calls early."

"The rest of the world doesn't run a bakery."

"Good thing, or we'd have too much competition."

Vic went to the kettle and checked the temperature before pouring herself a cup of tea. She sat down to join Erin. Orange Blossom meowed for attention, rubbing against Vic's legs. She bent down to scratch his ears. Marshmallow, seeing that the cat was getting attention, hopped over to Vic to get his long ears scratched too. Vic smiled at the brown and white rabbit and gave him some love as well.

K9 was stretched out on the floor beside Erin and looked up at Vic but didn't bark or go over to her. Orange Blossom didn't like the big shepherd. While K9 would have been perfectly happy to make friends with the ginger cat, Blossom had steadfastly refused to have anything to do with the dog. Unless he was eating a treat. Then the cat was right there to steal whatever crumbs he could snatch or lick off of K9's face.

"Do you know what I found when I was looking for the Christmas ornaments yesterday?" Erin asked, looking back down at her task list.

"Didn't you know you're not allowed to get out Christmas things until Thanksgiving is past?" Vic teased.

Erin ignored her. She hadn't gotten the ornaments out; she had just been inventorying to see what she would need to add or replace. There was nothing wrong with being prepared.

"I found a huge box of chai spices."

"From Clementine's tea shop?"

Erin nodded. Her aunt Clementine was the one who had left her both the house and the retail space that had been her tea shop, having no other kin after the death of Erin's mother years before. The bakery would never have been anything more than a distant dream if Erin hadn't inherited the little shop on Main Street. She'd barely been able to keep her head above water up until then, working whatever jobs she could find and never able to stick with something for very long. It was hard to believe how fast the months had gone and everything that had happened since she had moved to Bald Eagle Falls. Bald Eagle Falls, Tennessee was now home, even though she had spent most of her growing-up years in Maine.

"So I guess we're going to be drinking chai and nothing else for a while?" Vic suggested.

"I think I'd get tired of it before long," Erin said. She liked variety, and for the brief time that she had known Clementine and "helped" with the tea shop when she was a young child, she had developed a wide-ranging taste for teas. "And I don't think we'd be able to sell that much at the ladies' tea each week. People like their traditional teas. I suspect that's why Clementine ended up with a big box of spices in the attic."

"Strange foreign tea," Vic agreed, sipping her English Breakfast. "What will people think of next?"

"So I was thinking… Thanksgiving is a great time for nice warm, spicy baking. Pumpkin pie, gingerbread, all of those other great spice blends…"

"And how about using chai spices in something?" Vic suggested.

Erin nodded eagerly. "We have them, we might as well use them for something. We can offer chai tea at the ladies Sunday tea as well, but I don't think we'll be able to move more than a cup or two a week."

Vic pursed her lips. "But what can you put it in? People don't really bake with it, do they?"

"Actually, I was looking at some recipes online." Erin looked down at her lists, warming to the topic. "There are a ton of different recipes that you can use chai spices in. Cookies, muffins, apple pie, oatmeal raisin bars… really, anything that you might put cinnamon or pumpkin pie spice in. Just a little twist on some old favorites."

Vic raised her brows. "Well, that might work. Just don't expect everyone to be enamored with the idea. You might not have noticed, but we have a few rednecks around here who are a mite suspicious of anything… different."

Erin laughed. Her gluten-free baking and atheism and Vic's transgender identity had already raised more than a few eyebrows and attracted comments, lectures, and even threats. "Just a mite," she agreed.

Chapter Three

AT THE TINKLING OF bells, Erin looked at the front door to see who had just entered the bakery. The woman's slim, well-tailored figure and neat ash-blonde hair shot with gray were instantly recognizable. "Morning, Mary Lou."

Mary Lou's smile seemed brighter than it had been lately. She nodded to Erin and Vic in turn. "Good morning Erin, Vic." She took a long sniff of the air. "It always smells so good in here. I'm not sure I would have enough willpower to work here and not eat the inventory."

Erin knew very well that Mary Lou had iron willpower, so she didn't believe it for a moment. But she smiled at the compliment. "Thank you! How are you today?" She tried to guess at what might have put a genuine smile back on Mary Lou's face. "How is Roger?"

The smile dimmed. "Oh, he's about the same. They're changing his medications around again, hoping that he'll be more stable on a different cocktail." She shrugged. "I'm not sure how they can expect him to stabilize when they keep changing things around. I think he would be better if he was at home in familiar surroundings... but I know that's not an option. They're doing the best they can to help him, but I don't know if anything they do will make a difference."

"Oh, I'm sorry." Erin felt terrible for bringing up Mary Lou's husband. "You looked like you'd had good news, so I hoped..."

"We must have hope, but no." Mary Lou's eyes crinkled a little at the corners. "But you're right; I did get some good news."

Erin brushed a trace of flour from her apron and smiled in relief. "Great! What is it?"

"Campbell is going to come home for Thanksgiving dinner."

"Oh, that *is* good news! It will be so nice for you to have him home. I'll bet you're looking forward to that."

"I am. I was not looking forward to it just being Joshua and me for Thanksgiving. It's a little tough to do with just the two of us, and I was waiting for him to say that he was going off with friends for Thanksgiving to avoid it. But now that Campbell is coming, Josh will stay for sure. And Campbell said he will be bringing a friend along as well. So even though it's only four of us...

it feels like an event. An actual celebration instead of just Josh and me trying to figure out what to do with ourselves to make it not so depressing."

"That's wonderful," Vic contributed. She leaned forward. "So what are you planning to do for treats?" she asked in a conspiratorial tone.

Mary Lou chuckled. "You have a very astute employee there, Erin. We are definitely going to need to do something special. I can't just pick up a pie from the grocery store, and Roger won't be there to make anything."

"We've been discussing some ideas for Thanksgiving," Erin offered. "One idea that I had was to make a lot of tiny one-bite treats. Fairy cakes, tiny tarts, mini cookies, maybe some mousse or ice cream in little shot glasses. That way, people can have a taste of everything, instead of having to choose one big piece of pie at the end of the meal. And they would work well for get-togethers where people weren't having a full meal too. It would work for casual dos like an end-of-day party in the teacher's lounge, or a fancy-dress party."

"What a good idea," Mary Lou approved. "Then there is no fight over who gets their favorite this year. Everybody can have their favorites. And if they're small… maybe I'll even allow myself an indulgence this year, while I have both of my boys home."

Mary Lou was always a strictly no-sweets person, so that was a real coup.

"Why don't you text or email me their seasonal favorites," Erin suggested, "then I can make sure that I have something that they like. We'll probably do the same at Christmas too."

Mary Lou nodded her agreement. She looked into the bakery display case. "Of course, we'll also want some white buns to go with dinner and to make turkey sandwiches for the next week."

"Of course," Erin agreed.

"Can you believe that a couple of years ago, I would never have considered getting gluten-free baking for my boys. If Auntie Clem's had been the only choice in town back then, I would have made the trip into the city for my baking."

A couple of other customers entered the bakery behind Mary Lou. She blushed a little and patted her hair. She wasn't usually so complimentary. But the last few months had been hard on her and she had discovered that many of the women she had thought were friends had not stood by her through her challenges.

"For this week, just a loaf of rustic rosemary… and a few of those pizza pretzels that Joshua likes so much."

"Coming right up," Vic agreed, and started on Mary Lou's order. Erin rapidly tapped the entries into the till. Mary Lou was soon on her way, and Erin turned to the next customers.

"Are you and Willie doing anything together tonight?" Erin asked as she drove home with Vic at the end of the work day.

16

"No, I don't think I'm going to see him. He's been kind of… busy with other things lately."

Erin frowned. She didn't like to think that Vic and Willie weren't getting along very well together. They had been through plenty of ups and downs, with their gender issues, age difference, life views, and each being from old Tennessee clans who were at odds with the other. Not just feuding, but organized crime syndicates that were constantly at war with each other.

Willie had been sensitive about the friends that Vic had recently made on their Alaskan cruise, and if he'd decided now that he wasn't going to be there for her…

"You don't need to look quite so protective," Vic laughed. "He's not out chasing after women." She chuckled. "Or at least, he's only chasing after one woman."

Erin frowned. "What?"

"Theresa Franklin. He thought he might have gotten a lead on her in the city. So he's doing a little investigating to see if he can find her."

"Oh!" Erin let out a pent-up breath she hadn't realized she was holding. Of course Willie wasn't out fooling around. He and Vic hadn't broken up. He was trying to find the crazy woman who had injured Terry Piper and Detective Jack Ward during the course of an investigation. Erin wasn't sure whether or not she wanted Willie to find Theresa, but she supposed it was probably better if he did. As long as he didn't turn his back on her. "Terry will be glad to hear about it if Willie can track her down. He's pretty sore about her getting away."

"Willie will let Terry know if he finds anything. Right now, it's just rumor."

Erin nodded. "I think Beaver is still looking for her too. No one was too happy about her escaping after everything she did."

"Crazy Theresa," Vic sighed. "I'm just glad I haven't heard anything more from her."

"Do you want to come over for supper with me and Terry? It won't be anything fancy, unless Terry has taken up cooking to fill his time."

"I'm not sure. Okay if I see what I feel like after I've had a chance to shower and relax?"

"Fine with me. You know where to find us."

Chapter Four

ERIN TOLD TERRY ABOUT the news that Campbell Cox would be home for Thanksgiving dinner, and went on a little more than was necessary about the treats that she and Vic were planning on cooking up for the holidays. She was excited about putting her plans into action and was so happy for Mary Lou, knowing she would be able to have both of her sons with her for Thanksgiving Day.

"That is good news," Terry agreed. "I hope everything works out for her."

Erin shrugged. "As long as Campbell gets there, she'll be happy."

"That may be what she thinks right now, but we're talking about human beings here with real frailties. Campbell might be planning to come home, or he might just be saying that to make her happy. Even if he plans to come home, a lot of things could happen to prevent him. And if he does make it… I'm sure you know that not all happy family dinners end up being… happy family dinners."

Erin could attest to the fact that many family celebrations she had attended had not ended up going well. Especially where teenagers were involved. Some of them had been pretty disastrous.

"Well… I guess you're right. But we're going to do everything we can to help make it a successful event. And Campbell and Josh are good boys. Everybody says so. I'm sure they'll try to make it nice for her."

Terry nodded. "Just don't get your hopes up that this is going to be a happy reunion. It may not be. Don't get too invested in someone else's perfect day."

"Yeah. But we're going to have a good day too." Erin smiled at Terry and met his eyes. This year, she knew for sure that Terry wouldn't end up working on Thanksgiving Day. They would have a feast, and there would be lots of baked goodies for their table. Whatever didn't sell out at Auntie Clem's.

Terry smiled back, but the expression didn't quite reach his eyes and the dimple didn't make an appearance in his cheek. She still loved his ruggedly handsome good looks, but she wanted to see real joy in his expression. He had been happy and fulfilled when he was on duty. Convalescing did not suit him.

"Vic might come over for dinner tonight."

Terry nodded. He went to the fridge to see what was on hand. Erin wondered whether he had eaten anything during the day. He had been worried about putting on weight while he was recovering, since he wasn't walking a beat all day like he normally did. But his face had lost some of its fullness and she didn't think it was just his nightmares and restlessness that were making him look so gaunt. He'd lost the few pounds that he had gained on their cruise, and a few more.

"Did you get out for a walk today? How are you feeling?"

"Took K9 out a couple of times." Terry sighed. "Didn't go very far, though."

"Because you weren't feeling well? Is it your head?"

He knew that she was worried about his head injury, even though the doctor said that he would likely make a full recovery. That was what they said, but she couldn't help thinking about Mary Lou's husband, Roger, and how he had been damaged by his *accident*. Terry had taken a double-whammy, with Theresa choking him out and hitting his head. He might have had damage from both oxygen deprivation and the insult to his brain. The doctors said that his tests were promising. But they had told Mary Lou that her husband didn't need any specialized testing or supports, and that had turned out not to be true.

"My head was okay," Terry reassured her. He knew how worried she was about it. "I just... didn't have the motivation to go very far. It's different just going for a stroll. It's not like walking a beat."

"But you could set a goal, make a plan to walk a certain route... I know it wouldn't really be the same, but you could still get out there..."

"It isn't just a matter of not having a plan or something to do. I don't want... well, the way that people look at me now..."

Erin felt irritation—not at Terry, but the townspeople of Bald Eagle Falls. As much as she liked living and working there and felt like it was home now, as much as she enjoyed visiting with the friends she had made in her time there, she hated how small-minded and prejudiced some people could be. They had proven that Terry didn't have anything to do with Bo Biggles's death, and yet people still regarded him with distrust, as a policeman who had committed brutality, when all he had done was to arrest a dangerous criminal. He hadn't been found guilty of any wrongdoing, and everyone knew now who the real culprit had been.

But people still acted like he had done something wrong.

And the sad part was, they had both known that was the way it was going to end up. They knew that even if they proved Terry's innocence, there would still be people who thought that he had just gotten away with murder.

"Most people are not going to treat you any differently than before."

"I don't know about most. There may be a few who don't see me any differently than they used to... but the sideways looks that I get, and the whispers, and people turning away from me and blocking their faces when they talk to each other... I'm not imagining that, Erin. That's the reality. I've been marked. And people are not going to forget."

"We could go somewhere else. We could move somewhere people wouldn't have preconceived notions about you."

"And leave Auntie Clem's? What would you do? You've made a life for yourself here. This is where your friends and employees are. This is where your home and your bakery are. What would you do if we went somewhere else?" He shook his head. "It's not even worth considering, Erin. You know that. This is where we live, and I won't be run out by people who are... stupid and backward."

"Okay." Erin breathed out. She didn't like arguments or confrontations, and the conversation was getting too emotional for her. She felt trapped. She needed to back off and get some air. But she didn't want to walk out of the room and make Terry feel like he had said or done something wrong. He was expressing his feelings, and that was precisely what she wanted him to do. She just didn't want him to feel so bad. She busied herself with getting out plates and the rest of the things they would need for dinner.

"It's okay, Erin. It isn't you."

She glanced over at him. He could read her way too well. He was watching her with concern and regret on his face, ashamed at having upset her.

"I know that," she said. "You're upset at the people who are mistreating you. I'm upset about that too. It's one thing when people say stuff to me... I can handle that. It's when people attack my friends... you or Vic or anyone. Mary Lou, Adele. I hate it when my friends are treated badly. I want to fix it all and make everyone behave themselves."

"You're a nurturer."

He came up behind her and massaged her shoulders. His grip hurt, and she pulled away from him. "Ow."

"You're all knotted up." He caught her again, and his fingers were gentler this time, kneading the muscles and seeking out the sore spots, trying to loosen them up. "You're concerned about me going out for a walk and feeling better, but you need to think about yourself, too. You need to find a way to let some of this tension go."

"I know. It isn't that bad. It will be fine. I'll feel better when we sit down and eat. And cuddle after dinner."

He continued to massage her tense muscles. "Your job is physically demanding, and when you worry about me and Mary Lou and everyone else, it affects you."

He wasn't just talking about her knotted muscles. That was only one of the ways that the stress was affecting Erin. He was talking about the dreams and the other problems too. But those weren't caused by worrying about whether people were talking behind her back. Those were the product of the other things that had happened since she had moved to Bald Eagle Falls. Unexpected deaths, accidents, and threats to her house, her livelihood, and her life.

Terry was the police officer; Erin was the baker. She had never signed up to deal with dead bodies.

She knew that the next thing Terry would suggest was therapy. He was just as concerned about her as she was about him, and while he had avoided suggesting she see a professional for a while, she could always see it in his face.

Of course, if he suggested it to her, she would kick it right back at him. He had been injured in the line of duty. The department would want him to see a professional before he was allowed back on active duty. They would need doctors not only to sign off on his physical ability, but his mental and emotional state as well, certifying him as well enough to return to duty.

"I'm going to do something," she told him, heading off the suggestion of therapy. "I *am* taking care of myself. I'm going to try some meditation and see if that helps."

His hands relaxed, and he just let them lay on her shoulders for a few more moments, warm and reassuring.

"That's good. I'm sure it will help."

The next week when Mary Lou came by the bakery, she had a gleam in her eyes that told Erin she was still expecting Campbell to make it for Thanksgiving. Erin hoped against hope that Terry was wrong and that Mary Lou would get her special dinner with her sons and that things would go well for them. It could be the next step to healing their family. They needed some good news, a nice time together, sharing happy feelings and good food and enjoying one another's company without pressure or stress. Erin wanted them to be the happy family they had once been.

Even when Erin had first moved to Bald Eagle Falls, she had sensed that there were problems. While Mary Lou was always calm and collected, perfectly turned out, Erin had sensed the stress behind the mask. Mary Lou smiled coolly and was open about the challenges her family had been through, but had made out that everything else was fine. They were getting along alright. The boys were doing well in school and Roger was, if not recovering, at least in reasonable health. She didn't let the cracks show. The looks and comments that she had to endure from other members of the community. The real struggles that Roger was having at home or the boys were having at school. They continued to be leaders in the community, to get good grades and play on the school teams and to work in their spare time to help Mary Lou make ends meet, since they had lost the family breadwinner's earning ability.

And despite Roger finding solace and some ability to contribute to the family by making the Jam Lady jams, his mental state had been worsening, his anxiety and confusion building and leading to violence that Mary Lou had never expected.

It was a lot to expect one family to deal with. And then to be ostracized by most of her friends... Erin felt like it wasn't fair what Mary Lou had been forced to go through. Vic maintained that God didn't give any person more than they could deal with, but Erin was pretty sure that even if there was a God, that much was not true. She had seen people who had been given more than they could bear. Roger was one of them. She hoped that Mary Lou could rally and her family could heal, and she would not be another example of someone broken by the challenges of life.

Mary Lou gave Erin a reserved smile, but her eyes shone more than usual, giving away her excitement.

"How are things going?" Erin asked. "Are you ready to place your order for Thanksgiving Day?"

"Everything seems to be coming together," Mary Lou confirmed. "Campbell promises he'll be there. Josh doesn't say much, but he's excited about having his brother back, even if it is only for a day or two. He wouldn't go anywhere else and miss the opportunity."

"That's great. It will be so nice for you to have the whole family—to have both boys home."

Mary Lou's face blanked for a moment, but then she lifted her chin, gave another determined smile, and nodded her head. "It will be a good day. I'm not going to overplan it. No program or games or anything enforced, just a meal and spending some time being with each other."

"Yeah. They're getting to be more independent. It's not like when they're little kids, and you need to keep them entertained."

Mary Lou nodded her agreement. She leaned forward a little. "And it turns out that the friend Campbell is bringing home for Thanksgiving… is a girl."

"Oh!" Erin grinned. "Well, I guess now you know what's been keeping him away. That's wonderful. Do you know anything about her?"

"No, nothing. He only let it slip accidentally that she was a girl. I haven't drilled him for details, however much I want to know them. I'll just let him bring her, and introduce her, and…"

"Then you can grill her over dinner," Vic supplied. She was standing in the doorway behind Erin, drying a bowl with a red-striped towel.

Erin rolled her eyes. "Vic!"

"You'll have to, won't you?" Vic asked Mary Lou, giggling. "You need to find out everything about her!"

Mary Lou let out a chuckle. "You may be right. But I'm going to make sure I have her there at my table before I start asking questions. I don't want Campbell to change his mind and stay away because he thinks I'm being too nosy."

Vic and Erin nodded their agreement.

Mary Lou cocked her head slightly. "And how is Officer Piper doing? He is recovering well, I hope?"

She clearly felt that since Erin had been inquiring about her family, she needed to ask about Erin's. Erin wished that she hadn't.

"Yes… I'm not sure when he'll be back on duty, but the doctors say he'll make a full recovery."

"That's good news. I'm glad to hear it. He's been a good policeman in our little community. It's an important job."

Erin nodded. Mary Lou frowned, eyeing her. Maybe detecting that everything wasn't quite as rosy as Erin would like her to believe.

"He's having a tough time," Erin admitted, before Mary Lou could ask her anything more intrusive. "He has headaches and can't concentrate on things the way he wants to. He has nightmares. I'm sure he'll be fine, but it's hard for him. And not everyone is so keen on him getting back on the street. Some people are acting like he really did do something to Bo Biggles, in spite of all of the evidence to the contrary. I don't understand people being so stupid and… ignorant."

"We do have some… stubborn people in the community. I'm sorry that he's had to learn that the hard way."

"I think he's always known it… he grew up here, so he must know the way people think and gossip. But still, that's not the same as actually facing it."

Mary Lou sighed. If anyone had learned that, it had been her. Erin didn't know for sure what she had thought of the community and her friends before the tragic turns her life had taken, but she knew that Mary Lou had been sorely disappointed in the way that people had reacted to Roger's arrest.

Erin opened her mouth to tell Mary Lou not to pay attention to what any of those people said. Erin knew that Roger wasn't responsible for his behavior. But they weren't talking about Roger; they were talking about Terry, so she closed her mouth and left it unsaid.

"You must really be looking forward to Thanksgiving. I guess since you don't know anything about this girl, you don't have any idea what she's going to like or not like at the table. That makes it a little more challenging. But as long as we provide a variety, there should be something she likes."

"And they're small, so even if she is watching her figure, she can have just one or two bites and not be worried that it is all going to go to her hips." Mary Lou smoothed her blouse over her hips as if worried that she might have put on some weight herself. If she had, Erin couldn't detect it. The combination of stress and an iron willpower kept Mary Lou looking as slim and svelte as a schoolgirl.

Chapter Five

ERIN VENTURED OUT INTO the backyard as the air cooled and the sky started to darken. She was a little nervous about being seen, but Terry had gone out with Willie, and Vic had gone out with Beaver and Jeremy. Erin had begged off spending the evening with anyone, telling them that she was just going to rest and work on plans for the bakery.

She straightened her clothes and assumed the start position.

She had watched several videos on her phone, but even though she had no audience, she felt awkward and self-conscious.

She closed her eyes and focused for the first few minutes on her breathing, trying to calm her mind and be aware of her body. She slowly started moving through the forms that she had seen in the videos, trying to remember everything she had read and watched. She had practiced a few of the movements inside while watching them, but the various sites she had read had all advised on performing her practice outside in nature. She didn't buy any of the woo-woo stuff about aligning herself with natural forces, but she knew that it did help to calm her to be outside, and that was good enough. The whole point was for her to meditate and relax and to start to heal her brain.

She needed to let go of all of the nightmares and be able to find her center again. She'd always been an anxious person, but she hadn't always suffered from the nightmares and jumpiness and poor focus that she had been dealing with ever since Mr. Inglethorpe's death. Maybe even before that.

She could remember her foster sister Reg's nightmares. Erin didn't know all of what had happened to Reg, but she remembered the nightmares. Even during the day, Reg had been hypervigilant, paranoid about someone or something following her. She had confided in Erin about the presence that she believed followed her from place to place. She had sworn Erin to secrecy, not wanting to be sent back to the hospital for treatment.

Erin took long breaths in and out, focusing on her final pose, wondering whether the practice had done her any good. She didn't feel much different, and she hadn't exactly been able to stop her racing thoughts. She was a bit tired. Maybe a teensy bit calmer than she had been before she started.

She opened her eyes.

Vic was sitting on the stairs to her loft apartment, watching. Erin let out a startled cry.

"What are you doing here?"

"I live here," Vic advised dryly.

"I mean…" Erin tried to catch her breath and to slow her racing heart. So much for being calmer. "I thought you were out. You said you were going out with Jeremy and Beaver."

"Beaver ended up running late. Jeremy is going to drive out to the city to see her, but I don't feel like being out that late. I was going to come in and see if you wanted any company."

Erin blew out her breath noisily. "Come on over." She motioned to the house. "Let's go in."

"Are you done?"

"Yes."

"Didn't seem like very long."

"You're not supposed to do too much to start with. All of the sites say to start slow, with just a few minutes."

Vic stood up and started to descend the stairs. "So, what is this?" She waved her arms around randomly. "Yoga?"

"No, it's tai chi."

"Tai chi? Like martial arts?"

"I guess it is, but it's not like jujitsu or karate. It's not for fighting. It's for… health and meditation."

"How long have you been doing this?"

"I just started." Erin's cheeks heated. "This is my first time… going outside to do it. I thought you were out."

"Why? You don't have to hide it from me."

"I'm just self-conscious."

They walked into the house together. Erin automatically put on the tea kettle. Vic sat down at the table. Orange Blossom wandered in to see what they were doing and rubbed against Vic's legs.

"Well, now I've seen you, so you don't have to be self-conscious anymore."

"I don't know." Erin shrugged. "It's something different. I didn't know how you would feel about it."

"You could just ask."

"Well…" Erin slowly got out the mugs and tea tray and arranged them on the table. "How *do* you feel about it?"

"I think it's weird that you'd take up some foreign spiritual practice when you're an atheist. If you're curious, why don't you go to church? The ladies would be happy to have you attend over at First Baptist. Or one of the other churches, if you're interested in the competition."

"It's not a spiritual practice," Erin objected. "It's just... standing meditation. Something to help to calm me down. Get me centered. So maybe I can get rid of the nightmares and anxiety."

"Prayer," Vic said. "So why don't you just try a prayer or a psalm?"

"That's not what it is. It's like exercise. Except for the brain."

"Your brain or your mind?"

The kettle started to whistle. Erin poured it into each of their mugs. She wanted to argue that there was no difference between her brain and her mind, but she wasn't sure it was true. Was her mind, the person she was inside, just the function of a properly or improperly functioning organ? Or was her individuality more than that? Was it just the sum of electrical connections inside her brain, or was consciousness something separate? She sat down and stirred her tea.

"I don't know. It's all the same, isn't it?"

"Is it?" Vic raised one eyebrow.

"This is too philosophical for me. I'm just doing meditation. Something that might help me to feel better. To get over... these problems."

They were silent for a few minutes.

"I couldn't sleep after what happened with Alton," Vic reminded Erin. "I had a really tough time after that. Couldn't get to sleep at all without taking something."

"I remember. But you're doing a lot better now. So what did you do?" Erin figured they spent so much of their time together, she would have known if Vic were seeing a therapist.

Vic stared down at her tea. "Prayer. Talking to a priest. Just... getting it sorted out in my mind. That's why I say, you know, it could help."

"I don't think prayer works if you don't believe in it."

Vic opened her mouth to argue the point, then smiled and shrugged. "You do what works for you. If this Eastern meditation thing works for you... then I guess you go for it."

"I don't know if it does yet. I'm just trying it out to see."

"Because you don't want to take the next step."

They had talked about it enough; there wasn't really anything left to say. "I've seen enough psychologists before. I never really felt like they helped. I don't think they're the magic pill that Terry seems to think they are. Or that they have the magic pill. I'd rather do this my own way."

Chapter Six

ERIN LOOKED AROUND THE laden Thanksgiving table at her friends, her adopted Bald Eagle Falls family. It seemed like it had been a long time since they had all been around the table together. Since Theresa's attack on Terry and Jack Ward, it seemed like everyone had been going in different directions. She would see one or two of them, but they weren't together as often as she was used to. Maybe because Terry was not working during the day, people felt like they could drop in whenever they wanted to, rather than waiting until the evening when Erin would be home as well. Or maybe people like Adele didn't feel as comfortable dropping by when she knew Terry would be there as well. She was strongly introverted and preferred to meet with Erin one-on-one rather than in a group.

Willie and Beaver had each been investigating Theresa's disappearance, seeing if they could track her down and, although neither Willie nor Vic had said anything about going through a rough patch in their relationship, Erin sensed that Willie was still feeling uncomfortable about Vic's expanding circle of LGBT friends, people who shared experiences with Vic that Willie didn't relate with.

Or maybe that was just Erin's own anxiety, worrying that things weren't going to work out as they should. She found herself obsessing every time she and Terry disagreed about something or she found him to be irritable or out of sorts, terrified that he was going to break up with her or do something drastic.

But they were all there for Thanksgiving. Everyone had put aside their investigations and work schedules and had made the time to be there.

Vic and Erin had prepared the turkey, since they were used to being up early and could get the big bird started in time for a noon dinner. The herbs were from Adele's garden or wildcrafting. Beaver and Willie had each brought a store-bought dish with them. Beaver brought enchiladas, and Willie, a more traditional dish of roasted brussels sprouts. There were sweet potatoes and mashed potatoes with gravy, sweet peas and corn. And there were, of course, plenty of desserts from the bakery.

"This is really nice," Vic proclaimed, when Erin found herself tongue-tied, unsure of what to say for the occasion. "Our family is getting bigger all the time. I'm thankful for that. And for all of this plenty." She bowed her head and said a few words praising God. Erin wasn't sure whether it was an official prayer or not. Some around the table bowed their heads briefly, but most didn't. Then Vic smiled, looking around at them all, eyes sparkling. "We're going to be as stuffed as hogs on their way to the market. So dig in!"

There were exclamations of appreciation all around the table. Everyone grabbed the nearest serving dish and started dishing up.

"Everything looks and smells so good," Erin said appreciatively, drinking in the smells that were nearly as thick as the gravy. Now that the formal welcome was done and the spotlight was off, she found herself able to talk again.

"Sure does," Willie agreed. Almost twice Vic's age and with skin always stained dark from his mining and processing activities, he didn't look like a likely match for the beautiful and graceful Vic, but the unlikely couple usually got on well.

Terry carved the turkey and served everyone their preferred cuts, with Beaver adding an enormous drumstick to her plate. Erin would once have thought it impossible that the lean Rohilda Beaven could possibly eat that much and still have room for all of the side dishes too, but Beaver had proven her appetite in the past and Erin had no doubt the drumstick would be gone before Erin was even halfway through her own meal.

Jeremy, Vic's older brother, with shaggy blond hair falling to his shoulders and an expression that was always right on the edge of a laugh, had his plate piled as high as Beaver's. The two were a couple, with appetites to match.

There was a comfortable lull in conversation as everyone dug in. Silverware clinked and there were occasional comments and general approval, but the conversation lagged for a few minutes as the meal was enjoyed.

After a while, the conversation started to pick up again as everyone shared updates on what they had been doing. Since they had all been going in different directions, there was news from pretty much everyone. Erin kept her eye on Terry, whose thoughts seemed far from the table and his friends sharing the meal with him. Normally, he would have plenty of stories to share. News about Bald Eagle Falls, funny things that had happened while he had been on patrol, some new trick or skill that K9 had learned, complaints about politics or personality conflicts in the police department. But he kept quiet, listening to everyone else, or maybe not hearing a word they said.

Beaver was entertaining as always. While there wasn't much she could share about her government job, she still regaled them with stories of past investigations. People doing stupid things, trying to get away or to lie about what had happened. Parts she had played while undercover. Descriptions of people and their traits and flaws that were so colorful, Erin could picture them clearly. Beaver had a long nose and generous mouth, and had a knack for portraying the expressions of the subjects she told tales on.

Then Beaver switched to childhood memories. Thanksgivings past, family trips over holidays that always seemed to end with someone throwing up somewhere inconvenient, and even dinners celebrated in soup kitchens with the street people she worked with, masquerading as a junkie or someone else down on her luck.

Beaver looked around the table, eyebrows up, waiting for someone else to volunteer their Thanksgivings past.

Things were awkward and quiet for a few minutes. Beaver shook her head. "Now I know y'all have celebrated Thanksgiving in the past. Maybe it was good, and maybe it was terrible, but everybody here has something to share."

Erin could remember a few childhood Thanksgivings, but not a lot. Sometimes she had been with a foster family, and sometimes she had been sent to respite care while the family traveled or had a big family celebration without her. Once she had aged out, she had ceased to mark the holidays, preferring to continue as if they were regular days and not time to be spent with her nonexistent family or with friends who felt sorry for her. She would beg off, saying that she wanted to celebrate it her own way, and then have a sandwich and read or do something else that wouldn't make her feel unwanted or depressed.

Vic and Willie had both had traditional Tennessee celebrations with their big families, but since they were both estranged from their kin and were from rival clans, they might have felt awkward talking about it.

"We used to play football on Thanksgiving," Jeremy said, giving Vic a light punch on the arm. "You remember that? Always a family football game in the afternoon. Pretending we were all pros and knew what we were doing. Very serious. The kind you always end up getting covered in mud and grass stains from."

Vic smiled. "Yep. The family fight."

"Always," Jeremy agreed, grinning. "And you and me, we were determined to beat Joseph and Daniel one year. We figured we were catching up with them in size; we should be able to beat them. But it never happened."

"Almost," Vic said. "But Daniel cheated."

"Daniel always cheated!"

They both laughed.

Erin looked around the table. Willie was dishing up another serving of sweet potatoes and also snagged some turkey from the platter. He gave his meal great attention, projecting the impression that he was clearly too busy to contribute a memory of Thanksgiving past.

"How about you, Adele?" Beaver prompted. "How did you celebrate when you were a kid? Did you have a big family?"

Adele didn't look pleased to have been singled out. She looked at Erin and glanced swiftly toward the door as if measuring whether she could make a dash for it without being tackled by the retired football players. She shook her head.

"Just regular Thanksgiving dinners like any other family," she said. "Nothing special."

"And when did you become a witch? Did you start celebrating it differently then?" Beaver prodded.

Everyone shifted uncomfortably. Erin and Vic had always been careful to say nothing to anyone about Adele being a practicing Wiccan, as she had been run out of other small-minded rural communities in the past. Erin didn't know if Adele herself had told Beaver this detail, whether she had heard it from someone else, or figured it out for herself. But Beaver didn't have the best social graces and often made people uncomfortable.

Adele looked at the remnants of the food on her plate. She was normally unflappable, and Erin felt sorry for her being put in the spotlight, but didn't know what to say to make it easier for her.

"How about you, Terry?" Vic chimed in. "What's the weirdest holiday crime you can think of?"

Terry was far away. It was a few seconds before he realized that everyone was looking at him and that Vic had asked a question. He looked at Erin, then Vic, wetting his lips and opening his mouth to ask what he had missed.

He startled, putting his hand over his chest, and Erin's first thought was a heart attack. That was it. He'd gone from being active to sedentary, had filled up on a big, heavy meal, and now she was going to lose him.

But he slid his phone out of his shirt pocket to look at it, unaware of the scare he had caused. While he tried to remain impassive as he looked at the screen of his phone, it was clear that something had happened. He half-turned to look at K9 and get to his feet before remembering that he was no longer on active duty. Then he just sat there, looking at Erin, not sure what to do with himself.

"What is it?" Erin asked.

He looked at the phone again, trying to come to a decision.

Erin swallowed, nervous in anticipation, worrying about what could possibly have gone wrong now. He was apparently still on the police distribution list despite being on leave. A break-in at the bakery? Another fire? Someone else hurt or killed, and he didn't know whether to act as a first responder or stay out of the way and let someone else take it?

"I think... you should go by and see Mary Lou."

Chapter Seven

ERIN COVERED HER MOUTH.

If there was anyone who didn't deserve one more blow, it was Mary Lou. How much could one woman stand?

"Is it... did something happen to Roger? Is he okay?"

People got killed in prison. Or hung themselves in mental facilities. Something could easily have happened to Roger in his facility. Something horrible that his family would never recover from.

"No. Not Roger."

Terry flashed a look at Beaver.

The Thanksgiving dinner turned into a rock in Erin's stomach. Campbell? What could have happened to Campbell? He had made it home for dinner, Erin was sure of it. He'd arrived the night before, and all kinds of speculation were flying around Bald Eagle Falls about him and his girlfriend.

Not just a city girl, someone whose pedigree and history they could not explore, but a black girl. Tennessee might have legislated mixed-race marriages decades before, but the old prejudices still lingered. The whispers were flying thick and fast around Bald Eagle Falls.

For a few seconds, Erin was rooted to the spot. She wanted to ask all of the questions, to find out everything that Terry knew or didn't know. But he had already told her what she should do. She needed to go over to Mary Lou's house and see if she was okay. Mary Lou didn't have a lot of friends left in town, and if something had happened to Campbell, she needed Erin's support.

Erin leaned on the table, making the dishes rattle, and pushed herself to her feet.

"I don't know how long I'll be. Can someone make sure that the turkey doesn't get left out? We don't want to have to worry about food poisoning."

"We'll take care of the food," Willie assured her. "Vic, are you going to go too?"

Vic nodded. She was on her feet half a second after Erin. "Yeah. We can have dessert later. It will be better to have it after everyone's dinner has settled anyway. We'll enjoy it a lot more if we aren't all stuffed. Just make sure everything is covered so it won't dry out..."

Erin looked around for her purse, quickly made sure that everything was in it and that her phone was charged, and fished out her keys.

Vic was right behind her. "What do you think happened?" she asked, as she and Erin climbed into Erin's car and Erin crossed her fingers that the engine would start.

"I don't know. Campbell was home… I don't know what could have gone wrong. What could have gone wrong? I thought… Roger… but it wasn't Roger."

Nothing was very far away in Bald Eagle Falls, so they reached Mary Lou's house in just a few minutes. Fast enough that there were still police cars in front of the house. Erin looked at them, feeling ill. There was no ambulance, but that didn't necessarily mean anything. The police were first responders. And the volunteer fire department. A fully-equipped ambulance would have to come from the city, which could take an hour or more, depending on what kind of Thanksgiving Day emergencies had happened there.

Erin pulled into a vacant spot against the curb, and she and Vic got out quickly. As they headed toward the front door, it opened, and a uniformed police officer exited with Campbell Cox in handcuffs, escorted firmly by the arm. Erin knew Officer Stayner by sight, but she didn't know him personally. He had been hired on contract to help cover for Terry's position while he was off of active duty. He hadn't come from Bald Eagle Falls, but had been sent over from one of the other counties. A rookie, low man on the totem pole, with plenty to prove.

"What happened?" Erin asked. "What's going on?"

"Private matter, ma'am," Stayner said stonily. "Excuse me, please."

Erin and Vic weren't exactly blocking the sidewalk, but they each moved a little farther away. "Campbell?" Erin asked. "What's going on?"

She didn't know him well. They had only met once or twice. But Campbell knew who she was, knew that she was a friend of his mother's.

Stayner continued to hustle Campbell on, not letting him stop to talk to explain what was going on. He called out to her frantically as Stayner dragged him on toward the car.

"It wasn't me," he told her. "Tell her that it wasn't me. I'm sorry, I can't believe this happened! On Thanksgiving Day! Tell her I'm sorry!"

Stayner opened the door and shoved him into the back seat with a terse warning to watch his head.

Erin looked at Vic, her eyes wide. They turned back toward the door and continued to walk up the sidewalk. Erin felt removed from reality. It felt like a movie screening, like it was a drama or a joke or part of a bizarre family tradition and soon everyone would be talking about it and laughing about how she was naive to have believed that it was real.

"What's going on?" she asked Vic, even though she knew that Vic didn't have the answer.

"I don't know."

They mounted the stairs to the door and stood there, unsure what to do. The door was still open a few inches and there was a lot of activity inside. They hadn't been invited and Erin had no idea what the etiquette was for barging into someone's house when a member of the family had just been arrested. Was it like a funeral? Did one knock and go in? Ring the doorbell and wait to be invited? They hadn't brought a casserole or cookies.

Vic eventually knocked sharply on the door and pushed it open a few more inches, sticking her head in and yoo-hooing to let Mary Lou know that she was there. She paused for a moment, then pushed the door open the rest of the way and stepped in, motioning for Erin to follow.

They walked into the living room. The feeling of being on a stage set continued. Mary Lou was sitting on the couch, her eyes wide and her face pale, looking around her in distress. The turkey and fixings were still on the dining room table, barely touched. The chairs were pushed out around it. Josh sat next to Mary Lou, his arm around her shoulders, speaking to her in low, urgent tones. He looked up at Vic and Erin, relief flooding his features. He was only sixteen and needed another adult there to take over. Sheriff Wilmot stood in front of Mary Lou, notebook in hand. His look was one of compassion, but his lips were tight and his stance rigid and unbending. Erin could hear Tom Baker talking to someone else outside the room. The girlfriend, Erin supposed. He was trying to get her side of the story, whatever it was.

Vic swooped in and sat down on Mary Lou's other side, also putting her arm around the woman.

"Mary Lou, what happened? What's going on?"

Mary Lou just looked at Vic and shook her head. She and Vic looked at the sheriff, who flipped a page back in his notebook as if he had to refresh his memory on what had taken place there in the past ten minutes.

"Campbell Cox has been arrested for possession of illegal narcotics," he informed Vic.

Mary Lou was shaking. There were no tears in her eyes, but she had clearly been pushed past the point of being able to bear the news. Josh tightened his grip and leaned to press his head against his mother's as if trying to transfer strength directly from his brain to hers.

"It's okay, Mom. It's a mistake. It's just a stupid mistake. Please don't cry."

But he was the one with tears in his eyes. He let go of Mary Lou's shoulders to stroke her short, neat hair.

"It's okay. It's all going to be okay."

"But I don't understand. How could this happen?"

"Ma'am," Wilmot sounded like he was repeating something to Mary Lou for the third time. "We are impounding the boy's car. He will be taken to Moose River to be arraigned. It's a holiday today. He might be held for a few days before he can get bail. Okay?"

Josh nodded his understanding. "Yeah. Okay. He'll get out on bail, Mom. Everything will be okay. They just made a mistake."

The sheriff left the room to talk to the girl Tom Baker was with. Erin could hear the girl's tones getting more strident, but couldn't make out what she was saying.

Erin stood there, looking at Mary Lou helplessly, knowing there was nothing she could do, but longing to be able to help. After a while, Wilmot and Tom Baker left, and it was just the four of them.

Mary Lou looked toward the table, all set for the family's Thanksgiving meal. It looked like they had just started to serve up.

"What are we supposed to do now?" Mary Lou asked. "I suppose we still have to eat." She looked at Josh, trying to be the responsible adult but at a loss for what to say or do. "You must be hungry."

"No, Mom. Not really."

"But we have to eat." Mary Lou looked at Vic. "What about you? Have you eaten? We can't let it all go to waste."

"We ate. But we can sit with you while you have your dinner. Come on," Vic coaxed Mary Lou to stand up. "You might not feel like it, but at least have a taste. You need some sustenance to keep going."

Mary Lou shuffled like a zombie to her seat at the table. She looked around at the other empty chairs. "Brianna. She'll need something too. Where did she go?"

"I'll get her," Erin offered.

She went to the other room, a parlor at the back of the house, where she had heard the voices. She looked in the room. A young woman was sitting on a chair, her face in her hands, elbows on knees. Her face was smooth and unlined, very young, and streaked with tears and mascara.

"Brianna?"

Brianna looked up. "Who are you?"

"I'm a friend. Come on and eat. You'll feel better if you have something in your stomach."

Erin wasn't sure that was true. She was feeling rather nauseated and wishing that the Thanksgiving dinner wasn't sitting like a lead weight in her own stomach. But Vic said that they should eat, so Erin was following that script.

"Come on."

Brianna eventually rose from the chair. She had a round face and a body hidden under several layers of clothing. Her black hair was braided back from her face, quite dark-skinned. She picked up the backpack at her feet. They walked together back to the kitchen, and Brianna moved to her seat. She looped the arm straps of the backpack over the chair. She sat and stared at the empty chair at the place setting where Campbell had obviously been sitting.

Chapter Eight

O BEGIN WITH, THEY all just passed the dishes around and ate food mechanically. It wasn't like the dinner at Erin's house where everyone had been enjoying the food and saying how good it was. Erin supposed that they barely even tasted it.

Mary Lou swiped at her eyes a few times, sniffling.

"It will be okay, Mom," Josh told her again.

She sniffled, trying to force a smile. "I'm sure it's all just a misunderstanding," she agreed. She swallowed and looked around the table at her guests. "It will all be straightened out. It wasn't..." Her eyes settled on Brianna. "Campbell doesn't take drugs, does he?"

Brianna avoided her eyes. "I don't know, Mrs. Cox. I don't know what's going on."

"You don't know where these drugs came from? I don't understand how there could have been drugs in Campbell's car. And how the police knew they were there."

Brianna shook her head, staring down at her plate. She poked at the food, not eating.

"It wasn't anything to do with me," she insisted. "I don't do drugs. I wouldn't let them arrest Cam if they were mine."

Erin looked across the table at Vic. Their eyes met. Vic didn't believe it either. Neither of them knew Cam very well, but they were more inclined to believe him over the stranger. Yet Campbell was the one who had been arrested and Brianna had not been taken into custody.

Erin glanced over at Joshua and found him staring at Brianna, his expression openly hostile. Did he know something, or just resent the stranger for whatever her part might have been? It was easy to blame someone you didn't know and love when things went sideways. A lot harder to believe that it could be your brother.

"I'm sure it will all get straightened out," she said, lamely echoing what had already been said.

In the meantime, it was going to be a miserable few days for Mary Lou and Josh.

Mary Lou pushed her plate away from her. She had hardly made a dent in the modest amounts she had dished up, but clearly wasn't able to stomach it. She rubbed her temples, worry lines deepening across her forehead. She looked at Joshua's and Brianna's plates and could see that they weren't eating either.

"I guess we may as well clear up. When people get hungry, they can warm something up in the microwave or have cold turkey sandwiches."

The phrase *cold turkey* rang in Erin's ears, an unfortunate pun that Mary Lou had definitely not intended.

"Let us help with that," she offered, standing up and reaching for a couple of serving dishes after checking to make sure that Joshua and Brianna were in agreement and weren't going to want any more. As she took them to the kitchen counter to pack away, she saw the platter of one-bite desserts covered with plastic wrap. "Do you want dessert? Something sweet might go down a little easier?"

Mary Lou shook her head. Brianna and Joshua looked slightly interested.

"Would you like anything?" Erin addressed the two of them. "You can take a few, and then I'll rewrap the rest so they stay nice."

Brianna nodded and, seeing that he wouldn't be the only one, Joshua agreed as well.

"Yeah, just a little," he agreed. "Chocolate makes everything better, right?"

Erin took the platter and dessert dishes to each of them and Josh attempted to compliment the dishes.

"These are yours from the bakery, right? You've single-handedly kept us in desserts since you moved into Bald Eagle Falls."

Erin smiled and nodded. "We wanted to make sure you had a nice Thanksgiving."

After it came out, Erin wasn't sure that had been the right thing to say. Their chances at a nice Thanksgiving had gone down the tubes.

"Wow, it all looks so good," Brianna murmured, helping herself to a few of the bite-sized treats. Erin took them over to Mary Lou, but she waved the platter away.

"I'm sorry, I can't right now. You two have some. No point in them going to waste."

"We've got some at home," Erin laughed. "There are plenty to go around. I'll just make sure these are covered. You might feel like some later."

Mary Lou pressed a knuckle into her forehead. Standing beside her with the tray, Erin felt she should be doing something more to comfort her. She put her hand on Mary Lou's shoulder and gave it a little squeeze. Mary Lou patted Erin's hand, then she pulled away slightly and Erin let go.

"I'm so sorry. Is there anything else we can do?"

Vic was working quietly, helping to put the Thanksgiving dishes away.

"No, no. We'll be fine. There's nothing you can do. You should go home to your own families."

"We'll just get this cleared up first," Vic said.

Erin returned to the counter to help with the effort. Mary Lou stood up with a sigh.

"I'm sorry we're not very good company right now. I think... I may lie down."

Joshua nodded. Brianna looked quickly around. "What am I going to do?" she demanded. "Is there a hotel? I don't have any money. Where am I going to go?"

Her words hung in the air. Erin wasn't sure what to suggest. She had a free guest room, but she wasn't eager to invite a stranger over to stay, especially one who might be involved in illegal drugs.

"You will stay here, of course," Mary Lou said. "I'll make up the spare room."

"You go lie down, Mom," Joshua instructed. "I can do that."

"Josh, you don't need to do that..."

"My mother taught me how to make a bed properly," Josh told her firmly. "I know how to take care of guests."

She gave him a faint smile. "Okay. Thank you."

Mary Lou nodded vaguely at Vic and Erin and mounted the stairs.

Joshua popped his last bite of dessert into his mouth and rose to his feet. "Why don't you have a seat in the living room," he suggested to Brianna. "You can have a cup of tea while I get the room ready."

When he headed for the tea kettle, Vic shooed him away. "I'll do that. Erin and I will keep Brianna company while you do the real work."

Josh lifted his palms and shrugged, then followed Mary Lou up the stairs to get the bedroom ready for Brianna.

Brianna took her backpack from the back of her chair and went into the living room with it. She sat in one of the upholstered chairs, holding the backpack against her chest and looking at them with wide eyes. She had wiped most of the mascara and tear tracks from her face.

Erin didn't think it would be polite to ask for a recounting of what had happened and what the police had said to her that the rest of them hadn't heard. She sat looking at Brianna, unable to think of what to say to put her at ease. Vic bussed the tea over.

"Here you go. So where did you and Campbell meet, Brianna?"

Brianna looked awkward holding the teacup and her bag at the same time, but didn't seem inclined to put it down, looking as if she expected one of them to grab it. Erin understood Brianna's need to keep her possessions close. She knew what it was like to have little to call her own and the constant fear that someone else would get into it and steal or mess with her stuff.

Brianna sipped at the scalding hot tea, looking over the rim at Erin and Vic. "I don't know. Cam and I just... knew each other from parties. Same group of friends. We saw each other different places and just started talking."

"I don't really know Cam at all, but Mary Lou is a good person. She's had a lot to deal with, but seems like she's really devoted to her family. I think she's a good mom to them."

Brianna nodded. "Yeah. Cam doesn't complain about her. So I guess."

"For a family to go through everything they have had to, they have to be strong."

Brianna just shook her head. "What do you mean, what they've gone through? They seem like they've got it pretty good."

Vic and Erin exchanged glances. "Well, they don't own this," Vic pointed out. "It's a rental. They lost their house."

"They're not hurting. It's not like there's rats."

Vic kept her voice low, glancing toward the stairs to make sure that Mary Lou and Joshua were not within earshot.

"They lost all their savings and their house. Then Campbell's dad tried to commit suicide."

"Tried to? Because he didn't have enough money? Plenty of people worse off than this."

"He ended up with brain damage," Vic explained further, ignoring Brianna's comment. "He couldn't work anymore, so Mary Lou and the boys had to try to take up the slack."

Brianna considered this. "Cam never said anything about any of that." She scratched at a spot on her jeans. "So that's why he's in the hospital, or whatever that place is?"

"Well, partly." Vic looked at Erin, asking with her eyes whether she ought to say anything else. It wasn't like it was a secret. Everyone in Bald Eagle Falls knew. It had been in the papers. Even if Campbell hadn't told Brianna, it wasn't like she would remain in the dark once he brought her home. He would have to explain to her what had happened sooner or later.

Erin nodded and shrugged, hoping it conveyed her opinion that it wouldn't matter, Vic could tell Brianna if she wanted to.

"He went there because he killed a woman," Vic said gently. "And he tried to kill Erin too."

Brianna's eyes widened.

"He wasn't in his right mind," Erin hastened to add. "He wouldn't have done it if it wasn't for the brain injury."

"He tried to kill you? What did he do? Shoot you?"

"No. It was just spur of the moment. He didn't have a gun, he was afraid, and he tried to choke me."

"After he poisoned you," Vic reminded Erin.

Erin wriggled uncomfortably. Maybe they should not have opened the door to that conversation.

"Good thing they locked him up," Brianna declared. "Imagine having someone like that living in your house." She shuddered.

"I don't think he was a danger to Campbell and Joshua," Erin hurried to assure her.

But how could she know that? Just because Mary Lou and the boys hadn't chosen to share any incidents of Roger hurting or threatening any of them, that didn't mean they hadn't ever been in danger from him. They might have brushed off intentional poisoning as accidental food poisoning, or might have chosen not to share his more violent moments for fear of what would happen to him when it came out. Or how they would be treated in Bald Eagle Falls if people knew everything there was to know.

Mary Lou had said she didn't have any secrets. But no one was that transparent. Everyone held something back. Mary Lou had certainly never let Roger know she was aware of his infidelity. Maybe saying she didn't have any secrets was evidence in itself that her life was overflowing with them.

As Beaver said, everyone had secrets.

Vic sipped her tea. She didn't offer any more details. What more was there to share? Their knowledge of Campbell's experiences ended with when he had dropped out of school and left his mother's home. They had seen him once or twice since he had left Bald Eagle Falls.

There was nothing else to tell.

It was time for Brianna to reciprocate with what she knew.

Chapter Nine

$\mathcal{I}$T WAS SUPPERTIME WHEN Erin and Vic got back home. There had been nothing left for them to do, and they had left Mary Lou, Joshua, and Brianna, telling them to call if they needed anything, but knowing full well that they wouldn't. Erin's stomach eventually relaxed and she started to feel hungry. She eyed the dessert platter but didn't help herself to anything, knowing that she had a pile of treats back at her own house to dip into.

Terry and Willie were visiting in the living room, the TV playing the NFL football game. Terry stood as Erin and Vic entered.

"How are they?" he asked immediately.

"It's pretty tough, but they're hanging in there."

"What a thing to happen on Thanksgiving Day!" Vic exclaimed. "Poor Mary Lou."

Terry nodded. He hugged Erin and searched her face.

"Come sit down," Willie told Vic, indicating the space beside him on the couch.

Vic instead sat in his lap and put her arms around him. Startled, Willie returned the embrace to hold her steady. "It was so sad," Vic told him. "I just don't understand what happened."

"What exactly is unclear?" Willie asked. He had obviously managed to break down Terry's defenses to find out what had happened. "Campbell was caught in possession of illegal drugs. It's a pretty common story."

Erin loosened her hold on Terry, turning toward Willie. "Campbell was just here for a day. How would the police know he had drugs? It's one thing if they pull him over in a traffic stop and see something suspicious. But why were they looking in his car? How did they know he had any drugs to look for?"

Willie had no answer. Erin looked at Terry to see if he would explain. He might not be on active duty, but someone in the police department had sent him that text and might have given him details. Or he might have a guess based on his experience.

"I suppose they had a tip."

"Who could have tipped him?"

No one answered. Erin looked around the room. "Where's Beaver?"

Of all of them, Beaver was the one with the most intelligence on Campbell. He was her informant.

"She wouldn't have said something to the police, would she?" Erin asked. "She wouldn't have wanted him to be arrested."

"She's gone to Moose River to see to things," Terry said. "She was caught just as off-guard by this as any of us."

Erin nodded, but wasn't convinced. Maybe Beaver hadn't known what was coming down the pipe. But Campbell was her CI, wasn't he? Maybe she had known more than she let on.

"Did Jeremy go with her?"

There was noise in the direction of the bathroom and Erin turned to see Jeremy coming down the hall. He joined them, nodding a greeting to Vic.

"How is everyone over there?"

"Pretty rough shape."

"You didn't go with Beaver?" Erin asked, though the answer was patently obvious.

"You think she would let me go with her on business?" Jeremy shook his head. "I'm not an agent."

"You could go as a friend."

"I don't know Campbell. And Ro wasn't going as his friend. Or not entirely."

"They'll let him go if she tells them to, won't they? She can get him out."

Jeremy raised an eyebrow at Terry. Terry shrugged his shoulders. "I don't know what their exact relationship or Campbell's involvement was. If he's an important informant and the amount of narcotics wasn't too high, then she can probably talk them into dropping the charges and letting him go so that she can continue to build her case. Better to get the big fish than little guppies. But is he an informant? I don't even know that."

Erin considered the question. "I'm pretty sure he is. He's helping her with something. What else would it be?"

When they finally got around to getting out the desserts, Erin realized that they were also missing Adele.

"She didn't stick around for long after you left," Terry advised. "She likes you, but I don't think she's very comfortable with the rest of us. Or with too many people in the same room. It was probably an effort for her to come, and once you were gone, she made her apologies and headed for the trees."

"I'll take her some desserts. I don't want her to miss out, just because our meal was interrupted."

"Not tonight," Terry said, looking out the window at the gathering darkness. "It's not safe to be wandering through the woods at this time of night. You can catch up with her tomorrow."

Erin didn't like being told what to do. She had been in the woods after dark before and had been perfectly safe. But she had to admit to herself that she hadn't liked it and had been pretty freaked out by the experience. Walking through the dense woods in the daytime was one thing. At night, it became a totally different place.

"Adele goes out at night," she grumbled.

"Yes. And I'm sure that if she had a boyfriend in the police force, he would warn her that it wasn't a safe practice too. In fact, I have suggested that she not go wandering like that… but Adele has a mind of her own. And she's pretty good at getting around in the woods without being seen."

"Whereas I bumble around like a baby elephant?" Erin suggested.

"Well… not an elephant." Smiling, Terry looked at Vic for help. "What's smaller than an elephant?"

Vic had grown up hunting, fishing, and camping, and when she walked through the woods, Erin could hardly even hear her. Vic shook her head and didn't answer.

"A buffalo?" Erin tried.

Terry took a tiny pumpkin tart from the platter and hugged Erin around the shoulders. "I would never compare you to a buffalo. But will you wait until tomorrow? For me?"

"Yes," Erin grudgingly agreed.

"If not, I could go with you. Then at least I wouldn't be wondering if you were okay."

But Erin knew that Adele wasn't particularly comfortable with Officer Terry Piper. They'd had several encounters before and Adele had always been on the wrong side of the investigation. It didn't make her well-disposed to Terry, no matter how many times Erin tried to tell her what a sweetheart he was.

"No. That's okay. I'll wait until tomorrow."

It was a long day, and Erin was exhausted before it was over. After dessert, everyone went their separate directions. Only Terry stayed behind. He made sure that everything was cleaned up and the floor swept so that Erin wouldn't feel like she had to keep working. He suggested that she change into her pajamas and get started on her lists so that she could settle in and her mind would be quiet when she went to bed.

"Will you stay with me?" Erin asked.

"I'm here. I'm not going anywhere."

"I mean in bed. Not get back up and go watch TV until morning."

"I don't want to keep you up if I'm restless."

"I just want someone there with me."

Terry considered. "I'll stay until you're asleep," he promised. "But if you're asleep and I can't get to sleep in good time, I'm going to leave you alone so that you can get a sound sleep. Once I'm tired enough, I'll come back."

Erin knew that was as good as it was going to get, and that it was as much as she could ask for, so she nodded.

Hopefully, he would fall asleep at the same time as she did, and they would both sleep soundly, without any nightmares, and neither would wake the other up.

Chapter Ten

BUT THE DAY HAD been far too eventful for either of them to sleep soundly. Erin was restless, worrying about a dozen things even though she had written down her thoughts and made her lists for the next day before going to sleep. Sometimes, she hated to admit, even making lists didn't help to calm her anxiety. Terry seemed to get to sleep quickly for once and lay snoring beside her. But he had only been down for an hour when he awoke with a jump and was immediately out of bed looking for a threat.

"You just had a dream," Erin whispered. "It's okay."

"I heard something. Is the burglar alarm armed?"

"Yes. And I was awake. There isn't anything to worry about."

"There was a noise. I heard…" he couldn't seem to remember what it was that had alarmed him. "I heard something."

"I was awake. There wasn't anything. Just you snoring. You had a dream."

Terry wouldn't be convinced. He pulled on his pants and toured the house, gun in hand, looking for any threats. By the time he finally decided that no one had broken into the house or was lurking around outside, Erin was so wound up she wasn't sure she would be able to sleep at all.

"Maybe it was just a car backfire," Terry reasoned, sitting on the edge of the bed to pull his pants off again, and then sliding into bed beside Erin.

"It was just a dream," she repeated.

"Okay. It was a dream," he snapped.

Hurt by his tone, Erin didn't say anything else. She lay there, facing away from him, and waited for him to go back to sleep.

"I'm sorry," Terry apologized after wriggling around several times to get more comfortable. "You didn't do anything wrong. I'm just anxious."

"I am too."

"I know. I'm sorry. I should have better control. Okay?"

Erin nodded. "Okay," she mumbled into her pillow. Terry's arms tightened around her and he kissed her neck gently.

"I am sorry."

"I know. We should try to get back to sleep."

But there was no way either of them was ready to settle in to sleep, both thinking about the possibility of an intruder, about bad dreams, about the increasing number of sharp words and hurt feelings between them.

Erin was tired and knew that it was the worst time for them to have any kind of relationship discussion. Things would look better in the morning when they were both fresh and feeling better. At night when she was tired, things always looked their bleakest. She sniffled, tears running into her pillow, and she didn't talk to Terry, waiting for him to go back to sleep.

After another twenty minutes, he got up from the bed and left her there, sitting down in front of the TV to try to distract himself until he was too tired to stay awake any longer.

Morning came too soon and, although Auntie Clem's was closed for the day, Erin couldn't sleep much after her usual rising time, even if she had only gotten a few short hours of sleep. She felt the empty space in the bed beside her, and couldn't get back to sleep without knowing that Terry was okay. She slid out of bed as quietly as she could, but Orange Blossom heard her up and immediately started meowing and chatting with her about all of the things that he had done while she had been sleeping.

"Shh, shh. You're going to wake Terry up. Be quiet," Erin whispered to him.

As she walked past the spare room, she peeked in to see whether he was in the extra bed, somewhere he could sleep without worrying about kicking her or waking her up with his dreams. But the spare bed was empty, the coverlet unwrinkled. Erin used the commode before venturing out to the living room, where the TV was on, tiny voices from a peppy morning show playing to a sleeping audience. Terry sat slumped on the couch where he had fallen asleep watching some late-night movie.

There was no possibility of him staying asleep with Orange Blossom's maddeningly loud meows. He awoke as she moved past him into the kitchen, hoping to quiet the cat with a couple of treats. Terry scratched his whiskery chin and rubbed his eyes.

"What time is it?"

"Too early for you to be up. Go on back to bed. You need more sleep."

He grunted and groaned, moved around trying to get comfortable again. He scratched and groaned some more.

"Can't you shut that cat up?"

"I'm doing my best. Come on, Blossom."

"He needs a crate like K9. But soundproof."

"That would be something," Erin laughed. She skidded a few kitty treats across the floor for Orange Blossom to chase and eat. "Have you ever actually tried putting a cat in a cage?"

Terry grunted and cleared his throat. "Probably a lot more times than you have. I always had cats as a kid. They don't take to it quite as well as dogs…"

He finally got up off of the couch and shuffled toward the bedroom.

"I'm just going to knock off for a couple more hours."

"Sweet dreams."

He grumbled something else that she didn't catch, but she didn't need to hear it to know that sweet dreams probably were not on the program. He shut the bedroom door so that he wouldn't be able to hear the cat—or at least, not as well. Erin sighed and petted Orange Blossom.

It was early enough that Erin hoped to be able to catch Adele before she headed to bed after her night-time wanderings, so she packaged up an assortment of treats and went out immediately without putting the kettle on and having her usual cup of tea.

The morning was cool enough for a jacket, brisk and refreshing. Erin hurried across her property into the woods beyond the fence. Erin's woods, though she always thought of them as Clementine's rather than her own. Or even as Adele's woods, even though Adele was her tenant and groundskeeper. It was wildland, not groomed with walking trails and fire pits and picnic tables. Erin frequently saw deer as well as the birds and squirrels that twittered and hopped through the trees, and occasionally other animals, which scurried through the underbrush or froze at her approach, hoping not to be seen by her.

The pathway to Adele's cottage was becoming well-worn, with their trips to and from each other's houses, and it wasn't long before Erin was in the clearing that just a year before had been unfamiliar to her. She crept to the door and listened, trying to discern whether Adele was still up or whether she had gone to bed. She couldn't hear anything. She tiptoed to the window and tried to see past the curtains, looking for light or movement.

The door opened, making Erin jump. Adele stood looking at her, a slightly amused expression on her face.

"I thought I might have a burglar," she commented. "It's been a while since I had to run anyone out of the woods."

"Sorry. I didn't want to disturb you, but I thought you might not be in bed yet…"

"You were right." Adele opened the door wider. "Come in."

Erin entered. She presented Adele with the plate of goodies. "You missed dessert yesterday."

Adele took them without protesting that she was trying to lose weight or didn't eat carbs. She set them on her kitchen counter but didn't open them. "Things were a little busy yesterday. I didn't know how long it would be before you were able to get back."

"Yeah. We were at Mary Lou's for a few hours."

"Is she alright?"

Erin shook her head. "As okay as you can be when your kid is arrested in the middle of Thanksgiving dinner. I can't imagine what she must be going through right now. I wish there was more that I could do."

"She knows that. You're a good friend to her. You've stood by her and she won't forget that."

"It's so sad. She was excited about Campbell being home for their celebration, and them all being together again for a bit. And Campbell brought a friend with him, and she was tickled to be meeting this new... girl."

"Girlfriend?" Adele prompted.

"He says not, but I don't know. I don't think boys want to admit to their mothers when they are getting serious about someone. Not at first, anyway. He said they're just friends, but..."

"You got the feeling that they were close?"

Erin frowned, thinking about it. Campbell had brought Brianna home for the holiday, but he hadn't told her about any of the trials their family had gone through. Brianna had known nothing more than that Campbell's dad was in the hospital. If they were boyfriend and girlfriend, wouldn't he have at least told her a little more about his father's problems?

"I got that feeling that they were... involved with each other. But I'm not sure that they are..." Erin grimaced, trying to put it into words. "Emotionally close...?"

"Just sex, you mean."

Erin coughed. "Uh. Maybe. Yeah."

Adele nodded and didn't make any further comment. She motioned to the chairs and table for Erin to sit down, and put the kettle on the stovetop, bending down to light the kindling already in the stove. It would take a little longer for her kettle to warm than Erin's.

"I hope, for Mary Lou's sake, that it is all a mistake," Adele said. "But there are so many temptations for teenagers these days. For a boy Campbell's age, off on his own, without adult supervision... who knows what he might have gotten himself into."

"You think they were his drugs?"

"They were in his car."

"They could have been planted there. They could have been Brianna's. Or... someone else's. A friend's. Maybe Campbell didn't even know they were there."

"Because kids often store their drugs in other people's cars?" Adele asked wryly. "And planted by who? Not the police, surely, after all the time you spent recently arguing that the police department in Bald Eagle Falls would never break the law."

"I don't know. I don't know much about the new guy, Stayner. Maybe he thought if he could get a good drug bust, he could get a promotion. Be considered for a permanent position instead of just filling in until Terry can get back. I don't know him at all. Or maybe... someone planted them there and then called it in to make sure that Campbell got arrested. The police didn't just happen to walk by and see drugs in his car during the few hours Campbell was in Bald Eagle Falls. That doesn't make any sense."

"I'm not sure your story does either."

"Well... no. But I haven't really figured that part out. I'm just saying... I hope that there's some other explanation."

"An innocent reason for having illegal narcotics in his car."

"Yeah." Erin sighed. "Exactly."

The tea was hot, and Erin and Adele were both sitting at the table. The Thanksgiving treats had been opened, and each of them was delicately nibbling at one sweet, trying to make it last so that they wouldn't eat too many treats before the day had even started.

"Do you pray?" Erin asked. "I mean... I guess I know you do, but I mean... I get a little lost on the difference between prayer and meditation and... different people do different things and call it by different names. When you say a blessing, or say a prayer, are you talking to nature or God? Or to... something else? And... why? And what do you feel when you do?"

Adele was still, inspecting her mini cookie and thinking about Erin's spate of questions.

"You have a lot of questions for someone who doesn't believe in any god."

"I guess so. I'm trying to do some meditation. Tai chi. To see if it will help me to feel better... not so stressed out or... you know, to help with nightmares and... thoughts. Vicky thinks that it's spiritual, like prayer, but I just want... something to quiet my mind."

"There's nothing wrong with meditating if it makes you feel better. Whether you meditate sitting cross-legged on the floor, do tai chi, or kneel to the Christian god. What difference does a position make?"

"I figured tai chi would help me relax my muscles, because of the movement. I don't think I could sit still and meditate. But it's not really that... I was more bothered by the fact that Vic thought it was the same as prayer— except to a different god—and... well... that's not what I was doing. I don't believe in god. Not hers or any eastern tradition..."

"That's something you'll have to sort out for yourself."

Erin sighed and had another sip of tea.

"Did you feel like it helped?" Adele asked.

"What? Oh... I don't know. I think I have to do it a few more times before I can decide that. I wasn't really... it felt good while I was doing it, just kind of awkward and self-conscious. And then Vic saw me, so I felt even more self-conscious about it. She got me all stirred up with her questions, so I was more mixed up when I finished than when I started."

Adele nodded. "You probably need to practice for a while before you get the benefit out of it. Spiritual habits are often referred to as practices."

"So you do think it is spiritual? Tai chi?"

"I think you're mixing up religion and spirit. Whether you believe in any god or not, you still have your self. You're trying to find a place of calm and to heal your… center. And I would call that spiritual. You can call it what you like. Ego. Self. Mind. Personality. Mental health."

"Yeah. Okay. I find all of the different religious viewpoints a little confusing. Maybe that's why none of it ever made any sense to me. If everyone used the same language and there was one central belief system… that would make a lot more sense to me. But it doesn't make sense to me that there could be one god and hundreds of religions. Or even hundreds of gods, and still no consensus. If it was real, we would all see it the same way."

Adele popped the rest of her cookie into her mouth. She dabbed at her face with a napkin. "I think I might get a cat. Do you think that's a bad idea?"

Erin blinked at the change of subject. She considered for a moment, wondering whether Adele was trying to draw some parallel between Erin's opinion on religions in general and her opinion on cats, but she couldn't see a connection.

"I don't know." She looked around the cottage. "You don't have a very big place. I don't know if a cat would be happy to stay inside."

"What about allowing it outside? It would seem a shame to live in the middle of a wild space like this and to keep the cat confined to a little cottage. It would be happier outside where it could be in a more natural setting, wouldn't it?"

"Some people think that cats should be allowed to come and go as they like," Erin said reluctantly. "I have Orange Blossom outside sometimes, but only when I'm right there to watch him. I wouldn't want him getting lost in the woods, or killing birds and bringing them home, or getting killed by a cougar or a car. It's safer for him to be inside."

"Undoubtedly," Adele agreed. Erin didn't know whether that meant she agreed or not.

"Cats that live outside have much shorter lifespans. Probably just a few years, instead of the fifteen or more that an inside cat can live."

Adele nodded, thinking about that. "Perhaps I will have to rethink, then. I assumed that they would have a better life in a natural setting."

"I just don't think it's very safe."

Chapter Eleven

ERIN WASN'T WORKING AS many Saturdays as she had in the past, but a number of her workers were taking an extended long weekend for the Thanksgiving holiday to spend time with their families, so she had agreed to work both Saturday and Sunday.

As she had suspected, Saturday was a quiet day. She worked by herself, promising to give Vic a call if things got busy. Erin didn't think there would be enough work to justify them both being there at the same time, and she was right. A few people popped in for pastries or extra one-bite desserts to round out their weekend meals, but it was very quiet.

She worked in the kitchen on new batches of gluten-free doggie biscuits, and some softer treats she was developing for cats. Not that Orange Blossom didn't like K9's biscuits, but they were a little large and unwieldy for a cat to gnaw on. She had plenty of leftover turkey to experiment with.

The bells on the front door jingled. Erin wiped her hands on her apron and walked out to the front to see who it was. Melissa smiled and nodded at Erin, her dark curls bouncing.

"Hello, Erin. Did you have a good Thanksgiving?"

"Well, it was a little disrupted," Erin said cautiously. She didn't know how much the news of the arrest had spread through Bald Eagle Falls. It didn't usually take very long for gossip to make its way around the small town.

"Is it true that you were over at Mary Lou's when it happened?" Melissa asked in a low voice, looking around as if someone might overhear her. But she was the only one in the shop. No one was going to hear unless they had the place bugged.

"No, I wasn't there when it happened, but I heard and went over to see if there was anything I could do." Erin shrugged. "There really wasn't. I stayed over for a few hours, but I don't know if I was any help or comfort."

"Oh, I'm sure Mary Lou appreciated it," Melissa assured her. "She has a hard time showing her feelings. She's very reserved. But that doesn't mean she doesn't feel them. She just—doesn't show it."

As someone who was used to masking her own feelings when they were inconvenient, Erin could understand that. It wasn't easy for her to let herself be vulnerable, even to her closest friends. It was easier for her to mother Vic than to explain how she was feeling deep down. Easier to comfort Terry after one of his nightmares than to tell him about her own and the feelings of dread they always left behind, like an oily residue on her consciousness. And easier to wrap up Mary Lou's Thanksgiving dishes and put them away than to tell Mary Lou how concerned she was about Terry and his state of mind.

"I know. She was pretty shaken up. I wish there was more I could do for her."

"I can't imagine what Stayner was thinking," Melissa said, shaking her head. "The Coxes are such a pillar of the community. Whatever would possess him to search Campbell's car?"

Erin leaned on the top of the bakery display case. "I thought you would know whether the police got a tip. I can't see how Stayner would just stumble across something like that. Campbell's car on the street in front of Mary Lou's house. He surely wouldn't have left drugs in full view."

"I'm off work for a few days, so I don't know." Melissa helped part-time with administrative work at the police department and frequently let information slip when she should have guarded her tongue. But the Thanksgiving weekend was working against Erin. Melissa wouldn't be in the office until at least Monday. There was no way for her to know whether there had been an official tip called in unless Clara or someone else in the department told her.

"It has to be the girl," Melissa suggested. "Nobody knows anything about her. Who knows where she came from or what kind of history she has?"

Erin didn't like to throw around accusations, but she too had her suspicions about Brianna. It would make far more sense to her if the drugs were Brianna's than Campbell's. Brianna had just been too afraid to admit that they were hers. Campbell either didn't know where they had come from or wanted to protect Brianna. He had told Mary Lou that he and Brianna were just friends, but it was more likely that they were boyfriend and girlfriend. So, of course, Campbell would want to protect the one he loved.

"I don't know anything about her," Erin told Melissa. "She seemed like a very nice girl. But I didn't talk to her very much."

"Can you believe that Campbell would be going out with a black girl?" Melissa's eyes were wide. She shook her head. "I know that may not be such a big deal where you come from. Or even in Nashville. But around here? The courts may have passed *Loving* in the sixties, but that didn't have much effect on people's opinions on interracial marriages in these parts."

"There's nothing wrong with Campbell dating or marrying a black girl," Erin asserted. "But bringing her home for Thanksgiving dinner doesn't mean he's getting ready to marry her. He says they're just friends."

"So he says. He's got to know what folks around here would have to say about the matter."

Erin agreed, but she wasn't going to let Melissa think that she had anything against Campbell dating or marrying a girl of another race, which she did not. "Best we don't judge."

"Oh, I'm not judging. But if I had to pick which one of them is on drugs, it wouldn't be Campbell. And that's not because of the color of her skin, or his. That's just because I know Mary Lou and I've known those boys since they were babies. I just can't see Campbell getting into something like that. He has too much good sense."

Erin shrugged uncomfortably. It was hard to see anyone you had known since they were a baby taking up drugs or any other dangerous or criminal behavior. That was only natural. But it didn't mean Melissa was right. Erin knew from what Mary Lou had said in past months that she was worried about what Campbell might be getting into, and she was more likely to know than Melissa.

"So, what would you like today?" she asked, directing Melissa's attention to the display case. "Are you interested in some of our bite-sized Thanksgiving treats? Or are you looking for something for dinner today or tomorrow? Or one of your favorites?"

Melissa looked over the displayed treats, moaning about how good they looked. "I swear, you're going to make me gain ten pounds! Everything is always so good; I can't stop eating it."

"Maybe some of the little bites, then. You can have a few different ones, and it's like you've had one treat instead of three or four."

"Okay, how about a variety of those? Make sure you get some chocolate in there."

Erin knew that chocolate was one of Melissa's weaknesses. She nodded and got out a small box to put them in. "So do you have any plans for the rest of the weekend?"

"I'm planning on going out to Moose River—for a visit—this afternoon." Melissa avoided saying that she was going to see Davis at the penitentiary, but Erin knew what she meant.

She just smiled and nodded. She couldn't understand what it was Melissa saw in Davis, other than the fact that they had been friends when they were young. Erin never could see why women were attracted to men in prison. Those who became prison pen pals, especially to men on death row, made no sense to her. Why would they want a relationship with a murderer or some other criminal? And why have a relationship with someone they could never see except through bars or bulletproof glass?

"He's not as bad as you think," Melissa said. "I know that your experiences with him were not good, but he really isn't like that. He's just—that's how it's made him, the way that Angela treated him. Having to grow up like he did, without a father, knowing how he had died. He didn't have the kind of home life and opportunities that you or I did."

Melissa should have remembered that Erin's background was nothing like hers, and that having grown up in foster care, she hadn't had the home life and opportunities that Melissa referred to. Yet she hadn't found herself compelled to kill anyone she knew or to burn down any houses. Davis was where he belonged after making the choices he had, not as a result of something his mother had done decades before. He had still made his own choices to break the law and cause harm to others.

Melissa looked away from Erin and fussed with her wallet. Erin finished packaging the desserts and ringing them up on the register. She supposed that if she didn't want to hear Melissa was going out to see Davis, she shouldn't ask what her plans were.

After work, Erin decided to stop by Mary Lou's house. Mary Lou hadn't asked her to, and Erin hadn't said that she would, but she felt like it was the right thing to do. Mary Lou had a lot to deal with and if Erin could do anything to help her get through it, she wanted to do it.

Probably Mary Lou would assure her that everything was fine and they could get on without her. She had two other people in the house, not necessarily grown adults, but close enough to it.

But Erin felt she should check, just to be sure.

She had second thoughts while standing on Mary Lou's doorstep with her finger poised over the doorbell. Maybe it would be better if she just went home. Or if she called before showing up on the doorstep. She thought that the neighborly thing to do was just to go because, of course, if she called, Mary Lou would say that she didn't need anything. It was a friend's job to figure out what she needed and offer it. Something specific, not just an 'if there's anything you need, call me.'

She should have taken Mary Lou a casserole. Or at least buns. She could go back to the bakery and get the day's leftovers out of the freezer. She'd hardly sold anything,

The door opened and Mary Lou looked at Erin. She raised her brows.

"Erin?"

"Oh, I'm sorry... were you just going out? I wanted to see if everything was okay. If there was anything I could do for you."

"Come in; I didn't know why you were just standing there without ringing the bell."

"Oh." Erin entered, her face burning. "I realized I didn't have a casserole..."

Mary Lou laughed. "You don't need a casserole, Erin. Heaven help me, I'm going to have a freezer full of casseroles. I never knew that a drug arrest was a 'casserole' event."

They sat down in the living room. Erin glanced around. It was very quiet. As if they were the only ones in the house.

"Where are Josh and Brianna? Are they… resting?"

Mary Lou rubbed her forehead, looking pained. "I don't know. What I mean is… no, they're not sleeping. We got up this morning and Brianna was gone. She left sometime in the night, just walked out of the house. No message or note, she was just gone. I don't know whether to tell the police she is missing or just to be glad I don't have to look after her. She said she was stranded here without a car… but I guess she found some way around that."

"She didn't take your car, did she?"

Mary Lou looked at Erin for a long moment as if she were considering the question, then finally shook her head.

"No. My car is still here. And if she's taken someone else's car, no one has informed me of the fact. I just assumed… that she must have called a friend from the city to pick her up. I was just glad that I didn't have to do it. She made it quite clear that she didn't have a way to get around on her own."

Erin remembered how Brianna had whined about needing somewhere to stay on Thanksgiving. Like somebody owed it to her. But what else was she going to do? With no way to get around and no money, the only other option would be to live on the streets, as Vic had when she had first arrived at Bald Eagle Falls, trying to keep under police radar and remain invisible. Not so easy in a small town like Bald Eagle Falls. Not like it would be in the city. When a person didn't have any home or money, she had to learn pretty quickly to speak up for what she wanted or to take what she needed. There was no other way to survive.

"I guess that's a good thing, then. Joshua didn't know where she had gone?"

"If he does, he isn't telling anyone. He's gone out… I think he might be looking for her, but I'm not sure. I'm… not looking for her."

"No, I think you have enough on your plate right now."

Mary Lou nodded.

"Have you heard anything from Campbell today? I know that because it was a holiday, the sheriff said not to expect anything for a few days, but did you get a chance to talk to him or hear that he was settled…?"

"I'm told he's fine but that I can't speak to him. I'll have to wait until he's arraigned and they decide whether he will be able to get out on bail or have to stay…" Mary Lou's voice broke and, for a moment she didn't speak, trying to regain control. "Or whether he will have to stay there until his case goes to court. It can take a long time for cases to be heard, so I am hoping that he can make bail."

"I hope so too. I'd hate to see him having to wait for that long."

Mary Lou nodded. She looked around the room. "Can I get you some tea?"

"No. I just stopped in to see if you were okay. I should be bringing you something."

"As I say, I don't need any more casseroles. And there are still all of the Thanksgiving leftovers. We barely touched anything. And now it's just down to Joshua and me again."

"I could help you get some of it packaged up and put in the freezer. You don't want to have it going bad."

Mary Lou closed her eyes and leaned back in her chair. "That sounds like a good idea. I don't have the energy to do it myself, but it really should be done."

"Okay. Why don't you rest there for a few minutes and let me take care of that."

"I should get up." Mary Lou put her hands on the arms of the chair to push herself up.

"No. I can find my way around a kitchen. You just stay put. That's an order."

The other woman settled back into the chair again. "You can't give me orders in my own house."

"I certainly can. If I was a doctor, I could give you orders, couldn't I?"

"Perhaps... but you're not."

"Hush."

Erin opened the big fridge to look over the contents, most of which she had packed away on Thanksgiving. It didn't look like anything had been touched. She looked quietly through the drawers and cupboards to see where all of the necessary supplies were, and started running water to fill the sink so she could clean the dishes she emptied and not leave them for Mary Lou to do. The noise of the water running helped to cover up the clinking of dishes as she proceeded with the work. Mary Lou's eyes remained shut and, in a few minutes, Erin was sure she was dozing, if not flat-out asleep.

Erin finished getting everything put away for Mary Lou, transferring most of the food into the freezer and leaving a couple of plates for Mary Lou and Joshua ready for microwaving, and left while Mary Lou was still asleep. She probably hadn't slept much during the night and had been worrying herself all day with Campbell's arrest. It wasn't fair that she wasn't even able to talk to him on the phone to reassure herself that he was alright.

She headed for home, thinking that there was still plenty of food left over from her own Thanksgiving dinner, so she didn't have to make anything new, either. She could also just warm up some turkey and gravy and the other fixings and microwave them. Done and dusted.

Terry wasn't able to tell her any more than Mary Lou had about Campbell. He wasn't on active duty, but Erin had thought that he would at least have gotten word from the sheriff or someone else in the department and would know a few details. Likewise, he hadn't heard anything on whether the police department was looking for Brianna or wanted her as a witness for the drug charges against Campbell. Erin suspected that was exactly why Brianna had disappeared. She wasn't going to want to appear in court to testify against Campbell or to take the chance that they would decide the drugs were hers and turn around and charge her as well.

"Do you at least know whose idea it was to arrest Campbell? Or to look at his car? They must have had a warrant to search his car, right? They couldn't have looked at it otherwise."

"Unless he had the drugs in plain sight," Terry agreed.

"But he wouldn't have them in plain sight. That would be stupid."

"There are plenty of stupid drug dealers and users out there. How do you think we manage to get the arrests that we do?"

"Well, I suppose. But I don't think Campbell is stupid. I don't think he would leave them where anyone walking by could see them."

Terry shrugged. "I wish I could tell you something, but I'm not involved in the investigation, so I don't know."

"And if you were involved in the investigation, then you wouldn't be able to tell me."

"Exactly."

"What good is having a police officer for a boyfriend if he can't give you all of the details of a current investigation?"

Terry grinned. "Darned if I know."

"Well, at least you can make dinner!" Erin observed. She hadn't even had to microwave the turkey dinner herself. Terry had everything ready on the table. When she got home, she felt bad for a moment for having gone to Mary Lou's house after work and being held up there. It meant that Terry's timing had been off, as he'd expected her home half an hour earlier than she was. But the turkey was still warm, and nothing was dry or congealing. "Everything is great. Thank you so much for getting it all on. That was a nice surprise."

"Well, you and Vic made everything. All I did was warm it up. The least I could do."

Erin pushed Orange Blossom away when he stood up on his hind legs and tried to reach the plates of turkey with one of his forepaws. "Blossom! No! You'll get your own. Stay back from the table."

He dropped back to his feet and sat looking at her.

"No need to sulk, you'll get some."

"I probably should have fed him before dinner. Then he wouldn't be bothering you."

"He knows better. K9 is behaving himself. Why can't Orange Blossom be polite like him?"

"Because Orange Blossom is a cat, and cats are allowed to behave however they want."

"Not however he wants. I told him to get down."

"And he's going to do it again anyway," Terry pointed out.

Erin used her toes to push the cat down again. "If you do that again, I'm going to lock you in the commode," she warned.

Orange Blossom slunk away, his ears down.

Chapter Twelve

SUNDAY WAS A SLEEP-in morning, since all they had to do at the bakery was the ladies' tea after their Sunday services. Erin told Vic that she could handle it, but even if she couldn't, then Charley was going to stop by and would pitch in.

As she parked her car in the lot behind the bakery, she eyed the unfamiliar vehicle behind her. Customer parking was in the front and no one else should have been parked in back when Erin was the only employee scheduled to be there. She didn't recognize it as an employee's vehicle.

She got out of her car and, after taking a glance around, sidled up to the unfamiliar black car. It had out-of-state plates and was a lot nicer than what most people in Bald Eagle Falls drove around.

The windows were tinted, and she leaned in close to peer into the car for any clues as to who it might belong to.

Erin jumped when she realized there was someone inside, looking back out at her. "Oh! I'm sorry, I was just looking to see if…" Erin sputtered, trying to explain herself. "I didn't recognize the car, so I wanted to see…"

The man inside did not move. He didn't change his position or say anything. Erin stood there, frozen, looking at him and waiting for his response.

As she stood there, it gradually dawned on her that no one could stay that still for that long. Not if they were awake. The man had clearly fallen asleep. Maybe he had pulled off the highway because he was tired and had found his way into a quiet private parking lot so that he could sleep without being approached by a highway cop.

She knocked on the window to wake him up. There was still no movement from within. The man stayed just as still as if he were unconscious. Maybe he was sick. Maybe he had diabetes and had gone into a coma from low blood sugar.

Or maybe…

Maybe he'd had a heart attack. Or something worse.

Erin knocked a few more times, more and more loudly, with increasing anxiety over the lack of response.

Finally, her heart pounding hard in her chest and a knot tied in her guts, Erin slid her phone out of her pocket and dialed the police dispatch number.

In a few minutes, Officer Stayner was on the scene. Erin hated that it wasn't Terry, or even one of the other people in the police department that she knew. She wanted the comfort of it being someone she knew.

Stayner wasn't at all comforting. He climbed out of his car slowly, eyeing her, his body language projecting that he thought she was a hysterical female who was panicking over nothing. About the only thing missing was an eye-roll, and she was sure he had done that when he had initially answered the call.

Stayner was probably around her age, late twenties or early thirties. New on the police force, without very many hours under his belt. Perhaps just enough to let him operate on his own without a partner babysitting him. Just enough to be dangerous.

"Miss Price," he greeted.

"Hi, Officer Stayner. Sorry for bothering you…"

"Not at all. That's what I'm here for. To serve and protect. Or whatever the Bald Eagle Falls version is."

She could just hear the snide remarks he was making in his head about the little town, and how boring it was to be a policeman there. Nothing exciting ever happened in Bald Eagle Falls. Well, if he'd been policing there for longer than a few weeks, he wouldn't be thinking that.

"So what have we here?" Stayner asked. He looked in the window of the unfamiliar car and tapped on the glass with his big flashlight. "Buddy. Time to get up."

When there was no response to his initial knocks, he pounded harder. "Hey! Are you drunk or stoned in there? Wake up! Let's see some ID."

There was still no response from the man. Erin watched Stayner, waiting for the moment when it would finally occur to him that there was something wrong. Something was very wrong.

Stayner stood there for a minute. He looked at her. He looked back at the unmoving man. Then he finally did what Erin hadn't dared to do and lifted the door handle.

Chapter Thirteen

ERIN BRACED HERSELF. BUT she still wasn't prepared for what she saw. The man's skin was white. That hadn't been obvious from viewing him through the tinted window. In fact, his skin was shockingly white. As if all of the blood had been drained out of him. Vampire white.

But not everything was white. His shirt was red. A nice dark red. It was, Erin thought, a white t-shirt originally, with a band logo stenciled on the front in black. It had been stained a deep, dark blood red, and Erin didn't think it was a fabric dye. There was a faintly sweet smell. His deodorant or the beginnings of decomposition.

Stayner reached out to shake or steady the driver, but stopped with his hand an inch away from the man's shoulder.

"Uh…"

"You should probably put on gloves," Erin said in a small voice.

Stayner cleared his throat. He seemed unable to move or to act. While Erin wasn't happy about the situation, she was just a little bit pleased to see his superior attitude disappear. He had answered the call thinking that she was panicking over nothing, but when it came down to it, he was the one who had frozen up.

"Gloves?" Erin suggested again. "Or maybe you should call the sheriff?"

Bobbing his head, Stayner finally reached for his shoulder-mounted radio and clicked the button. He placed the call in a calm voice, but Erin suspected it was more the consequence of shock than of feeling collected and in control.

"Are you okay?" Erin asked him. It was much easier to focus on Stayner and his reaction than on the man in the driver's seat. Her eyes stole back to him. He had on a black ball cap and dark glasses, so she couldn't see his eyes. He appeared to be in his early thirties. Well-built. She couldn't tell how tall he was sitting in the car, but his seat seemed to be pushed back, so he was probably a good height.

"I'm a cop," Stayner snapped. "I'm fine."

"Okay."

"Did you touch anything?"

"Just the window. I just knocked on the window to wake him up. Like you did."

Except that he hadn't used his hand and left prints on it. Erin tried to remember whether she had leaned on the car. Had she left prints on the top or the side when she was bending down, peering in the window?

"I don't think I touched anything else. I didn't open the door."

Stayner had been the one to open it. His prints would be on the handle, maybe obscuring the prints of whoever had last opened the door. Unless that person had been wearing gloves and had not left prints.

Erin didn't get close enough to see how the driver of the car had been injured. She didn't want to add whatever bullet hole or stab wound might be visible to the catalog of images in her head. Her brain already had plenty there to keep her up at night.

Sheriff Wilmot pulled into the parking lot in his squad car. Once out of his car, he met Erin's eyes, raising an eyebrow.

"Miss Price... what have you done now?"

Erin gave a laugh that was more of a sob. "It's not my fault that bodies keep showing up. Can't these guys find somewhere else to die?" She laughed again, feeling a little giddy.

The sheriff glanced in the open door of the strange car, but didn't get close. "Let's get you out of here first. Have you opened up the bakery yet?"

"No."

"Where are your keys?"

Erin looked down at her purse. She knew she must have just put them away and they should have been sitting right on top, but they weren't. She dug down deeper into the purse, shifting things around. She didn't hear the jingle of the keys. She patted her pockets and found a lump. She handed the ring of keys to the sheriff. He took her by the arm and escorted her to the back door of the bakery, looking through the keys to find the one that would unlock the back door. He opened the door and took her into the kitchen.

"Have a seat, Miss Price. Have you had anything to eat this morning?"

"Yes." Erin pulled one of the stools back from the counter and sat. The muscles in her legs started to twitch. She hadn't even realized how she had been shaking until she sat down.

"Good. Can I get you a drink of water? Do you want to put on the kettle?"

"I need to make tea for the church ladies. I have a boiler." Erin indicated the tall, stainless steel electric boiler.

Sheriff Wilmot eyed it. "I'll just get you a glass of water for now, and you can operate that thing. But only when you're sure you're steady." He found the coffee mugs and filled one with cold water from the tap. He handed it to her.

"Sit for a while and sip that. Will you be okay here for a few minutes while I go deal with that?" He made a motion toward the back.

"Yes."

"You're not going to faint?"

"No. I'm okay."

"Don't try to do anything yet. I'll have someone check on you in a few minutes and take your statement. Until then, stay put."

She stayed put. She knew that she needed to get things ready for the ladies' tea, but she didn't know if the sheriff would even let them go ahead with it, or if he would keep the whole place closed down until he had finished their initial crime scene review.

Erin wanted to call Terry and tell him what was going on. But the sheriff probably wouldn't like her talking to anyone until she had told them everything she knew—which was nothing. But he still wouldn't want anyone else talking to her about it.

Eventually, she got bored with sitting on the stool without doing anything else. She got down and started puttering around, getting things prepared for the ladies' tea in case it was allowed to go ahead. There wasn't a lot of preparation that had to go into it; they often had leftover treats from the freezer rather than her making anything specially for the event. Desserts and hot water for the tea were the only things that were needed. Though she might make coffee for the sheriff and the other officers too. She knew they preferred coffee over tea.

"We have a few questions for you now, Miss Price."

Erin startled at the voice behind her. She hadn't heard the door open while she'd been rattling dishes. She turned quickly and saw Officer Stayner. She wished that Tom Baker or the sheriff had been assigned to question her instead. At least she knew them and that they would be fair to her.

"Uh, okay."

"How do you know the victim?"

She looked at him, blinking. "I don't know him. I've never seen him before in my life."

"Are you sure of that?"

"Of course. He had out-of-state plates. I didn't recognize the car. I knew it was out of place as soon as I got here."

"You're from out of state."

"Well… yes. I guess. But I don't know him. I've never met him before."

"Then what was he doing in your parking lot? If he was waiting for someone, why would he be behind the bakery? He was waiting for you, or for one of your employees."

"I don't know him," Erin repeated.

"It can be difficult to recognize someone… in that condition."

"Dead, you mean?"

"Yes. People's faces look different when they aren't… animated."

"I have seen dead people before."

He lifted his eyebrows. "So I understand."

"I didn't mean that. I meant... funerals and things like that. I've been to funerals and seen open caskets before. People look different, but not that different. I don't know the guy. I swear."

"So you don't have any explanation of why he would be here in your parking lot."

"As far as I know, he just randomly pulled in there to rest."

"And someone just happened to come by and kill him while he was resting there. If Bald Eagle Falls had a night stalker serial killer, I might believe that, but there isn't exactly a history of random murders here."

Probably more than he realized.

"I don't know him or why he stopped here. That's all I can tell you."

"Start at the beginning and tell me how you found him there and what you did."

Erin sighed. She moved around the kitchen, making preparations and walked him through the sequence of events from pulling into the parking lot to calling the police and Stayner's arrival.

"And that's it. All I did was try to wake him up, and when he didn't wake up and I thought there might be something wrong, I called the dispatcher. That's what I'm supposed to do, isn't it?"

Stayner was making notes in his notepad. He nodded grudgingly. "Yes, that's what you're supposed to do. You know the drill. Been here before, haven't you?"

Erin just looked at him. She couldn't see how he could think it was her fault that someone had been killed in her back parking lot. She hadn't had anything to do with it, and if she had been out to kill someone, why would she have done it right there on her own property? Wouldn't it make more sense to do it somewhere farther afield? Maybe where they wouldn't connect it with her? Unless she was some lunatic who liked getting the attention of the police and being put under the microscope again and again.

"We would like you to come to the police department to make an official statement and sign it."

"I just made a statement. I have the ladies' tea soon. It will have to wait."

"Are you being obstructive?" he challenged.

"No. I'm running my business."

Stayner glared at her. Erin made a motion to indicate the kitchen and what she was doing. He couldn't be that blind. He knew that it was her bakery. She couldn't just drop everything.

The man wasn't going to get any deader.

"Did you identify him?" she asked. "I assume he must have had some ID On him, or the car registration, maybe...?"

"He's been tentatively identified by his ID, yes. We'll have to get that confirmed through fingerprints or medical records."

Erin waited for more information. The man had died in her parking lot, after all; she deserved to know something about it. But Stayner didn't look like he was going to offer any more information without prompting.

"Was he someone known to the police? Did he have family around Bald Eagle Falls?"

"We'll have to follow up on all of that," he snapped.

That told Erin that the victim wasn't known. Stayner would have been more likely to tell her it was none of her business if he knew but didn't want to share it.

"So nobody knows him? That's pretty weird."

"I suspect your friend Campbell Cox knows something about it."

Erin opened her mouth to object. Campbell Cox? What did the stranger have to do with Campbell Cox?

"Awfully coincidental, don't you think, that we have this sudden crime spree when he gets in town?"

"Crime spree? You arrested him for drug possession and someone we don't know shows up dead? That's a spree?"

"It's pretty unusual around here, wouldn't you say?"

"No… I wouldn't. We've had several unusual deaths, and they didn't have anything to do with Campbell. And I don't know if I believe that he was in possession of drugs, either. I think that smells like a set-up."

Stayner advanced toward her, his expression grim. "*What* did you say?"

Erin took a step back. She looked toward the back door, hoping Sheriff Wilmot would appear. "I'm saying I think someone set him up. How did you know there were drugs in his car? Were they in plain sight? Did someone call in a tip?"

"Listen, Miss Price." He continued to advance until he was right inside her personal space. "I don't like these accusations. Do you think I would act without due cause? That I go around arresting whoever I feel like? Campbell Cox was arrested because he was in possession of a large amount of illegal narcotics. Not because of any personal feelings I may or may not have toward him."

"Okay." Erin held up her hands, trying to keep him from advancing any farther or touching her. "I didn't mean to imply that you had done anything wrong, just that there might be someone who had an axe to grind. Someone else could have called in a tip and set him up."

"Do you think that I'm not qualified to investigate something like that? I'm just some backwoods inbred cop who just got the job because no one else wanted it?"

"No."

"I have the training. I have the experience. They wouldn't have put me in this job if I hadn't."

"No, of course not."

"You think that your sweetheart is the only one who can investigate anything around here? You think he's God in these parts and no one else can possibly measure up to what he does."

"Officer Stayner…" Erin protested, tears of frustration springing to her eyes as she tried to stop the verbal assault.

He just looked all the more enraged by her attempts to stop him. There was a sound at the door, and Stayner whirled around.

Tom Baker touched his cap in greeting at Erin. "Miss Price." He turned to Stayner. "Sheriff wants us to do a canvass of the block, see if anyone saw or heard anything last night…"

"No one would have witnessed it. Bald Eagle Falls shuts down at nine o'clock. There wouldn't have been anyone in any of these stores."

"Some of the stores have residences over top," Tom pointed out. "Or they might have stayed late to do their books or inventory. You never know what people might have been doing."

Stayner grumbled and headed for the door to go out to do the canvass with Tom. After he was gone, Tom nodded to Erin and left, pulling the door shut behind him.

Chapter Fourteen

HE LADIES' TEA WENT ahead as scheduled. Erin had everything ready and hadn't been told by the sheriff that she would have to remain closed or shouldn't have anyone into the shop.

By the time the women got into the bakery, they knew most of the details about the death already. More than Erin could have shared with any degree of certainty.

"We pigged out at Thanksgiving," Cindy Prost said as she selected a couple of treats from the platter of goodies. "I really shouldn't be having more sweets today! Christmas is still coming, and I don't want to put on extra pounds before that. It's hard enough to lose the Christmas weight in January."

"They're so small," Erin assured her. "And the tea is hardly any calories. That's not enough to cause any weight gain."

"I don't know how you can bake all day and stay so slim."

"Do you think Mary Lou is going to come today?" Melissa asked.

Erin was shocked by the question. "Oh, I don't think so. She's having a hard time holding it all together. If I was her… I certainly wouldn't be making it to tea."

"She didn't make it to church," Melissa confided. "I thought she would at least do that. Where can you go for solace if not to church?"

Erin smiled and shook her head. If she were looking for peace and quiet, a place where she could really heal the hurts, it wouldn't be to church where everyone would be whispering about her and talking about her behind her back.

"Maybe I'll stop by there after the tea," Melissa offered. "A few of us could go, give her our regards, let her know that we were there for her whenever she needs us." Melissa looked around at the other ladies and got nods and murmurs of agreement from a number of them.

"We should take something over, though," Lottie Sturm reminded them. "I can't imagine she's up to making meals, and she has a teenager. That poor woman. I can't believe Campbell would put her through all of this after all she has been through already. It's like a stab to the heart."

There was a sharp intake of breath and everyone looked at her.

"Oh!" Lottie covered her mouth dramatically. "I didn't mean it that way!" She let out a high-pitched giggle. "A stab to the heart! Oh, my goodness. It must have been because I was already thinking of…"

They all looked toward the back of the bakery, though of course there was no way for them to see what was going on through the walls. They had all seen cop shows on TV. They could imagine everything that was going on.

"Do they know anything yet?" Cindy asked Melissa. "They must at least know the identity of the man who was…"

"I won't know anything until tomorrow! This is one long weekend when I wish I hadn't got the whole time off. There has been so much going on, and I don't get to hear any of it because I'm just sitting around at home. I even asked at the penitentiary yesterday, but they weren't letting anyone see Campbell. I can't imagine what he's going through, the poor boy. He can't even see any visitors!"

"Why not?" Cindy demanded. "Even criminals are allowed to have visitors!"

"They said no one could see him," Melissa reiterated. "I even told them I was with the Bald Eagle Falls PD, and they just shook their heads and said there were no exceptions! I was shocked. If one of them wanted to come and see one of our detainees, I would let them."

"You don't exactly make the rules for the police department," Lottie pointed out. "I don't think it would be up to you! Besides, why would they want to see one of your inmates, except to transport them to Moose River? You wouldn't exactly stop them from doing that!"

Melissa's cheeks turned pink. "I was just saying, we would never treat them that way. Like they were just a name on a list. We would consider the circumstances. In a little place like Bald Eagle Falls, we don't just rubber stamp everyone and treat them the same way. We understand that circumstances vary. And someone like Campbell… well, it isn't like he's a dangerous criminal. He's just a boy. And not one of those violent psychopaths that you see on TV, up for murder before they're eighteen. He's just a nice young man. They should take that into account."

Erin worked her way around the room with a teapot to see if anyone needed more hot water. It was a smaller crowd than usual, and if they were planning to visit Mary Lou before heading home to make their families' suppers, then it would be a short day at Auntie Clem's.

"So we don't even know who it is yet?" Cindy asked. "It wasn't anyone from Bald Eagle Falls. Some outsider. That's what I heard."

"Clara couldn't make it," Melissa observed. "She's almost always here for the tea, but they called her in to work. On a Sunday! She'd be able to give us the details, but with everybody busy over there right now, she's not going to be able to give us any information." Melissa shook her head grimly. "Sheriff doesn't like to think that people are gossiping about the cases."

And yet, the gossip always got out anyway. Erin looked the ladies at the tea over, wondering which of them would manage to pry information out of Clara first. Clara might be worked within an inch of her life at the police department, doing all of the administrative work demanded by the three policemen, and Sheriff Wilmot might hover nearby making sure that she didn't spill the beans over the phone, but one way or another, Clara would still get the information out just like a town crier. Everyone would know what had happened long before the weekly paper was circulated.

The bells on the door jangled, and Charley burst into the bakery. She always had to have a dramatic entrance. To make it look like she was overworked and just barely keeping it all together. One would think that she was the one running the bakery instead of Erin. Charley liked to think she ran the bakery, but it was all for show. She really didn't have a clue about most of the day-to-day running of the business.

"Oh, Erin. I'm sorry to be so late getting here! You would not believe what a day it has been! If it's not one thing, it's another! I meant to be here in time to help you get everything ready to go, but there has been no end of interruptions today! I was wondering if maybe we should arrange to take some things over to Mary Lou Cox's house. You heard about her son, right? I couldn't believe it when I heard that he was arrested. That poor woman."

"I was there," Erin said. "On Thanksgiving. And yesterday. To help her out with a few things. You can talk to Melissa about what arrangements the ladies are making. I'm sure you would be a big help to her."

Charley's nose wrinkled. She did not like being told what to do. If there were a rescue mission, she wanted to be the one leading it, not the one following orders. "Oh, of course," she agreed. "Do let me know what you're doing, Melissa, and what you need."

"Come sit down and we'll talk about it," Melissa said, inviting Charley into the circle of women and their discussions about what would need to be done for Mary Lou and Joshua, and about the latest word on the man who was stabbed.

"What?" Charley's voice rose above the rest. "Who was stabbed?"

They all looked at her, and Charley immediately knew she had made a mistake.

"I didn't make it to services today," Charley explained quickly. "You know how it is when you're planning for an event like this; I needed to be here. I had a list of things that Erin would need…"

She glanced at Erin, hoping that her big sister wouldn't give away the lie. Not that anyone believed her anyway. If Charley had needed to prepare anything for the women's tea, then she would have been there before it started, not halfway through.

"There was a man in a car in the back parking lot," Erin told her.

"And he was... stabbed? By who?" Charley looked around at the other women as if expecting one of them to jump forward and explain their part in it. Maybe that was the way it had worked in her old life in the Dyson clan, but that wasn't what happened in Bald Eagle Falls. The man had probably been stabbed by another outsider. It was a crime that had just happened to take place in Bald Eagle Falls. It didn't actually have anything to do with anyone who lived there.

"We don't know that," Erin told her. "They're investigating. It just happened this morning. It wasn't like someone was standing over him with a knife or who confessed to it already."

"Who was stabbed? Was he injured? Killed? Did he know who had done it?"

"He's dead," Melissa said. "Discovered by your sister."

"By Erin?" Charley shook her head at Erin. "How is it that you keep stumbling across bodies? You're bad luck!"

"I just... he was in the parking lot. It isn't my fault that whatever happened had to take place in my parking lot. I didn't plan it that way, I can assure you!"

"I hope not!" Charley agreed. She shook her head in mock dismay. "She looks like such a quiet, harmless little thing. But under the surface... still waters run deep."

Melissa laughed, tossing her head of bouncing dark curls. "You're always so funny, Charley."

Charley frowned, maybe deciding that 'so funny' wasn't the image she wanted to project. She was supposed to be a tough chick from a crime family. An entrepreneur and business owner. Not a clown. She looked around at the little group.

"Where is everyone today? Is Vic in the kitchen?"

"Vic is off with Willie today," Erin reminded her. "That's why you were supposed to be here to help in the kitchen."

"Oh right, I forgot she was off this weekend. I'm just so used to seeing her here all the time. And Terry? Does he know yet that you found another body?"

Chapter Fifteen

𝒥 T WAS A QUESTION that Erin didn't know the answer to. She suspected that if Terry knew about her latest discovery, he would have been there at the bakery to at least make sure she was okay. But he was also off of active duty and might have thought it was best to stay away so that the on-duty officers could take care of the investigation, knowing that he would be in the way if he were there. It was a weird feeling, not having him and K9 on duty, making their rounds, always there at the end of the ladies' tea to help Erin to clear up so that they could spend the rest of Sunday afternoon and evening together.

The ladies' tea was not interrupted by the police canvassing the neighborhood. They probably wanted to catch each of the women alone. But since they were going to Mary Lou's to check on her, they broke up a little earlier than usual, and Erin was left to tidy up herself.

Charley, of course, had gone with the others to Mary Lou's. Hopefully, she wouldn't make a nuisance of herself.

The bells on the door rang, and Erin looked up, expecting to see one of the policemen there. Or maybe Terry, there to help as he usually did. But it was Rohilda Beaven.

"Oh, Beaver. I'm afraid you're a little late. The ladies' tea wrapped up early. They headed over to Mary Lou's house to see if she needed anything."

Beaver chewed on her mouthful of gum, nodding. "I know. I saw the convoy."

"I hope they don't stay there too long. They'll wear her out."

Beaver said nothing. Erin paused in her work, wondering what to say. Beaver was clearly not there for the ladies' tea. So what was she after?

"Guess you had some more excitement this morning."

Erin nodded slowly, wiping a few crumbs from the tables. "Yeah. You heard. Did you know anything about it? Is he... one of yours?"

"One of my what?" Beaver laughed. "I didn't leave a dead body in your backyard, if that's what you're asking. I wouldn't be so messy."

"No... I guess I mean, was he a drug dealer you knew of? Or an informant? Anybody... from your world?"

Beaver chewed for a few more minutes, considering Erin's question. Erin didn't think that it was that complicated a question.

"We might have a line on him," she said slowly, "but I can't say that I know for sure who it was yet. For one thing, the police department has not asked for my assistance."

"That doesn't mean you can't go in, does it? Can't you ask, if you think it's related to a case of yours?"

"A person has to be careful of politics between departments and organizations. I don't want to step on any toes. I wouldn't be surprised if the sheriff asked for help, but so far he seems to think this is something he can take care of on his own."

"Can he?"

"I don't have any reason to tell him he doesn't. Unless, of course…"

"What?"

"Well, if it is someone who is known to us… then that could put a different spin on things."

"But how will you know he's known to you unless they identify him and pass that information on to your organization?"

"It's a bit of a Catch-22," Beaver agreed, chewing.

"Do you think you know who it is?"

More chewing, no response.

"Do you think I can tell you something about him?" Erin tried.

Beaver gave a wide smile. "Well, if you're offering…"

"You know I'll always help you out if I can."

Beaver leaned forward. She looked around the bakery and apparently changed her mind. She flipped the front door sign over to 'closed' and turned the bolt to lock it.

"Back door locked?" she asked.

"No, I think it's still open. The police were in and out."

"After all that has happened, I would think you would be more careful about securing doors."

"The police were here. What's anyone going to do?"

"You don't know until it is done, and then it is too late."

"I don't want to become completely paranoid. I already have to fuss with the burglar alarm at home, even if I'm in. I don't want to be the town crazy lady."

"Oh, I think that position is already taken."

"By who?" The thought gave Erin pause. Erin herself, because she kept stumbling over dead bodies? Beaver, an outsider, who was aloof and knew things that no one else did? Mary Lou because her husband was crazy, so she must be too? Adele? Charley?

Beaver shrugged. She pulled down the blind that covered the window.

"Let's go in back. Less chance of being seen or overheard there."

71

"No one is going to overhear us out here."

But there was no point in arguing about it. Beaver walked around the counter and into the kitchen. Erin followed her, wondering what was going on.

"Tell me everything you can about finding the stabbing victim," Beaver instructed.

Once more, Erin went through the story. She didn't remember anything significant that she hadn't told the police. She was going to have to go into the police department to tell it once again and to sign her statement, so it wouldn't hurt to practice telling it one more time to Beaver.

Beaver didn't interrupt, listening carefully to every word. Erin finished with her call to the dispatcher, looked at Beaver, and shrugged.

"Can you describe him?" Beaver asked.

"White guy. Thirties. He looked well-muscled. Can't exactly tell how tall he was. T-shirt with a band name or something on it. Blue jeans."

"Any identifying features?"

"No… I don't think so…" Erin tried to replay the moment in her mind. She had seen the man pretty clearly. She hadn't been standing far away. "He had… like a black, patterned bandana around his neck. He had on dark glasses and a cap, a black cap, so I couldn't see much of his face."

"Long hair, short?"

"Short. Maybe buzzed."

"Tattoos?"

"Uh… yes." Erin closed her eyes and tried to picture the areas of skin she'd been able to see. "I think there was something on his neck, under the bandana, but I couldn't see what it was. And he had one on his arm."

Beaver nodded. She waited while Erin tried to remember what the tattoo had looked like.

"It might have been a homemade tattoo. A little fuzzy."

"All black?"

Erin nodded.

"Colors are harder to cook up in prison," Beaver said.

"You think it was a prison tattoo?"

"Do you remember anything else about it?"

"I'm trying."

"Was it a word or a symbol? Or a picture?"

"There might have been a word under it. But I don't think it was English. Maybe Greek or Russian, those kinds of letters."

"Cyrillic."

Erin thought for a minute, then shook her head. "I can't think of what it was. I was… trying my best not to look at him. I have enough nightmares already; I didn't want anything else to add to them."

"Sure," Beaver agreed. "That's fine. I'll ask the police department. See if they mind telling me what they know. The guy's identity should be released within a few days. It's just nice to get a head start on it if it happens to be related to one of my cases. Since the big drug bust, I'm the person who is sort of responsible for... keeping an eye on things in Bald Eagle Falls. Making sure that the bad elements don't start creeping back in."

"Well, this guy looked..." Erin fished for the right word. "He certainly could have been one of them—a drug dealer or organized crime. But I don't think he was from around here. Not from one of the clans."

"Not with a Russian prison tattoo," Beaver agreed.

"Are they gone yet? Have they taken him away?"

Beaver went to the back door and cracked it open to peer out. "Still here. From what I understand, transport gets a little tricky out here. And on a Sunday... they probably have to call someone in who wouldn't normally work today."

"With Bo, they had to wait longer than twenty-four hours. You don't think we'll have to wait that long, do you?"

"We could always strap him into a seatbelt and do it ourselves," Beaver suggested. She laughed at Erin's alarm. "The medical examiner wouldn't like that. Chain of custody and all. Let me see what they have to say."

Beaver opened the door the rest of the way and walked through the parking lot to where Stayner was positioned to guard the scene until the victim could be transported to the medical examiner's office in the city. Erin could hear her inquiring tones. "Erin wants to know when..."

Erin figured Beaver was probably happy to have an excuse to get closer to the scene and see what she could find out from the officers. Erin looked out the door to see how Beaver was being received, but she didn't want to see any more of the body, so she only took a quick look and then went back to cleaning up. Stayner didn't appear to get aggressive toward Beaver like he had been to Erin. He'd have a shock if he did antagonize her. Beaver was more than capable of defending herself. She wouldn't put up with any nonsense from Stayner.

When Erin got home, she was expecting Terry to be watching anxiously for her. He would have heard about the dead man in her parking lot and would want to know if she was okay. But he didn't come to the door as she walked up to it, not watching out the window for her. He wasn't in the living room when she walked in. Erin frowned.

"Hello? Anybody home?"

There was no answer. The house was quiet. Quiet enough for Erin to hear Orange Blossom jumping off of the bed and coming down the carpeted hall toward her.

"Hey, Blossom. How are you doing?" She bent down to scratch his ears, and saw Marshmallow watching her from behind a chair. "Where's our friends? Where are Terry and K9? Did they go out?"

The cat meowed, which didn't help Erin at all. She straightened back up and looked out the front window. Terry's truck was still parked against the curb, so he hadn't gone out for a drive. He was probably just taking K9 out and would be back soon. It was such a change for them to be at the house most of the day, instead of out on patrol, always moving.

Erin didn't know what to do with herself. She had anticipated having to tell her story and answer all of Terry's questions. Instead, she was in an empty house with no one to talk to.

"I guess… I'll work on my plans for next week," she told Orange Blossom. "It's nice and quiet, so I should take advantage of that while I can." Soon enough, she would be hearing from Terry and Vic and everyone else who learned about the demise of the unknown man in her parking lot.

Blossom rubbed against her encouragingly. It was comforting that he didn't care about the dead man. As far as he was concerned, it was a perfectly normal day.

Chapter Sixteen

ERIN WAS STARTING TO get worried about Terry not getting home. He knew what time she usually got finished at the bakery, and she had expected him to be back. They liked to spend time together Sunday afternoon and evening; it was a special time that they tried to set aside for each other.

Maybe he thought that since he was at home all the time now and they had more time to spend together, she wouldn't expect him to make time for her Sunday night.

But he wasn't usually out for so long without letting her know where he was.

She couldn't help but think of Mary Lou's Roger, wandering away, getting lost, how the whole town had turned out to search for him. But that was different. There was nothing wrong with Terry. At least, the doctors said there wasn't. They said he would fully recover. There was nothing to worry about.

Erin looked out the window, hoping she would see Terry walking toward the house with K9 at his side. There was no sign of him.

An anxious knot in her stomach, she finally pulled out her phone and texted him. A text would be less intrusive than a call. She wouldn't sound like a nagging wife. He would know that she was home and waiting for him, but he wouldn't have to give excuses or explain where he was.

She watched anxiously for his reply.

Eventually, Erin gave up on waiting for Terry or anyone else to get home. She was her own person with her own life, and she didn't have to wait around for Terry to finish having a beer with the guys or whatever he was doing. Since there was no one else around, it was a good time for her to practice her tai chi.

There were a lot of thoughts she wanted to clear out of her mind.

She padded out to the yard in her bare feet, keeping a lookout for any stray offerings from K9. He was good about using the run that Terry had built along the fence for him, but she didn't want to get sloppy and end up putting her foot into something she would regret later.

She found a nice flattish area in the grass under a shade tree, and stood still for a few minutes just breathing and grounding herself. She could do it. She could heal her brain and stop having dreams and distressing thoughts, could quit jumping at every little thing, and could get a good night's sleep and be a support for Terry rather than his having to always come to her aid. All it took was a little self-discipline, a few minutes of standing meditation every day. Just like she had to eat and sleep to nourish her body, she needed some quiet time to meditate for her brain. Then she would be able to banish the effects of the traumas.

She focused on the forms she had learned from watching videos. She was, she was sure, not doing them quite the right way. If she had a trainer who knew what he was doing, he would correct her posture and tell her the right way to do each form, but she didn't, so her imperfect movements would just have to do. She didn't believe that there was any magical alignment of her body's energy fields that she needed to achieve. It was just a matter of quieting her mind and relaxing her body. Meditation would slow her heart rate and breathing, and that in itself would bring benefits.

Erin was nearing the end of her practice when she heard the back door of the house open. It slammed shut again.

"She's out here!" Terry called back into the house.

Erin opened her eyes and turned as he hurried across the yard toward her.

"I came home and you weren't there, I was worried sick that something might have happened to you!" Terry told her, his voice edgy and irritated.

Erin pulled her arms in and rested her feet flat on the grass and looked at him. "I was worried about you too. You didn't leave a note or tell me you were going out. We always do Sunday afternoon together, so I thought you would be here."

"Willie needed a part, and asked if I wanted to go into the city with him for a change of scene. I did message you."

"I guess I didn't get your message," Erin said calmly. She thought she was doing very well not to get upset by the conversation, by his panicky and accusatory tone.

"I wouldn't just leave without letting you know what I was up to!"

Erin raised her brows. "And I didn't either."

"You weren't in the house!"

"I was still in the yard. I would have been back inside in a minute, I was just finishing up. It wasn't like I left for hours on end."

"I sent you a message," Terry grumbled. He stood there for a minute, looking at her, his face a confluence of mixed emotions. Worry, irritation, relief, defensiveness. Everything but the smile and dimple that she liked to see there. Things just hadn't been the same since he'd been injured.

Erin put her arms around him, and he hugged her back fiercely, squeezing just a little too tightly and rocking her side to side. He kissed her head and neck and she felt his body start to lose some of its rigidity.

"Hey, if you guys are done out there…"

Terry released his hold on Erin, and she looked past him to Vic, standing at the back door grinning at the two of them.

"Looks like everybody is home. Did you go into town for parts too?" Erin asked her.

"I had some other things to take care of while the men did their manly shopping. Maybe we should have waited for you. I didn't think about taking Terry away from you. We just thought he might like to get out."

"I didn't need to go into the city. But it would have been nice to at least know where everyone was."

Vic grimaced. "Sorry. You're right. It was just spur-of-the-moment, because Willie's auger broke, and he needed it if he was going to—well, you know. It was an emergency. I didn't think we'd be so long, but apparently there aren't a lot of auger shops open on a Sunday."

Erin walked back across the yard and into the house, with Terry behind her, Vic withdrawing into the house and leading the way to the living room where Willie was already sprawled on the couch, his legs stretched out in front of him and a beer in one hand. He smiled and nodded at Erin. "So, any excitement at the ladies' tea today? I imagine there was a lot of chatter about Mary Lou's problems."

"Yes, that and the dead guy in the parking lot."

Chapter Seventeen

HE ROOM WENT UTTERLY silent. Erin held back a self-satisfied smile. She had been waiting to tell them all about it ever since she had left the bakery, and it was reassuring to see that she had not misjudged the situation. They hadn't heard about the appearance of Mr. Dead Guy because they had been out of town. They were in Willie's truck, so they didn't have Terry's police scanner along. And apparently, no one had bothered to call or text them. Probably everyone assumed that Terry would be the first to know, and the police department preferred to get their tasks done without his interference while he was off-duty.

Terry was standing behind Erin. He put his hands on her shoulders and turned her around to face him. "What?" He searched her face. "Is this some kind of joke?"

Erin shook her head. She couldn't find the words to say immediately, halted by the expression on his face. She shook her head again, blinking her eyes to avoid the tears that threatened suddenly. "No. Not a joke."

She had been strong all day. She had not fainted. She had called the police. She had reported to the police and held the ladies' tea and talked to Beaver about it, all without any show of excessive emotion. But in Terry's arms once more, looking up into his concerned face, the emotions welled up in her and her throat was hot and tight. She cleared her throat and shrugged.

"Come sit down."

Terry took her over to the couch. Willie sat up straighter so that she had enough room, and she and Terry sat down together, cuddled close. He encircled her with a strong, protective arm.

"What dead guy in the parking lot?"

"When I got to the bakery today, there was a car parked back there. It's private parking, and no one is supposed to be there except for me and my employees, but sometimes people pull in there because it's convenient to somewhere else they want to go."

Terry nodded. He knew that as well as she did. Who did she call when there was someone parked there illegally?

"It had tinted windows and I could see that there was someone inside, but I couldn't see any details. That he was... not just asleep."

She gave them the details of realizing that there was something wrong and calling the dispatcher, of talking to Stayner and the sheriff and Beaver. She only touched briefly on the ladies' tea; there wasn't really anything in that part of the story that would interest Terry or Willie.

"Have they identified him yet?" Terry asked.

"I don't know. You'd have to talk to the police. I don't think they had yet when I came home. But that was a few hours ago."

Terry shook his head. "I'm so sorry I wasn't here. I had no idea!"

"I know. I didn't think there was any point in calling or texting you, since you couldn't be involved in the investigation."

"But I still would have liked to know what had happened to you. You're the one that I'm concerned with."

Erin felt warm. She snuggled against him. Orange Blossom decided that he was missing out on all of the cuddling and jumped up onto Terry's lap and started kneading with needle-sharp claws. Terry winced and repositioned the cat, eventually managing to get him settled, half on his lap and half on Erin's.

"I'll check with Beaver," Vic declared. "The police department might not like you getting involved when you're not on active duty, and they for sure won't tell one of us anything. But I think Beaver will."

Erin nodded her agreement. Vic pulled out her phone and tapped in Beaver's number.

Beaver didn't have a delicate, ladylike phone voice. Vic's volume was turned up high enough that even a few feet away from Vic, she could hear Beaver's voice clearly.

"Evenin' Miss Victoria. I'm not far away. Do you want me to come over?"

"Yes," Vic laughed. "We're just at Erin's."

"I expected a call long before this."

"Well, we just got home. Erin's been here alone all afternoon."

"Be right there."

Vic slid her phone back away, shaking her head.

They mostly just looked at each other, not sure what to say, as they waited for Beaver to get there. As she had said, she wasn't far away, so they didn't have long to wait. She gave a quick rap on the door and let herself in.

Erin studied Beaver as she slouched into the room, lazily chewing her gum and looking around at them. Beaver always looked lazy and relaxed, but Erin was starting to recognize little tells. She looked around at them, not with the expression of someone who was bored with the situation, but with the interest of someone who was excited and had news to share. Her excitement was hard to detect, but it was there.

"So, you solved it yet?" she drawled.

"We don't even know who it was yet," Erin pointed out. "Have they identified him?"

"I have," Beaver said smugly.

"You have?"

Beaver looked around at the rest of them, as if expecting someone to jump in and say that they already knew. But nobody else knew what she had found out.

"Well?" Vic said impatiently. "Who was it?"

"I think Miss Erin has more of a right to be impatient than you do," Beaver pointed out. "You just barely even found out there *was* a victim."

"Just tell us what you know," Erin insisted.

"Volkov."

"What?"

"That's who it was. The victim's name. Valerie Volkov."

"Valerie?" Vic giggled.

"He's Russian," Beaver said, allowing a small smile of amusement. "Valerie is not an uncommon man's name."

"Valerie," Vic repeated again. "So, what do you know about Valerie Volkov?"

"He's a pretty unsavory character." Beaver nodded to Erin. "Like you and I thought, he has spent time in a Russian prison. That was a good catch."

Terry turned his head to look at Erin, frowning. "You figured out he had been in a Russian prison?"

Erin laughed. That had been Beaver's observation, not her own. Or Beaver had deduced it from what Erin had told her. And she would have figured it out quickly enough when she saw the body and saw the tattoo for herself. "It was a joint effort," she said. "He had tattoos, Beaver figured out that they were probably prison tattoos. And there was Russian lettering. So…"

"So Russian prison," Terry said. "And he was?" He turned the conversation back to Beaver.

"He was. In and out a few times. Maybe not Russian mob, but definitely a gangster. And then he shows up in the United States."

"And continued his life of crime," Terry suggested.

"Yes. Involved in all kinds of unsavory practices here."

Erin was sinking into the couch against Terry. She leaned away from him slightly. "What kind of things? What was he doing in Bald Eagle Falls?"

"What he was doing here. That's the question." Beaver looked off into the distance, her eyes unfocused. "That's the ten million dollar question."

"If he's Russian, than he's not one of the clans, right? So what was he up to?"

"He's into the drug market. Human trafficking. Prostitution. I've just barely identified him, so I can't tell you what he was doing yet. Just where he has experience."

"We got rid of the drug dealing. So it can't be that."

"Well…" Beaver trailed off.

"You busted that big drug network," Erin maintained.

"We did that. But that doesn't mean all of the drugs are gone from Bald Eagle Falls. There will always be drugs for sale, no matter where you go. You're not going to get rid of them all. You know that Bo Biggles came back here to deal drugs. At least, that was part of his reason for coming back. And then... there's Campbell."

"Campbell wasn't dealing drugs," Erin said with certainty. "And since he's your informant, you know that. Maybe he's here posing as someone selling drugs, but you know that he isn't really dealing."

Beaver tried to shrug it off, but Erin held her gaze. "You *know* Campbell isn't selling drugs."

Beaver sighed. "And *you* know I can't talk to you about that."

"You're the one who brought it up. I'm just saying... he's not really dealing drugs."

Beaver said nothing.

"So..." Terry cleared his throat. "Maybe this Volkov was here to scope things out. Or maybe he was here to... see someone? Not Campbell, surely. He's just a little fish."

Erin opened her mouth to protest, then just shut it and shook her head.

"It might have been something to do with Cam," Beaver agreed. "What... I'm not yet sure. I don't know how Cam would have attracted a big-time scumbag like Wolf. But sometimes there are things happening underneath the surface that you don't see."

"Wolf?"

"Volkov means wolf. That was what his tattoo was a picture of," Beaver advised.

Erin suddenly remembered the tattoo.

"Not a very good one," Beaver said. "I can understand you not even being sure what it was a tattoo of, but that's his name and that's his tag on the street. You know, it's supposed to strike fear into the hearts of his enemies."

"Of course," Vic said.

Beaver nodded.

"So he didn't have any known associates in Bald Eagle Falls?" Terry asked. "I don't ever remember hearing his name before. There are not a lot of Russian mobsters around here, so I think I would have remembered that one."

"We don't know yet who he was here to see. I assume that he was here to see someone—which is why he was in Erin's parking lot when he was killed. It's a good place to rendezvous. It's quiet and out of the way, but close to Main Street and a quick route out of town. Easy to find, easy to stay out of sight, easy to get out."

"See? It's not anything to do with *me*," Erin said.

Everyone looked at her. None of them responded.

"I don't think anyone suggested that it was anything to do with you, Erin," Willie reminded her.

Erin rubbed at her ear, her cheeks getting hot under their scrutiny. "Well, that's not what Stayner thought. He figured it had to be something to do with me. Thought I should know who the victim was and what he was doing there."

Beaver rolled her eyes. "Give him a break, Erin. He's still green."

"Give him a break? Tell him to give me a break!"

Erin felt tears threatening again. Not because she was upset about Volkov being killed in her parking lot, but because she was angry with Stayner. Furious, in fact. And no one else had been there to see how he had treated her. She swallowed a couple of times and rolled her eyes up to the ceiling, trying to head off the tears.

"Erin...?" Vic asked.

"He was acting like I orchestrated the whole thing," Erin complained. Maybe it was an exaggeration, but not much of one. Stayner had acted as if she'd had something to do with it. When the only connection she had to the man was that he had died in her parking lot. That had been his bad choice, not hers. "I didn't even know the guy. Why would I have killed him?"

"You wouldn't," Vic said. "We know that, Erin. If Stayner was acting like you did, he doesn't know anything. You wouldn't have anything to do with it."

"I didn't," Erin agreed.

"Of course not!" Terry agreed. "And if it had been one of the others of us talking to you about it, you wouldn't have been treated like that."

"I know," Erin agreed. "I was wishing that it was the sheriff. But he was busy with the crime scene."

"Probably a good thing, too. I don't know how many crime scenes Stayner has processed. You don't want to get it wrong in a case like this. End up with contaminated evidence or things being thrown out because chain of custody wasn't properly preserved... you can lose a whole case. And when it's murder..." He looked at Beaver. "It was murder, wasn't it?"

Beaver nodded. "It was homicide," she agreed. "Of course, there's no ruling yet; it will be days before the medical examiner confirms anything. But the guy was stabbed in the chest. That's pretty clearly homicide to me. It wasn't in the middle of a fight. Not when he's sitting inside his car. Not like it was a fight, heat of the moment."

Erin remembered the dark red stain down Volkov's shirt, and closed her eyes for a minute, trying to erase the image from her mind. She didn't want to be seeing that in her dreams. She already had Mr. Inglethorpe's bloody death scene in her nightmares. She didn't need another.

Terry rubbed her back. "It's alright," he soothed. "I'm sorry you had to see that... again."

"I didn't see much," Erin dismissed. Not like with Mr. Inglethorpe. That had been completely different. It was understandable that she would react to such a gruesome scene. But Volkov's death hadn't been nearly so gory. She could get over that, push it to some corner of her mind and not think about it.

"So, if I had to choose between assigning Stayner to question a witness or process the crime scene, I would have made the same decision," Terry went on. "If there is a problem with a witness statement, you can always get it straightened out later. But once you get physical evidence thrown out... that's the end of the case. You can't recover from that. Not unless there's a lot of other evidence that you can still use."

"He didn't put on gloves before he opened the door," Erin remembered. "He might have messed up any fingerprints under the door handle."

Beaver shook her head. "Stupid rookie mistake. Underneath handles is prime real estate in a scene like that. Whoever stabbed him probably did open the door. And you'd be amazed at how many people don't think to put on gloves before they kill someone."

Terry chuckled. "There's just no pride of workmanship these days."

Beaver grinned. "You said it," she agreed. "So... maybe he already destroyed some of the evidence at the scene. Best to get him away from it and keep him from destroying anything else. But I am sorry that he upset you, Erin. That wasn't professional."

Erin realized that she had been pretty lucky up until that point. With the number of murders that she had been connected with since coming to Bald Eagle Falls, she hadn't been railroaded or abused by the police. She'd certainly been a suspect, but even when she was the chief suspect in a case, the police had not bullied her. Terry, Tom, and the sheriff had always been courteous and careful. Even Jack Ward in Moose River had been gruff but not pushed her around.

"I guess there was no harm done. I told him I'll go in later to sign a statement. He thought I should go in and do it right away. But I had the ladies' tea to deal with."

"Of course." Terry smirked. "The ladies' tea has to take precedence over a little thing like a murder in your parking lot."

"He wasn't going to get any more dead," Erin shot back.

Vic giggled. "I can just see you telling Stayner that. I'll bet he just loved that."

"He wasn't too happy, but what's he going to do? Arrest me for saying I'll do it later?"

"He could have threatened arresting you for obstruction."

"He might have said something like that. But they were the ones who were obstructing me, not the other way around. I called them, gave them my statement, and said I would sign later."

"It's not like it's going to have any material effect on the investigation," Beaver said, shaking her head. "Since Erin isn't the one who stabbed him and didn't see whoever it was that did… She can't really tell them anything that she didn't already—that she found the guy in her parking lot, already dead."

"You didn't stab him, right?" Vic teased.

"I didn't see anyone around," Erin said, looking at Beaver. "Not that I remember. But what if I passed someone on the street and didn't even realize it? Just walking or driving down Main Street wouldn't have been suspicious… I wouldn't even notice."

"You didn't. The blood on his shirt was dry. He wasn't stabbed right before you arrived. It would have been hours earlier."

Erin was relieved. "Good. So it was probably sometime in the night, while it was still dark."

Beaver nodded. "That kind of thing is much easier to do under cover of darkness. Most stabbings don't happen at ten o'clock on a Sunday morning."

Chapter Eighteen

SUNDAY WAS A RESTLESS night. Erin was glad that she'd slept in Sunday morning. She at least had some reserves in the bank. She was exhausted by the excitement of the day, but her brain was still busy trying to process all that she had learned about Volkov's death.

She had the morning shift with Bella, who Erin hadn't spent a lot of time with since coming back from the Alaskan cruise. Bella was back in school. That meant she couldn't put a lot of time in at the bakery, but she still scheduled shifts in when she could. It was a week off at school, so she had a few shifts to cover while she was off.

"It feels great to be back here," Bella enthused. "I forget how much fun it is when I'm at school."

Erin laughed. "It is work," she reminded Bella, "It's not all fun and games. But I do enjoy baking."

"I do too. And getting money for it, too. And I want to be in business and run my own company, so it's good to have the experience and to see how you're doing things and how it all works."

"So you know all the things not to do?" Erin teased.

"You shouldn't put yourself down! You've done really well in getting the bakery off the ground and making money. It's hard for a specialty shop like this to be profitable, especially in a small town where there isn't a big population of people who are gluten-free."

"I don't know if I would be able to if there was still a traditional bakery here, a lot of the customers are a captive audience because it is a small town. If they want freshly-baked bread, they have to go into the city."

"But they wouldn't buy yours if it wasn't any good."

Erin shrugged. "Well, I'm glad you're in today too. I've missed working with you."

Bella smiled. She was an attractive young woman, heavier than society's ideals, but in a way Erin thought was pleasing. Her round face, surrounded by curling locks of shoulder-length blond hair was attractive and made her seem approachable. Erin noticed that customers spent more time talking with her than they did other employees.

"I really do enjoy it."

They were quiet for a few minutes as they worked on getting everything arranged for the morning rush.

"It was so sad to hear about Campbell," Bella said, shaking her head. "I can't believe that he would have anything to do with drugs. He was never with that crowd in school. Neither of them was."

Erin rested for a moment, nodding. "I know that you can never know what people are like in their private lives… someone who looks perfectly normal can be capable of all kinds of horrible stuff… but I'm with you, I never would have thought it of him, and I still don't think they're right."

"But Officer Stayner really did find drugs in his car? I mean, they didn't just misinterpret something he said or believe something that someone else had said about him, they actually found drugs?" Bella frowned and sighed.

"I guess so. It's pretty hard to believe."

"If they weren't his drugs, then they must have been the girlfriend's. And she took off? Just disappeared in the night?"

"Yes. Mary Lou doesn't have any idea where she went. Back to the city, I guess. We can't accuse her when we don't know anything about it… but I don't know what else to think."

"The police must not be too happy that she's gone. Isn't this one of those cases where they tell you 'don't leave town'?"

"I don't think they can actually do that. That's just TV. They can ask you questions, but if they're not arresting you, they can't make you stick around."

"Huh. Well, there you go. I guess if I got in trouble with the police more often, I'd know that."

Erin found herself blushing, and hoped that Bella didn't notice. It was always hot in the kitchen with the ovens on, no matter how hard they ran the AC, so she had an excuse to be flushed.

"Have you been over to see Joshua?" she asked Bella. "I know a bunch of the church ladies went over to see Mary Lou, but I don't know if anyone has really focused on Joshua. I gather things haven't been very good at school."

Bella considered this. "No. I haven't seen him. It's not like we were great friends, though; it might be kind of awkward for me to go by there. I wasn't ever very popular. He was nice to me, but…" She shrugged.

"It's up to you. I just thought he might be able to use some support."

"I'll think about it. Maybe I'll take some leftover cookies to him at the end of the day."

Terry texted Erin partway through the afternoon that Campbell had been granted bail and Mary Lou had gone to pay it and bring him home. She and Bella decided to go by the house after work together to see if the family needed anything. Then it wouldn't just be Bella and Joshua trying awkwardly to make conversation. With luck, Mary Lou and Campbell would be back from Moose River by the time the bakery was closed and cleaned.

Erin had rearranged the cookie tray at least three times, anxious about possibly intruding on the family when they just wanted to be left alone. But they didn't need to stay if they got the feeling that Mary Lou or one of the others wanted them to be on their way. Bella cocked her head at Erin and gave her a knowing look.

"They don't care how the cookies are arranged, you know. Stacked or overlapping, all of one kind together or in a random assortment; they really aren't going to even notice."

"I know."

"Are we ready?"

Erin nodded. She took a deep breath and let it out. "Okay. Let's go."

They each had their own cars, but wanted to arrive together. Erin paused as she opened her door to get into her car, looking at the spot where the Russian's car had been parked the day before. It was an odd place to park. Had he been hiding? Napping?

"Erin?"

"Yes, I'm coming," Erin agreed hurriedly. She slid into the driver's seat and pulled the door shut. She was flustered and managed to stall the engine once before reversing out of her parking space. She swore under her breath. Terry kept telling her that she had enough money to get a new car, and she should get one before hers broke down and left her stranded somewhere. But Erin was used to not having money and had a hard time with the idea of spending money on a new car before she had driven the old one into the ground. He was right, of course. Getting stuck in the middle of the city where there were cabs and buses was one thing. Getting stuck in the middle of Bald Eagle Falls, she'd be able to walk home from wherever she was. But if she got stuck on the highway or in some remote area one day, that would be another story. She really should listen to him and replace the car before it gave up the ghost.

She got to Mary Lou's without incident. Bella pulled her car in against the curb behind Erin's. Erin was glad to see that Mary Lou's car was at the house, so she knew Mary Lou and Campbell were back home.

Erin rang the doorbell and, when Mary Lou answered, presented her with the plate of cookies.

"Oh, Erin." Mary Lou looked tired. "You don't need to bring any more food."

But she stepped back to allow them to enter, and led the way into the living room and dining room area. A meal was spread out buffet-style across the table.

"It's a repeat of Thanksgiving dinner," Mary Lou said, as if embarrassed by the fact. "But with paper plates this time. I can't bear to even think about clean-up. We will be using disposable until further notice."

"Nobody cares, Mom," Campbell said. "And anyone who does, can go—"

"Campbell!"

"—jump off a cliff," Campbell finished, grinning at her. He looked happy and relaxed. Erin admired his ability to bounce back. It was clear that he was glad to be home with his family and going about normal activities like teasing his mother.

"We're not going to tell anyone you're using paper plates," Erin agreed. "Why would anyone even care?"

Mary Lou shook her head, unable to explain. "It's just… what people must think…"

Campbell was standing by the table and heaped a plate high with food. "I don't think people are going to be criticizing the paper plates. I think it's the fact that your son is going to prison that they're going to be talking about."

"You're not going to prison," Mary Lou said firmly.

Campbell snagged an extra piece of turkey from the bowl on the table and popped it in his mouth. "You wouldn't believe the kind of food they serve there. If I had to eat like that for ten years…" He shook his head. "I'd waste away to nothing. I wouldn't feed that… crap to a dog." He sat down at the table to eat. "Guess I'd better get used to the idea."

"You are not going to go to prison," Mary Lou reiterated. "We're going to figure this out."

"I hope so."

Campbell began to eat. Erin's eyes slid over to Joshua. He had stopped filling his plate, watching his brother, but now that Campbell was sitting down and eating, he started to move again, as if waking up from a dream. Bella moved toward him, awkward and uncertain.

"Hey," Joshua greeted, acknowledging her.

"Hi. We just came by… to see how you were doing. All of y'all. I can only imagine… it must be tough."

"Nothing happened to me. I guess I'm fine."

"But it still must be stressful." Bella looked over at Campbell. "Having something like this going on over the holiday, when you thought you were just going to have a nice family meal together…"

Campbell snorted and continued to shovel food into his mouth. Erin could see Mary Lou restraining herself from criticizing his table manners. Of course all she wanted to do was enjoy a family dinner together, to celebrate having her son home again, for however long it might last. She didn't need anyone else there poking their noses in and asking questions.

"Well, we don't want to keep you. Just wanted to make sure you got home safe and to see if there's anything you need."

Mary Lou shook her head. "Nothing that time won't cure," she said without enthusiasm.

Campbell was watching Bella as he ate. They were close together in age. Erin wasn't sure whether they were in the same grade or a year apart. They both seemed so young and so mature at the same time. Had she ever been that young and naive? And yet mature and knowing everything?

"Miss having you around school," Bella said, noticing his attention. "It's weird, you not being there."

"Yeah." He chewed more slowly. "Maybe I should have stuck around. Wouldn't have gotten in this trouble."

Erin didn't look at Mary Lou. How many times had she told Campbell that he should be going to school and not going off on his own? How many times had she begged him to come home and to stay away from whatever trouble he was getting into in the city? Erin didn't know if she'd be able to handle having kids. Not when they got to be independent and you couldn't stop them from getting in trouble by sending them to their beds anymore.

"Maybe you could come back now," Bella suggested. "Are you going to stay around here? You could show the judge that you were back in school and being a good citizen, maybe that would help your case."

"I have to stay here," Campbell said. He stuck his leg out and pulled his pant leg up, showing off an ankle monitor. "I go anywhere else, and they revoke my bail."

"So you could go to school."

"I can't go more than two hundred yards from the house, so I don't think so."

"You could do home study. They have that."

Campbell shook his head. "Yeah, I don't think so."

Mary Lou put a few bites of food on her paper plate and walked away from the table, toward Erin. "Why don't you sit down and visit for a few minutes, Erin. Let the kids... talk."

Erin obligingly sat down across from her. Mary Lou poked at her food, obviously not that interested in it. Erin searched for something to say.

"Have you seen Brianna?" Campbell asked Joshua.

Mary Lou cocked her head slightly, not turning to look at the boys, but clearly listening in.

"No. Don't know where she took off to. I looked around a bit, but she's not around here. I figure she must have gotten back to the city. Called someone or hitchhiked."

"Stupid. She should have stayed around here."

"She probably figured she was next. The cops would pick her up as soon as they had something they could pull her in on."

Campbell shook his head. "What's wrong with girls?" He looked over at Bella. "No offense. I know you're not like her. But why can't they just be sensible? We wouldn't be in this mess if it weren't for her."

There was silence in the room as everyone considered this statement. It was Bella who finally spoke. "So the drugs were hers?"

"They weren't mine. I didn't know they were there, so you tell me how the cops would know? The whole thing stinks. I don't think Bree put them there. Doesn't make any sense. If she had drugs with her, they would have been in her backpack and she wouldn't have let it out of her sight. She wouldn't leave a crap-ton of drugs in the car. Even she wouldn't be that stupid."

"Well, if you were set up, then she could be set up just as easily," Bella pointed out. "I'd probably run too. Get as far away from this as possible."

"She can't run away from it," Campbell muttered.

There was another period of silence. Campbell was making good headway in cleaning all of the food from his plate. Erin wouldn't have thought it was possible with the amount he had taken, even if he hadn't had anything to eat from the time he was arrested until the time he got home. But it had disappeared in short order. Teenage boys had an amazing capacity.

"You could call her," Joshua suggested. "Find out what's going on."

"I already know what's going on."

Erin waited, wishing that she could ask him to explain further, to unfold the whole thing for them, but knowing that the minute she gave any indication she and Mary Lou were listening in, he would clam up completely. She glanced at Mary Lou, who shook her head slightly, and Erin knew she was thinking the same thing. It must have been killing her to be so shut out of her son's life. To only hear these things because she happened to overhear him. She had always seemed close to her boys.

"What are you going to do, then?" Joshua asked. "It's not like you can go into the city and find her."

"Nope," Campbell agreed. "I just have to sit here and do nothing."

Chapter Nineteen

C OULD I ASK YOU for a favor, Erin?" Mary Lou asked as Erin and Bella prepared to leave.

"Of course, I'd be happy to help out any way I can."

"I have a casserole dish that belongs to Rohilda Beaven. I know she usually stays with Jeremy when she's in town, and I wonder if you could drop it off there…?"

"Sure. No problem."

Erin waited while Mary Lou retrieved it. It was the only casserole dish on the counter, and Erin remembered Mary Lou saying how many they had in the freezer. Maybe everyone else had used disposable pans so that they wouldn't be without them while waiting for Mary Lou to eat the casserole and return them.

Mary Lou handed it to her, flushing pink. At Erin's look, she blurted out an explanation. "It was fried chicken. Not homemade, you could tell it wasn't actually cooked in the dish, and I know she just got it at the family restaurant and put it in her own dish. To tell the truth… I dumped it all out. After her involvement in getting Campbell into this trouble, I didn't want her peace offering. And I don't want to return it in person."

Erin nodded and took it from her. She felt her own cheeks warming at Mary Lou's explanation. She liked Beaver and hated for Mary Lou to think that Campbell's trouble was her fault.

"I don't claim to know all of what happened… but I think Beaver was trying to look after Campbell and keep him out of trouble. I don't think it's her fault that Campbell was arrested. She wouldn't have… put drugs in his car or told him to do anything to break the law…"

Mary Lou looked at her for a minute. Erin looked down.

"Like I said. I don't know."

"She should not have had anything to do with him. He's not even an adult. She didn't have any business getting him involved in her investigation."

Erin nodded. "I'll run this by Jeremy's apartment," she promised.

When she got into her car, Erin called Vic. "I need to go by Jeremy's. Do you want to come along?"

"Sure," Vic agreed. "Always happy to have a reason to check up on him and harass him a little for his housekeeping. Are you going now?"

"I think I'd better, because once I get home, I'm going to crash. I'm not going to want to go out again."

"Okay. Just pull in front, and I'll be right out."

They headed over to Jeremy's together. Erin didn't tell Vic the details Mary Lou had confided about throwing the fried chicken out and blaming Beaver for what had happened.

Jeremy was surprised to see them, but didn't seem upset about the unexpected visit. He opened the door wide and invited them in, with a caution that he wasn't prepared for visitors.

The apartment was disorderly, but no more than any other bachelor's basement suite. Erin imagined Beaver probably ensured it didn't get too messy when she stayed over.

Erin and Vic made space for themselves in the living room area, moving a newspaper, laptop, and stray charge cables out of the way.

"I guess Beaver probably isn't too happy about all of this stuff with Campbell," Erin suggested, wondering whether Beaver or Jeremy knew anything of Mary Lou's animosity toward Beaver for the way things had turned out.

"Ro doesn't talk much about the things that bother her," Jeremy said. "But don't think that means that she doesn't worry just as much as the next person."

"She always seems so cool and unaffected by things," Erin said. "I'd love to be like that. To just be able to go with the flow and not be bothered."

"She's like that about some things," Jeremy admitted. "She's been through a lot of difficult stuff, so the little things aren't a concern. She knows that in the big picture, they really aren't going to matter, so why worry about them? But the big stuff…? It still bothers her just like anyone else."

"And she's worried about Campbell?" Erin asked.

"Of course. She took him under her wing and was helping him out, and now look at the trouble that he's in. He could end up in prison. And for a long time, not just probation or a few months in some minimum-security place. She feels responsible for that."

"But it's not Beaver's fault," Vic pointed out. "She's not the one who got him in trouble."

"No…" Jeremy said uncertainly. "But she's not saying how much he was already involved in and how much she might have nudged him forward so that he could feed her information for her investigation. You know he's been acting as an informant."

"But she's not the one who put him into the situation," Erin said, feeling her way along. "He was already involved with these people in the city. Mary Lou said that she didn't know what he was involved in and who he was staying with. She knew he didn't have a job or any money, so he was obviously involved in something… shady. Or he was living off of someone else. That's not Beaver's doing."

"I don't know what he was already involved in and what Ro might have gotten him into. And now she's taking flak from her bosses. They are not happy about her involving someone so young in her investigation."

"Didn't they know?"

"I guess when you're an agent, you don't always pass all of the details on to your superiors… you tell them what they need to know and keep the rest to yourself. So they might have known that she had an informant, and what kind of information he was giving her, but not that he was still a minor."

"And she's not supposed to use a minor?"

"I don't know if there are hard and fast rules. But I guess once that minor gets arrested and accused of serious trafficking charges… they might question your judgment."

Erin nodded. She hadn't ever been comfortable with the idea of Beaver using Campbell to get what she wanted. Campbell had seemed happy to work with her and for the sense of accomplishment and maturity that it gave him. But teenagers, especially teenage boys, had immature brains. Their judgment was impaired. Had Beaver taken advantage of Campbell's youth, getting him into something that he wouldn't have been involved in otherwise? Was he involved with drug dealers, and that was why drugs had been planted in his car?

Or was it even worse than that? Erin had seen a lot of the nastier elements on the street when she was younger. She had never been entirely homeless and on the skids, but she had been close, and her closeness to that life had taught her a lot of lessons that she would rather not have had to learn. Kids on the street were vulnerable. They thought that they were in control of their own lives. They thought that they were invincible. But they were easy victims.

"So… is Beaver in big trouble?" Vic asked. "Or is she just being asked to justify what she did?"

"She doesn't say much about it. You know, she can't give me any details, so she's pretty careful about what she says. But I gather… it could be a career-ending mistake. If Campbell goes to prison or they decide that she was out of line in using him as an informant… her job could be down the toilet."

"Oh, no…" Erin tried to imagine Beaver in some other job. She was made to be an agent. It was a job that fit her like a glove. She was a treasure-hunter as a hobby, but what would she do for a job that would fulfill those needs? Erin couldn't picture her as anything else.

"She'll be okay," Vic said. "You know Beaver. She'll come out of it smelling like a rose."

Jeremy nodded, but his eyes were distant. "I hope so. I don't know what she would do if she lost her job."

Chapter Twenty

I T HAD BEEN A long day. Erin was relaxing on the couch watching TV and dozing on Terry's shoulder when the back door slammed open, and Erin just about rocketed out of her seat. Terry was on his feet right behind her.

Vic strode through the kitchen and had started her tirade before she even reached the living room.

"What is wrong with men?" she demanded. She saw Terry. "No offense, Terry, but why do men have to be so thick-skulled? Is it in the rule book? Can't they listen and be sensible? Why do they have to always be right about everything?"

Erin's heart was still racing. She tried to calm herself down. Whatever was bothering Vic, it wasn't a real emergency. She wasn't being chased or attacked. She was just riled up about something that Willie had done. She swallowed and tried to answer Vic calmly.

"What happened?"

"Nothing happened. And nothing is going to happen if he is going to keep being so hard-headed and acting like he can't trust me! What have I ever done to make him think I would be unfaithful to him? I've never given him any reason to think that I would wander!"

"I know," Erin soothed. "I don't know what happened, but it will blow over. The two of you are just... passionate. You're going to butt heads sometimes. But you love Willie, and he loves you, the two of you can work it out..."

"I'm prepared to be reasonable. He is the one who isn't! I'm perfectly happy to talk things through and work them out."

"What exactly is bothering him?" Terry asked. He sat back down on the couch where he had been before Vic's dramatic entrance. He put his feet up on the coffee table, and Vic shook her head at him.

"What?" Terry demanded. "I don't have my shoes on and this isn't your coffee table. It's Erin's, and if it doesn't bother her, you don't need to act like I've committed a capital offense."

"It's not that." Vic shook her head, rolling her eyes at her own response. "I'm just wound up. It's not you. I need to talk to Erin. Someone who understands."

"Come to the bedroom," Erin invited. "You can say whatever you like without being overheard." She glanced over at Terry. "As long as you lower your voice. You are… a mite loud."

Terry snorted. He didn't offer to be the one to leave the room so that they could talk in private. He was in the middle of watching a show, and there wasn't a TV in the bedroom, so Erin couldn't very well insist.

"Come on," she repeated, motioning to Vic.

Vic followed her down the hall to the bedroom and, once she was in, Erin shut the door. Vic threw herself down on the bed, sprawling on her back, and groaned loudly.

"Can I go back to being a kid again? I'm tired of dealing with relationship crap. I want to go back to just… making mud pies and shooting squirrels."

"I don't think you'd better be shooting anything while you're in this mood." Erin thought about the fact that Vic was almost always carrying a concealed weapon since the house had been broken into, and that it was within reach when she was so angry during her argument with Willie. The thought made her queasy. All it would take was Vic losing control once… She had never given any indication that she would, but it was a frightening thought. "You need to calm down."

Vic sighed. "I'm just blowing off steam. I'm not going to do anything. I just get tired of being reasonable and patient and answering the same questions over and over again."

"You're okay?"

Vic nodded. "I'm okay."

Erin sat down on the edge of the bed, sighing. "So tell me all about it. If you want to share, I mean."

"He's just… you know, everything used to be good between us. I never had to worry about Willie getting jealous. I think… for the first little while, it just took so much to get used to me being transgender, that he didn't think about me being interested in anyone else, or anyone else being interested in me. It was just working out whether we could be compatible or not."

"Or you were just in the honeymoon phase."

"Maybe that was it. I don't know. But the last little while… you'd think that he caught me stepping out on him. Every little thing sets him off. I talk about one of the friends that I made on the cruise, and he thinks I'm going to run off with them or start sneaking around behind his back. And heaven forbid I should mention Theresa."

"Well," Erin said reasonably, "you can see how Theresa might be a sore spot with him. She is an ex, after all. You have a history."

"But I broke up with her. I'm not interested in getting back together. I'm not the one who started writing to her; she started writing to me. And I haven't had any contact with her since the whole thing blew up. But just mention her name and Willie…" Vic shook her head and blew out her breath. "I asked him if he'd found any trace of her. You know both he and Beaver have been trying to track her down. And…" Vic drew her hands out expressively, "you'd think that I said I wanted to get together with her. I didn't ask him because I want to see her. I asked because I want her to be brought to justice just as much as anyone else. I don't want that crazy chick running around all over Tennessee, and I especially don't want her in my backyard. What happens when she decides she wants to see me again? What if it's me with her arm around my neck in a chokehold next time? I don't want to be with her; I want her behind bars."

"Did you tell Willie that?"

"No. I blew up. Freaked out. Tore up one side of him and down the other." Vic closed her eyes, shaking her head. She held the heels of her hands over her eyes, groaning. "And now he's going to think that he struck a nerve. That the reason I'm protesting is that I'm secretly in love with her. When I'm just tired of him thinking I'm interested in other people when I'm not. Maybe he's the one who is attracted to someone else. Maybe he's just looking for an excuse to break up because he wants out."

"I don't think so."

Neither of them said anything for a while. Vic sighed.

"I don't want to lose him. I know he thinks that I've got better prospects with the LGBT crowd, but that's not the way it is. I like talking with them, sharing life experiences, things that Willie can't really understand, but I want to go home to him. It's nice to have friends who can understand what I've been going through. That part is great. But I really am happy with him. I'm not looking for someone new."

"So tell him that."

"I have. A hundred times."

"Men are hard-headed," Erin reminded her. "It might take a few hundred more."

Vic uncovered her eyes, stretched, and sat up. "What makes you so wise?"

"I'm not. It's just easy to give advice when it's someone else's problem."

Vic looked at her and laughed. "I can relate! Do you need advice about anything? Any problems of yours that I can solve?"

"I wish there were." Erin was thinking of her continuing nightmares and Terry's unhappiness. There wasn't anything Vic could do about either issue. And then there was Campbell… It was nice to try to solve someone else's problems instead of her own, but she had no idea what to do for Mary Lou and her family. She hated the thought of Campbell going to prison. He was a teenager. Prison would eat him up. Guilty or innocent, they would change him from a good kid with some family trouble and who was testing his limits into a bitter, hardened criminal. If he went to prison, he would be a different person when they let him out, whether it was two years or twenty. *That* kid would be gone.

They had to figure out who had set him up. If it was Brianna or Stayner or someone else, Erin had to figure it out and keep Campbell out of the system.

After a bit more girl talk, Vic and Erin left the bedroom and went back out to the living room. Vic had intended to apologize to Terry for blowing up and treating him like he was part of the problem when she was just upset with Willie, but when they got out to the living room, they saw that Terry wasn't alone. Willie, his skin darkly stained as always, sat at the other end of the couch, watching along with him.

"Oh. Hey." Vic swallowed and looked down at Willie. "Umm… sorry for going off the deep end. I guess I just lost it."

"It was my fault," Willie offered, sitting forward as a precursor to getting up. "I know I've been overly sensitive about you… being interested in other people lately. That's on me, not you."

"It's okay for me to have other friends."

"I know. You're right."

"I'm not seeing anyone else. I'm not looking for anyone else. I just have some friends that you don't know very well. I'm not running away with anyone."

"Of course not," he agreed, voice gruff. "It's just that… I'm so much older than you are, and I don't fit in with that crowd in any way. I don't want to lose you to them."

"You're not going to."

Willie stood up. He offered Vic a hug, and she stepped into his arms. Her next words were muffled.

"And you're not losing me to crazy freaking Theresa, either, okay? I want to know where she is so that I know she's not going to show up at my door someday. Not because I want to see her again."

Willie chuckled. "Yeah."

"Good. So no more jealous boyfriend?"

"I'll… do my best. No promises."

Vic drew back to look at his face. She shook her head and looked over at Erin. "Why do men have to be so hard-headed?"

She and Willie headed back toward the back door and Vic's apartment. Terry waited until he heard the door close, and turned to Erin.

"Maybe because he has to be strong enough to survive butting heads with *her.*"

Chapter Twenty-One

ERIN AND VIC MADE a trip into the city to do a supply run for the bakery and, after getting everything they needed, headed over to the food court to grab a bit to eat before driving back to Bald Eagle Falls. Looking across the bustle of the food court at the mall, Erin saw a couple of familiar faces.

"Erin? Erin!" Vic tugged at her sleeve. "I was just asking you—" she followed Erin's gaze and saw the two boys. "Oh. There's Jeremy and Campbell."

"Joshua," Erin corrected. "Campbell is on house arrest."

Vic studied them across the milling lunch crowd. "Yeah. You're right. It's Joshua. What are they doing here? I didn't think they even knew each other. Jeremy is still new to Bald Eagle Falls, and he wouldn't have much opportunity to run into Joshua, when Jeremy's working and Joshua's at school."

"I don't know," Erin said slowly. The two young men had their heads together and were looking around surreptitiously. It was a good thing they weren't the ones working with Beaver, the way their furtive looks drew attention. "Something is going on."

"Shall we crash the party?" Vic suggested, grinning.

Erin wouldn't have dared if it weren't Vic's brother, but she figured Vic knew what she could get away with. They worked their way through the tables and throngs of people, and Jeremy and Joshua were so thick in conversation that they didn't notice the two women until they were only a few feet away.

"Vic!" Jeremy's face flushed instantly. "Hey, what are you doing here?"

"Erin and I needed to pick up some supplies for the house and the bakery. And what are you two up to? You've got to be the worst spies ever. You stand out like a strawberry in a bowl of peas."

"We're not doing anything," Jeremy protested. "Just happened to run into each other and were discussing the Cowboys and their chances at—"

"Oh, give me a break," Vic interrupted. "You were not talking football. I can read you like a book. Fill us in. What are you up to?"

Jeremy and Joshua exchanged looks.

98

"Are you going to get something to eat?" Erin suggested, figuring that maybe once everyone relaxed, she and Vic might have a better chance at getting the truth from Jeremy and Joshua.

Vic flashed her an irritated look, but Erin ignored it and continued to look at the boys for their response. Jeremy and Joshua eventually nodded.

"Great. I'll grab us a table before they all fill up."

She gave Vic a bill and her order, and everyone split up to get their food. Vic brought back a tray laden with both her lunch and Erin's and divided it up accordingly. The young men joined them with their fat burgers and supersized fries, and everyone settled in.

"So," Erin said after a few bites. "What are you guys up to?"

Jeremy rolled his eyes. "I should have known this was just a ploy. You," he pointed at Erin, "are devious. Much subtler than my sister here."

Erin just raised her brows. "We all needed to eat, didn't we? Why sit at different tables?"

Joshua looked at Jeremy, and then at the women. "Okay... I wanted to see if I could find Brianna. Get the story out of her. Find out what she knows about what happened."

"I see." Erin had suspected as much. She chewed slowly on her sub sandwich. "So... does Beaver know what you guys are doing?"

"I don't think she'd approve," Jeremy contributed. "I didn't tell her."

"Easier to get forgiveness than permission?"

"I don't need her permission to take a look around and ask some questions. I'm just showing some concern for a missing girl. If you were missing, you would want me to look for you, wouldn't you?"

Thinking of the times that she had been in trouble, Erin nodded. But Brianna wasn't in the same situation as Erin had been. She hadn't been attacked or kidnapped. She had run away out of fear of the authorities.

"I would, but that's not exactly our job, is it? You should leave it to Beaver and the police department."

"Do you really think they're looking for her?" Joshua asked. "I don't think anyone is looking for her. She's a runaway, not the victim of a crime. Police don't look for runaways. Especially when she's not even in town. If we try to report her missing in Bald Eagle Falls, the sheriff knows they're not going to find her there. If we try to report her missing here... they'll say the last place she was known to be was Bald Eagle Falls. And if she did come back here, then she's home, and she's not missing. People like her don't get the attention of the police. Not as missing persons."

"People like her?" Erin repeated.

Joshua looked around. He apparently didn't see anyone that concerned him, so he answered. "She doesn't have a permanent address. She moves around, so the cops are just going to say that she's moved on somewhere else. They don't look for homeless people. There's no indication of foul play. And she doesn't want to get arrested, so she's going to stay away from any cops she sees."

"How much do you know about her?" Vic demanded. "She's Campbell's girlfriend. What did he tell you? Did he tell you where to look for her?"

"He doesn't... exactly... know that I'm here."

"Not exactly," Vic repeated dryly.

"Okay, maybe not at all. I didn't exactly tell him. Just like Jeremy didn't tell Beaver. Campbell has said enough that I know a few places to look, people to talk to. I knew he wouldn't want me getting involved."

"But you got involved anyway."

"You think I want Cam going to prison?"

Vic shook her head, her expression softening. "I don't want him going to prison either. I don't think he's done anything bad enough to be sent to prison. But I don't want you getting hurt, either. What exactly are you guys poking your noses into out here? Drug dealing? You talk to the wrong person or say the wrong thing, and you could end up with a bullet between your eyes."

"I'm not going to let that happen," Jeremy said with certainty. He patted his side where, Erin had to assume, he had a concealed firearm.

"Going after drug dealers with a gun isn't exactly safe!" she protested.

"Shh." Jeremy frowned fiercely and looked around. "Watch what you say. We don't want to attract people's attention. I don't exactly have a permit for a concealed carry."

"Then what do you think you're doing? You think this is a good idea?" Erin shook her head and looked at Vic. "What about you? Tell them that's just stupid."

Vic shrugged. She didn't comment on the issue of weapons. She *did*, Erin knew, have a concealed carry permit, so at least she couldn't be arrested for that, but she had to believe that the boys going after potentially violent criminals was a bad idea.

"How much do you know about where she might be or who she might be with?" Vic asked. "If we can talk to her alone, without alerting anyone else, I don't see how that could be a bad thing." She gave a little grimace in Erin's direction, knowing that Erin was not going to be happy with her answer.

"We've got a few places to look," Jeremy said cautiously. "Between what Ro has said and what Campbell has said, we have a pretty good idea where to find her. But as far as talking to her alone without attracting anyone else's attention... that is a bit of a problem. And the fact that she probably won't want to talk to us or to have anything to do with us."

"Then, why are you here?" Erin asked, exasperated. It didn't seem like they had thought their plan through very well.

Jeremy fixed Erin with a penetrating gaze and raised one eyebrow. "Because you wouldn't ever consider doing something on your own, would you? *You* wouldn't investigate a crime without the police. Ask a few questions here or there to try to solve the crime?"

"I don't do that. I've just gotten… mixed up in things before. I wasn't really *investigating.*"

"Uh-huh. And when Terry was facing charges? You didn't investigate that? Try to get him off, even though the police were already involved and told you to stay out of it?"

"I just…" Erin tried to think of some excuse or explanation. "That was different."

"Because it wasn't a drug dealing?"

"It wasn't… it wasn't dangerous…"

"No. Terry and Jack Ward just happened to fall down and get tangled up in some rope, and to injure themselves in the process. And Bo just happened to die in custody, nothing to do with no one."

"But it wasn't organized crime, that was just crazy—"

"As far as you knew, it could have been one of the clans. You didn't know whether it was an official hit or a revenge killing or what. You knew it wasn't an accident, that it wasn't Terry."

Erin looked down at her plate, wishing that she could argue with his analysis, but it was impossible. She didn't think it was the same as looking for Brianna when she might be in the company of drug dealers or some other criminal element. Erin hadn't ever gone looking for trouble. She had just been following the clues.

"So where do we look first?" Vic asked.

Jeremy looked at her. "Not you. This is just Joshua and me. We're not getting… a couple of women involved."

"That doesn't stop a couple of women from joining you. You think it's okay to involve a teenager in this but not a couple of grown women? You know my skills are just as good as yours."

Vic's skills with a gun were considerable. But Erin hoped that those skills would not be required.

"Maybe we should rethink this," she suggested.

Jeremy rolled his eyes. "Look. Vic and I know how to protect ourselves. We're not going to run into anything dangerous, just see if we can find Brianna and talk to her. If she wants to come, then fine." He shrugged. "And Joshua knows more about this than anyone, so he's coming too. She's more likely to talk to him. He's less threatening, and Brianna knows him. She doesn't know me from Adam, and she's only seen Vic once. If you don't want to come, don't feel like you have to. We didn't plan on going in with a whole group. You get what you need and head back to Bald Eagle Falls."

There was no way Erin was going to leave them to find and confront Brianna by themselves. Jeremy, the oldest of the three, had just turned twenty-two. They might know how to handle firearms, but their brains weren't fully mature. Not the part that governed judgment and impulse control, which was exactly what they were going to need if they ran into trouble.

"I'll come… but you have to promise that you'll be careful and won't do anything dangerous. Those guns don't come out… unless we're in mortal danger. Everyone needs to stay calm and not overreact."

"Of course," Jeremy agreed, and the others nodded. "We're not expecting any gunplay. We're just taking precautions."

"I still don't like it."

"Then like I say… go home. There's nothing wrong with that."

"No. Someone has to keep an eye on you guys."

Chapter Twenty-Two

THEY DIDN'T DISCUSS IT any further as they ate. They talked about other things and laughed and didn't address the fact that they might be going into a dangerous situation and properly prepare for it. Once everyone was finished eating their meals, they discussed vehicles, deciding they should all go together in one car rather than splitting up. They could leave Erin's beater at the mall and return for it after they had talked to Brianna.

"Unless she's coming back with us," Erin said. "Will there be enough room for all five of us?"

Jeremy shook his head in disbelief. "First, she's not going to come back with us. We'll be lucky if she says anything at all that will help us. She's not going to go back to Bald Eagle Falls now that she's put it behind her. And second... you can put more than four people in a car."

"I just wasn't sure whether you had enough seatbelts..."

"I do. Not that it would kill anyone not to have a seatbelt on driving back to the mall."

Erin thought about the rollover that had killed her parents and put her in the hospital. "It could," she said. "That's the whole point."

Jeremy looked at her for a moment, then shrugged it off. "Doesn't matter. It's not going to be an issue. So. Are we ready to go?"

He and Joshua discussed where to go first, and they were soon on their way. Erin watched the streets they drove through change from clean, upscale commercial buildings and homes to rougher, dirtier, darker streets. There were more people out and about, walking or biking from place to place rather than driving cars, panhandling, talking, and conducting various transactions right out in the open. She swallowed and looked over at Vic.

"It's okay," Vic assured her, though her eyes were a little wider than usual. She was farm born and bred, and her only exposure to street life had been the short time she had been homeless in Bald Eagle Falls before Erin took her in. Bald Eagle Falls had little to no street crime. "We'll be just fine. In and out. We're just going in to talk, nothing else."

Erin wondered if she would say the same thing if she knew where Theresa was. They had walked into Theresa's web once; it wouldn't do to step into the nest of someone as bad as or worse than she was.

103

"You think Brianna's here?" Erin asked Joshua. "We're getting close?"

Joshua was looking down at his phone. Erin assumed he was trying to navigate where they should go rather than playing Pokémon or checking Facebook.

"Yeah. If we turn into the alley up here," Joshua pointed, "we should be able to get in and out without any trouble."

Erin looked around as Jeremy followed Joshua's instructions and pulled off of the main street, parking as close as he could to the building, behind a cluster of garbage bins. "You think this is a safe place to park? The car will be here when we get back?"

"It will be fine, Erin," Jeremy laughed. "You're being melodramatic."

He, like Vic, had no experience with the seamy underbelly of the city. The two of them might think that they had learned everything they needed to from their father and the rest of the Jackson clan, but operating under the protection of an organized crime family was utterly different from having to fend for oneself on the street.

Joshua led the way into the apartment building through the back entrance, up the stairs instead of the elevator, to a door that he counted off, since there were no numbers attached to them. He rubbed his hands on his jeans to wipe off the sweat.

"Are you sure this is the right one?" Erin asked.

"Sure… no. As sure as I can be. Campbell just mentioned it once. I wasn't taking notes or planning on coming here myself then."

Erin nodded. "Is this where she lives?"

"Sometimes?" Joshua's voice went up, making it a question. "There are a few places she could be; I'm just hoping… that we'll hit it lucky the first time." He glanced around the hallway, the dingy walls scarred by graffiti, and a thick, sweet smell in the air that Erin knew was rats. Along with the cooking smells of everything that had ever been heated over a hot plate in the place.

"Let's go," Jeremy encouraged, motioning for Joshua to knock on the door.

"We're going to make him do this?" Erin asked. "The youngest one in the group?"

"The least threatening," Vic reminded her.

Erin shook her head. She raised her fist and rapped on the door. Not a quiet, tentative knock, but the sharp, authoritative kind that said they meant business. Vic looked at her in surprise, an eyebrow raised.

"I'm not very threatening either," Erin said. "But if I act like someone's mom, maybe they'll show me some respect."

She was hoping that everyone inside the apartment was as young as Brianna was. Erin wasn't old enough to be the mother of anyone over the age of ten, and she didn't have the experience. She'd had enough foster moms that she hoped she could get the attitude and the look right. If they believed the act, maybe Erin could find something out.

She was raising her fist to bang on the door again when they heard the sound of a bolt sliding, and the door was opened a crack. Someone around Erin's height, her face darker than Brianna's, put her eye to the crack.

"Who are you?"

"I'm looking for Brianna," Erin told her in a strong, authoritative voice. "Is she here?"

"She don't live here."

"Maybe not, but she stays here. Open this door. I want to see her."

The girl on the other side of the crack didn't move. "Who are you?"

"I'm here to talk to Brianna."

"You a cop?"

"Do I look like a cop?" Erin demanded.

There was no reason she couldn't have been a cop. Beaver was a federal agent. There were plenty of female police officers. Most were probably taller and more muscular than Erin, but she still *could* have been. But most cops wouldn't be surrounded by a cadre of young adults, either. Eventually, the door opened wider, and Erin could see the girl who had answered it. She was a dark-skinned black girl with tightly-braided hair, wearing a halter top with nothing underneath it and short shorts. The spindly legs that stuck out from under the shorts were scarred, and she had a black eye and lump on her cheek that probably kept her from seeing anything out that side. She was wearing makeup, an orangy lipstick, and the mascara on her good eye had run down her face. She'd probably washed away the mascara on the other side with cold compresses.

"Who are you?" she asked again, looking over the group.

"I'm Cam's brother, Josh."

The girl's eyes went to him, and she nodded. The boys looked very similar, and she would have to have both eyes blackened shut not to recognize the resemblance. She backed up and let them in.

"Is she here?" Erin asked.

"I haven't seen her."

"You haven't seen her today?"

"Haven't seen her since she went home with Cam. She never come back."

"She didn't stay in Bald Eagle Falls. She didn't call you for a ride? Say she needed someone to pick her up, that she needed somewhere to stay?" Erin asked.

The girl shook her head. "She never called me." Her eyes went to Jeremy and Vic, then back to Joshua. "She wouldn't call me for a ride no-how. I don't have a car."

"How do you get around?" Joshua asked, looking concerned.

The boy had never seen that kind of poverty before. He had no idea how the world worked for people who didn't have all of the advantages that he had.

"I walk," the girl said, with a laugh of disbelief. "I get rides with someone. Sometimes. I never had a car."

"Oh." Joshua stared at her with open curiosity. "What's your name?"

"What's it to you?"

His eyes stayed on her. Erin wondered if that was how it had been with Campbell and Brianna too. That he'd been so fascinated with the novelty of her life that he'd been drawn in. He wanted a different experience from the one that he'd been living, and there it was. As different from him as if she came from a different country, all the way around the world.

"I'm Kim," the girl finally said, apparently deciding that Joshua wasn't going to come up with a good reason for asking, but there was no reason not to give it to him. "So what do you want with Brianna?"

"Campbell is looking for her."

"They have a fight?"

Joshua pursed his lips. He apparently didn't want to lie to her, but he didn't want to tell her the whole truth, either. If he told her that Brianna had run away and that the cops might be trying to get her on a drug charge, or that Campbell might change his mind and decide to testify against her, then Kim wouldn't have any reason to help them out. She'd know why Brianna had run. "They had... a misunderstanding. He had to go out, and she left in the middle of the night. He's worried about her. Something might have happened to her."

Kim studied him suspiciously. "He hit her?"

"No! Campbell wouldn't do that! He's not that kind of guy."

"Everybody is that kind of guy, sooner or later." Kim pinned Vic down with her gaze. "Mark my words," she warned. She looked again at Jeremy, distrustful. She had determined that Joshua wasn't a threat, but she wasn't so sure about Jeremy. Older, wiser, bigger, and more of a threat.

"Not everyone," Vic said softly.

Kim rolled her eyes. "Who do you think knows more about it? You or me?" She indicated her black eye. "I know what they're like."

"Can I use your bathroom?" Joshua asked. "I'm sorry, I wouldn't ask, but the gas station down there," he indicated the way they had come. "I didn't think that would be the safest place to stop."

"You'd be right," she agreed with a snort. She shrugged. "Go ahead. But mind your own business. Keep your nose out of mine."

Joshua nodded and went in the direction she indicated. Not that there was anywhere else to go. They stood in the combination kitchen/living room area, and the bathroom and bedroom could only be through the hall on the other side of the living room. The living room was filled will all kinds of trash. There were clothes and old bags of fast food, flies buzzing around the bags and bouncing against the glass of the dirty window. Erin deduced that other people were living there. Not just Kim. Not just Brianna. Probably a few more of them, sleeping on the couch and the floor as well as whatever mattress or bed was in the bedroom.

Erin heard the bathroom door bang shut. There was the noise of the handle turning and jiggling, and the door banging against the doorframe a few times. Then Joshua apparently figured out that it wasn't going to latch properly, and quickly attended to his business before someone could barge in on him. He was back a couple of minutes later, sweat on his face, complexion pale. He nodded to Kim.

"Thanks. So… you know when Brianna will be back?"

"I told you she wasn't here." She gave him a knowing look. Of course she knew that Joshua's only reason for going to the bathroom had been to provide him with an opportunity to check out the rest of the apartment that he couldn't see from the doorway.

Joshua shrugged in embarrassment.

"I don't know when she's coming back or if she's coming back," Kim said. "Your guess is as good as mine."

"Do you know where else she would go? Is there somewhere else she can stay?"

"I don't know where she would go. She doesn't report to me."

"Does she have a friend? Someone other than Campbell or you? Who would help her out if she was in trouble?"

"What trouble?"

"Nothing. Just if she was in trouble? Where would she go?"

"She wouldn't come back here. She'd go away. Somewhere you couldn't find her."

"She'd have to go to someone. Someone who could help her out."

Kim shook her head. "She wouldn't have to. She knows how to look after herself. She could get herself some cash and a fix and be all set."

Joshua looked at her for another minute, then shrugged, unsure of how to proceed. He looked at Jeremy for help. None of them had any suggestions. Eventually, Joshua led the way back out the door, and Kim closed the door and slid the bolt behind them. Joshua led the way back to the car in silence, and Erin was relieved to find that it was still there and in one piece. They all piled back in.

"So there wasn't anyone else there?" Vic asked.

"There were some others in the bedroom. Not Brianna." Joshua shook his head slowly. "I can't believe people live that way. Why would anyone choose to live like that?"

"Not everyone has a choice," Erin said. "You make do however you can."

"But they could go to a shelter. Salvation Army. Get help from social programs. There are lots of social programs, lots of people out there to help."

"Most of them won't take addicts. And working girls take pride in being able to help themselves. Even if they've got a pimp taking most of the money and controlling everything in their lives. Not everyone has a choice."

"Campbell was out here by choice. Why would he do that? This can't be the kind of life he wants to lead."

"I don't think it is," Erin agreed. "I think he just wanted something different. He wanted to get away. He's probably not living somewhere like that. He's got friends with jobs who can make the rent on a decent place. He couch surfs. Crashes here or there for a few days. He probably saw the way Brianna was living, and…"

"And brought her home for Thanksgiving," Joshua finished. "He wanted to save her." He thought about that for a few minutes. "He kept saying that she wasn't his girlfriend. Maybe he just wanted to get her out of there. To show her a different kind of life. To try to help her."

Jeremy shifted the car into drive and cleared his throat. "You said you had a couple of other ideas. Where else?"

Joshua hesitated. "I don't know. We should probably just go home. If they're all like that…"

"We came all the way out here. Might as well do the job right. If Brianna knows what's going on, if she can help get Campbell out of trouble…"

"I don't think any of her friends are going to be able to help. Not people like her."

"They won't all be like Kim," Erin said. "She probably has a few people she can touch when she needs something. People who feel sorry for her and give her a bit of help now and then."

"I don't know…"

"Give me the next place," Jeremy said firmly. "We're going to check."

Chapter Twenty-Three

THE NEXT PLACE JOSHUA knew about was a second-story flat over a dilapidated bar. No matter how many times they knocked or called out, they couldn't get anyone to answer the door. Jeremy tried to peer in the windows.

"I'm sure there's someone home. We could break the glass…"

"We're not breaking any windows," Erin told him.

"I might be able to do something about this lock," Jeremy said doubtfully, studying the hefty-looking bolt. Erin had caught him using a bump key before, and doubted that he had much experience or skill with a pick. That security bolt would need more than a little skill. It would be simpler to break the door through the unreinforced wooden frame than it would be to pick it. But they weren't going to do that.

"Let's just go," she said. "If there's someone home, they aren't going to let us in, and they aren't going to stay put while someone breaks the door down. You'll get a shotgun blast in the chest if you try. I don't think Brianna's here."

"She could be," Vic disagreed.

Erin wasn't sure why she was arguing. Erin was pretty sure Vic wasn't going to stand for breaking into someone else's house either. So what were they going to do? Wait out there until someone decided to come out or go in?

"If Brianna saw Joshua out here, she would come out to talk to him," Erin told Vic. "She'd come tell him to get lost, or to tell Campbell to stop harassing her. She's not here. Probably another girl like Kim, cowering in there, waiting for us to go away, so she knows she's safe again."

An apartment over a bar like that—there were probably several girls living there, providing cheap entertainment to the patrons. Working all night and trying to sleep during the day.

"Let's go. Is that the last place?"

"No… I got one more." Joshua sighed. "Ten minutes, and we'll be done."

Joshua and the others looked relieved when they saw the next place Joshua directed them to, but Erin got a tight feeling in her chest. It was a nice place, an upscale hotel with a manager at the desk who watched them like a hawk. The carpet in the lobby was plush, with no stains or burn marks. The elevator appeared to be modern and fully operational—nothing like the abject poverty of the first two places.

Erin eyed the suspicious manager. "Do you know which floor?" she asked Joshua in a murmur. She didn't want to have to ask the staff. They would just run them out. They needed to act as if they knew exactly where they were going and had been invited. Anything less would end up with them out on their butts on the street. Maybe the police would be called as well, just to make sure they hurried on their way.

"Yeah, fourth floor," Joshua said, looking at the plaque beside the elevator. There were meeting rooms, a business center, and a fitness room on the first couple of floors. Nothing was marked for the fourth floor, just regular rooms.

They got on the elevator and Vic punched the button. They were silent as it rose to the appointed floor.

Everything was quiet. No shouting. No noise from behind the corridor of closed doors. Erin shifted anxiously. Everything looked perfectly fine. Clean, well-appointed, no foul smells. So completely opposite from any of the other places that Brianna might have run to. Erin was afraid of what they were going to find.

She didn't knock on the door. Jeremy gave her a questioning look, then stepped forward and knocked himself. They didn't have to hammer on the door and call out this time. Within a minute, the door handle turned and the door whispered open. This door was also opened by a young woman, but one who looked a lot better than Kim had. She wore a kimono dressing gown, but her hair and makeup were immaculate. Erin could smell the fresh scent of soap and shampoo, but no heavy perfumes. The girl looked over the visitors and raised an eyebrow.

"How may I help you?"

"Uh…" Jeremy cleared his throat. He put his hands behind his back, awkward and unsure what to do with them. "We're looking for Brianna?"

Her brows drew down. "Brianna?" She paused, thinking about it. "You'd better come in."

She led them into the living room of a large suite. She called toward the bedroom. "Mickey? We have company."

There was a muttered curse, then the squeak of a desk chair, and in a moment, an older man entered the room.

The smell of his cologne hit Erin like a punch in the gut. She looked back toward the door they had entered through, measuring the route to escape. She grasped Vic's arm. "We've got to go."

Vic resisted, giving Erin a puzzled frown. Erin turned to Joshua. "Come on. Let's get out of here."

He shook his head. They all looked at her as if she had just sprouted two heads. Erin's heart was racing. She couldn't understand why they didn't feel it too. The man was dangerous. She had known something was wrong going into the apartment, and her senses were all ringing alarm bells with the man's entrance.

"What is all this?" he asked. He looked at the four of them, and then at the girl, snapping something at her that Erin didn't understand. Erin was still holding on to Vic's arm. She dug her fingers in, hanging on for dear life.

Mickey was a medium height and build, giving the impression of compact efficiency. His neatly trimmed hair was graying around the temples. He was dressed in business attire, not a hood like Volkov, but he spoke with a Russian accent.

Jeremy was only then starting to get an inkling of the danger they were in. He licked dry lips and addressed Mickey.

"We're looking for Brianna. Someone said that she might be around here. That she came here sometimes."

"Brianna." Mickey looked at the girl. "Which one is she?"

The girl in the dressing gown looked at them, then back at the Russian. "The black girl. With Wolf. The one who—"

"Why are you looking for her?" Mickey cut across the girl's words. His gaze fixed on Erin. "Why would she be here?"

"She might have thought she was in trouble," Erin said, stammering for an explanation. "She disappeared and we just wanted to make sure she was okay. That nothing happened to her. Someone thought that she could have come here. I don't know; maybe she does some work for you…"

His eyes drifted away from Erin, discounting her. He took a step closer to Joshua, studying him carefully.

"You are the boyfriend."

"No. No, that was my brother. I mean, he wasn't her boyfriend, but he's the one who knows her. We look a lot alike."

"Where is your brother now?"

"There was some trouble. He couldn't come. But he was worried about Bree. I thought… I'd help him out."

"You go in the bedroom," Mickey told the girl. "Leave us alone."

She didn't argue. She walked out of the room, and Erin heard the bedroom door click behind her. She pulled on Vic's arm, desperate for them to get out of there. Vic used her other hand to pry Erin loose. It was clear from her expression that she was starting to get uncomfortable with the situation as well. Mickey ran his eyes restlessly over the group.

"Brianna is not here. You can see that. She doesn't live here. She does not…" his words were overly precise, "hang out."

Erin nodded and moved an inch closer to the door.

"It was a mistake to come here," Mickey advised.

"We're sorry," Erin said. "We'll go now."

"You," Mickey pointed at Jeremy. "And you." He pointed at Vic. "Remove your weapons slowly and put them on the table."

Jeremy and Vic looked at each other. Erin didn't know whether she wanted them to obey the Russian or to pull their guns to cover the group as they tried to leave the hotel room. Mickey didn't have a weapon trained on them, but Erin had felt threatened from the instant he walked into the room. He was probably armed. There were probably others close by—if not in the hotel suite, then in one of the rooms next door or across the hall. Mickey might have already given them a signal. They could be listening to what was going on in the room through a bug or an earwig. There could even be video surveillance. It would be impossible to spot the tiny spy cameras that were available to anyone who wanted one, certainly to the Russian mob.

But there was no one else in sight; it might be their last chance to make a break for it and get out of the hotel room. Erin watched to see what Jeremy and Vic would decide to do. The instant they made a move, she would be ready to act.

Jeremy first raised both hands to chest height, palms toward the Russian to show that he wasn't a threat. He pulled his jacket aside and then his shirt up to display the concealed carry holster at his hip. With the other hand, he slowly reached across his body and used two fingers to pull out the handgun. He bent over and laid it gently on the coffee table. Erin breathed a sigh of relief that he hadn't tried to shoot Mickey and that Mickey had not done anything to him.

Yet. Once Jeremy and Vic were both disarmed, he would have the four of them at his mercy.

Jeremy straightened up. He lifted his shirt and spun in a full circle to show that he didn't have a second holster in his waistband.

"And yours," Mickey told Vic.

Vic followed Jeremy's example, carefully removing her gun from a holster snugged up to her bra. Erin wondered how Mickey had seen either one of them. Even knowing that the two were armed, she hadn't been able to see either holster. But the Russian probably had a lot more experience in the matter than Erin did.

The four of them exchanged glances. They were now defenseless, at Mickey's mercy. Best case scenario, he would send them on their way. Erin wasn't expecting the best. She closed her eyes and tried to regulate her breathing.

Her thoughts went to Terry. Was she ever going to see him again? If Mickey killed them, would Terry even know what had happened? Or would they just disappear and he would always be left wondering what had happened in those final moments?

"Sit down," Mickey ordered. Erin opened her eyes and saw him pointing to the couch and chairs in a conversational grouping. He bent down and picked up the two guns and casually moved them across the room, leaving them on top of the minibar out of everyone's reach.

As they nervously sat down, Mickey looked over his shoulder toward the bedroom that the girl had retreated to. There had been no sound of the door opening, and likewise no noise from the TV or shower to indicate what she was doing. Was she lounging on the bed reading a book or having a nap, unconcerned with what happened to their 'guests,' or was she perched there, knees drawn up to her chest, tensely awaiting the sound of gunfire or cries for help?

Mickey went over to the window and looked out, his back to them. Erin glanced at the others for their reactions. Should they make a break for it while his back was turned? Or was that what he was waiting for them to do? Then he would whirl around and shoot them, or his goons would be waiting outside the hotel room door waiting for them?

No one made any move.

Mickey turned around and looked them over, leaning against the windowsill behind him.

"What happened to Brianna?"

They all looked at each other, trying to figure out how to answer him. His voice was neutral, his face an impassive mask. He wanted to know how much they knew. Or did he really want to know about Brianna?

He could have shot them all when he'd picked up their guns. There were enough bullets in those two guns to shoot them all several times over, making sure that he had done a thorough job. If he were a Russian mobster, he could probably put a bullet into each of their foreheads before they knew what was happening.

Those guys didn't play games.

"Tell me," he prompted. "You come here to find her, so you tell me what you know."

Joshua was the first one to give in. "She was staying at our house. She came for Thanksgiving. When Campbell got arrested, Mom told her she could still stay there. Until he got out on bail and they could figure out what to do. Brianna said she didn't have a car or any money. And there are no hotels in Bald Eagle Falls. A couple of B&B's, but she couldn't have afforded them even if they agreed to take her, and they wouldn't."

Mickey was watching Joshua intently. "Because she was black?"

"Black, homeless, an addict. The whole package. No one would want her in their house."

"Except your mother."

"She would do that for Campbell. She'd do anything for him. It wasn't anything for her to put up Brianna for a couple of nights. She just wanted Campbell back, and if she helped his friend when she was in trouble, that would go a long way to convincing him that she just wanted him to be happy."

"Then what?"

"That was it. When we got up Saturday morning, Brianna was gone. She didn't leave a note, but she didn't steal anything either. Just managed to find a way out of Bald Eagle Falls. She must have called someone or hitchhiked."

"Why do you say that?"

"She wasn't anywhere in Bald Eagle Falls. I looked around. It isn't like living in the city; there's nowhere to go. Nowhere she could be overnight. And she didn't have any friends."

"Did she know anyone? Meet anyone?"

"Just us. Me and my mom. Erin and Vic came over when Cam was arrested, so Brianna met them, but she didn't go to their house."

Erin and Vic shook their heads in unison.

"And where else? Did she know where you worked? She could not just disappear without help."

"We work at the bakery," Erin explained. "My bakery. She wasn't there." She rubbed her temples, trying to soothe the pounding.

Mickey paced back and forth across the room, slowly, deep in thought. He turned around and faced Joshua.

"What did Beaver say?"

Chapter Twenty-Four

J OSHUA'S MOUTH HUNG OPEN, shocked. Erin was sure she looked pretty much the same as he did. She tried to adjust her thinking. Mickey knew Beaver?

"What does Beaver say?" Joshua echoed.

Mickey leaned in slightly. "What did she think? That Brianna ran? That something happened to her? Is she looking? I don't understand what you are doing here, looking for her. A bunch of kids. Isn't she already in enough trouble for using Cam?"

"How do you know about that?" Jeremy asked.

Mickey shrugged. "It is my business to know. Everything that goes on here."

"Are you an informant?"

"I... have information," Mickey said cagily.

"And you know Ro? Beaver? You give her information?"

"You are getting off track. Why is *she* not here? Why has she not called me? What has happened?"

"You know about Volkov," Erin said, finding her voice.

Mickey looked at her. "The baker," he said flatly. "Would Brianna go to you? No. She did not know you. But maybe she knew where the bakery was. Maybe Cam pointed it out to her. So she told Volkov to meet her there."

"And...? Then what?"

"You tell me the rest of the story." He folded his arms and leaned back slightly, adopting a casual stance. "Go ahead."

"I don't know. None of us know. Was Brianna connected to Volkov? Was he her drug dealer?"

"He was... many things to her."

Erin swallowed. She tried to read Mickey's face, but it was impossible. He didn't twitch. Didn't give anything away.

"*You* were there," she said finally. "Why don't *you* tell us what happened?"

"Erin!" The cry came from Vic, a yelp of protest. A warning.

"Mickey was there?" the Russian gave a chuckle. "What would Mikhail be doing there? There is no reason for me to be in Bald Eagle Falls."

115

"Maybe *you* were the one she called. Not Volkov. Maybe you went to meet her. Or maybe Volkov called you, because he figured you would want to know that something was up. Maybe there was a reason you would want to know that Brianna had left Campbell's house and was trying to get out of Bald Eagle Falls."

"Why would I care? She is nothing to me. Just a used-up junkie."

"Then why were you there?" Erin asked.

Mickey chuckled. "I like this one," he said to no one in particular. "And you knew the minute I walked into the room. I could see that. How?"

"The smell. Your cologne or aftershave. I could smell that when Stayner opened Volkov's car door. Just for an instant."

"So he uses the same cologne. It is Russian. Why not?"

Erin shook her head. He had as much as confirmed that he had been there. Had he seen Volkov before he died? After? Had he been the one to kill him?

Mickey gazed at her steadily, his face still expressionless, and she wondered if he were trying to think of the best way to kill her and dispose of her body.

"Where is Campbell?" he asked.

"He's at home." Joshua was the one to answer. "He's on electronic monitoring; he can't leave the house, or go more than two hundred yards, anyway. If he came here, they'd put him back in jail."

"So he told you to come here? Told you where to go, that you might find Brianna here?"

Joshua looked around at the others. He hadn't been very forthcoming up until then about how he had gotten the information from Campbell. But it was no longer a matter of just looking around in the city to see if they could discover where Brianna had disappeared to.

"I talked to him before. Sometimes. While he was in the city. He'd call late at night or early in the morning, when he was mellow, and he'd talk about what he was doing. Who he saw and where he'd gone, what things had happened. He didn't always remember what he'd talked about the next time. I guess maybe he was a little buzzed."

"So he didn't tell you where to look. He said that he'd been here," Erin said.

Joshua shook his head. "He said that Brianna had come here. Not him. He'd followed her to see what she was doing. But he didn't get inside."

Unsurprisingly, Mickey did not jump in to tell them what Brianna had been to his hotel room for. Erin thought about the things that Beaver said the Wolf had been involved with. Drugs, prostitution, other human trafficking. Who knew what else. She suspected by Mickey's demeanor that he was not just a street soldier, low down on the totem pole. He was one of the bosses. Pricey hotel room, girls at his beck and call, whatever else he wanted. Had Brianna been there to entertain him? To run drugs? Maybe the drugs in Campbell's car *had* been her delivery, and she just hadn't had a chance to pass them on to whoever they were supposed to be going to. Volkov, waiting behind the bakery? Falling asleep because he'd had to wait for so long without any sign of her? And then...? Who had killed him? Mickey? Erin couldn't connect it up.

Mickey sat on the edge of the arm of the couch Jeremy and Vic were sitting on. He reached into his pocket, and Erin couldn't help holding herself tense, waiting for the inevitable weapon. Now that he had their story, now that he knew everything that they knew and whether he was safe or not, he could dispose of them.

But he pulled out a phone. Propped there on the arm of the couch, he tapped in a number and held it up to his ear. It didn't ring for very long. With the length of time that it sometimes took cellphones to connect, Erin suspected that it probably hadn't rung more than once on the recipient's end.

Looking at Erin, Mickey spoke into his phone. "We have a problem."

Chapter Twenty-Five

IME STOOD STILL. NOT entirely still, but it ground down to such a slow speed that Erin could feel every one of her heartbeats and the space in between, even though her heart was thumping fast in anticipation of danger.

The voice that answered the other end was loud enough to hear across the room, and it was a voice that Erin recognized.

"What's up, Mickey?" Beaver asked.

"Got some kids sneaking around here. Asking questions, poking their noses where they don't belong. You know I don't like people poking their noses in my business."

"What are you worried about? What kids?"

"That's just it. One of them looks like the one you were running. Cam."

They all looked at Joshua while they waited for Beaver to answer. She didn't respond immediately. Several long and painful heartbeats passed before there was any response from Beaver. A little quieter this time, the first sign that she was concerned.

"A kid that looks like Cam? Maybe his younger brother?"

"Yeah. How do you want me to get rid of them?"

"Don't say anything to them. Just tell them to mind their own business and get out of your way," Beaver suggested sensibly.

"They're asking about Brianna. I thought you said she didn't have anything to do with Wolf's death?"

"She didn't." Beaver cleared her throat.

"You're sure?"

"There's no evidence that she was at the scene. No fingerprints. No one saw her. No one who has connected the two of them."

"She called him."

"If she did, they were both using burners. And he didn't have it on him when he died."

"Because she took it."

"Mickey…" Beaver's voice was reproachful. "You're paranoid. I told you, there's no evidence that she called him. Where would she get another phone? She had no money, and any she did have went straight into drugs."

"He give it to her." Beaver couldn't see his shrug. "He decided he wants to keep her on the hook. So he gives her a hit. Gets her a phone. Tells her to call him if she needs anything. Your boy gets arrested for drug possession, so she calls. *Help me get away from this place before they arrest me too.* So Wolf goes. And…"

"And what?" Beaver repeated. "She kills him? Why would she? He's her meal ticket. He gets Brianna her next job, her next fix. She has no motive to kill him when he shows up to help her. And she needed a car, so why didn't she take his car?"

"Where is Brianna?"

"Where? How am I supposed to know? She took off. She's in the wind."

"I don't like these kids showing up."

"No," Beaver agreed. "Neither do I. They shouldn't be interfering. They're going to put themselves in harm's way, just by being around there. Tell them to go home if they know what's good for them. I'll talk with Joshua. Tell him to leave this alone or he's going to end up in a cell next to Campbell."

Joshua swallowed, looking green.

"I have to go," Mickey said. He tapped the phone screen to end the call.

For a few minutes, Mickey just sat there looking at them. He slid his phone back in his pocket.

"You coming here was stupid. If others had been here… there is only so much I could do. You do not want to end up killed," he said baldly. "You do not want these ladies," he indicated Erin and Vic, "to end up in the game. You think it cannot happen? One taste of China Girl, maybe two, and they will do anything to get another dose. A-ny-thing," he said it as if it were three words. "Beaver has been on this for months. You think you can come in here and blunder around and not screw everything up? She will not thank you for ruining a case they put hundreds of man-hours and millions of dollars into."

Erin put her hands over her burning eyes, the headache that had started in her temples banging behind her eyes. Everyone was deathly quiet.

"So go home," Mickey said finally. "Now I have to figure out how to clean up this mess."

He looked toward the bedroom, scowling. The girl who had let them into the hotel room had seen all of them and could put them together with Mickey. She had heard them inquire after Brianna. She hadn't witnessed anything beyond the initial introductions, but Mickey was going to have to figure out how to keep word of their visit quiet.

They got up, all moving slowly, still worried that anything they did could set Mickey off and make him change his mind. Just because he had told them to go home, that didn't mean he wouldn't do anything if he decided they were too big of a risk. He might be helping Beaver out, but he would still be running his illegal business operations as well. He had to stay involved to give her any help.

Jeremy took a short step toward the minibar.

"No," Mickey snapped. "Leave them where they are. Do you know how stupid it is, coming in here armed? You think you are Magnum PI? Maybe you lose your guns, you think twice about where you take them next time."

Jeremy looked toward his gun, then looked at Vic. She sighed and shrugged. It wasn't worth the risk for either of them to disobey him to see how serious he was. They all walked single-file to the door.

"Have a nice day," Mickey told them.

They let the door shut behind them and left the building without speaking to each other.

Chapter Twenty-Six

HEY WERE A SUBDUED group as they drove back to the mall to get Erin's car. They agreed to drive back to Bald Eagle Falls separately, in the same configuration as they had arrived, so as not to arouse any suspicions. Jeremy would drop Joshua at home, and then he would meet the girls at Erin's house.

Erin and Vic drove back to Bald Eagle Falls with little discussion of what had just happened. Erin wondered whether Vic understood what kind of an organization Mickey and Wolf and Brianna and Campbell were involved with. Vic had been on her own for only a very short time before Erin had rescued her, and before that had grown up on the farm, which Erin had to assume was sheltered from the type of street life that went on in the big city. She might not have understood as well as Erin, who had seen more of life on the streets, what kind of danger they had put themselves in.

Vic wiped at her face and sniffled, looking out the side window. Erin realized she was crying and swerved momentarily, looking for a tissue or some other way to comfort her friend.

"It's okay," she assured Vic. "We're going to be okay. If he was going to do anything to us, he would have done it while we were there. As long as we stay out of the way, he'll leave us alone. And anyone else... Beaver's already got an eye on it, and we'll set the burglar alarm, and Terry is right there if anything goes sideways..."

"I'm not worried about him coming after us," Vic sniffled. She searched in her purse and found a tattered tissue, which she dabbed at her eyes, trying not to mess up her carefully applied makeup. "It's just... I guess it's just hitting me, how close we came..." She took a deep breath and let it go. "If he hadn't been working with Beaver... or like he said, if there were other people there and he couldn't do anything to protect us... We were unarmed and totally at his mercy."

Erin nodded.

"And Brianna?" Vic asked, her voice going up questioningly. "Do you think... do you think she's dead too?"

121

"I don't know." Erin exercised all of the willpower she had to keep Vic's tears from making her break down too. She was driving, trying to keep up with Jeremy's reckless highway speeds, and she couldn't afford to let her eyes blur. "I don't know if she left on her own, or if something happened to her..."

"What if she's the one who killed Wolf?"

"Like Mickey said... why? If he was the one who supplied her with drugs and helped her, why would she kill him?"

"Because it happens all the time, Erin. Lovers get into fights. Pimps beat up their girls, and maybe she tried to defend herself. People on drugs do crazy things that don't make any sense logically."

"Well... yes. But Beaver doesn't think that's what happened."

"Neither of them knows where she went."

"Maybe that's good. Maybe it means she's safe somewhere, where no one knows where she is."

Vic sniffled and nodded. By the time they got back to Mary Lou's house, everyone was dry-eyed and appeared calm. Vic had managed not to wash away too much of her makeup, so that her moment of tears was undetectable. "And don't you dare tell Jeremy I cried!" she warned Erin.

"Why would I tell Jeremy?"

"I don't know. Just don't."

They dropped Joshua off at home. They watched him in to make sure that he was safe. And then they drove on to Erin's house.

Erin was glad to be home. It was getting late and the street lights were starting to come on. The lights inside the house were bright and warm and inviting. Erin was looking forward to a warm bath and hot cup of tea, and then to a long, undisturbed night's sleep.

She could wish, couldn't she?

She led the others into the house, feeling the tension fall away from her. She was home, and she was safe. She could cuddle with Terry and fall asleep in his arms. No more thinking about Mickey and what he might have done.

She was expecting to find Terry sitting on the couch, watching TV and waiting for her to get home. He would be wondering why they had been held up for so long in the city when they had just gone to look for a couple of things. Erin had texted on the way back that they had been held up but were on their way, but she would need to think of something to tell him to explain the delay.

But it wasn't Terry sitting on the couch; it was Beaver. And for once, she wasn't grinning and cracking her gum.

Chapter Twenty-Seven

IC AND JEREMY ENTERED behind Erin. They had both been talking in lowered voices, but stopped when they saw Beaver.

Beaver sat on the couch, one foot up on the coffee table and one foot on the floor, knee jutting out at an angle. On one hand, she looked completely relaxed and comfortable, but on the other, she was intense and serious, so far from what was normal that they knew they were in big trouble.

"Did y'all have a nice day shopping?"

Erin swallowed. The others didn't answer either. What were they going to do? Lie to Beaver? She clearly knew what had happened already.

"Doesn't look like you bought very much," Beaver noted. "Day ended up being a bust?"

"Yeah," Jeremy agreed, trying to force humor into his voice. "Looks like we're busted."

"And not just by me, either."

Jeremy shifted uncomfortably. "I'm sorry, Ro. We didn't mean to get in the middle of anything. I hope... we didn't screw up your op."

"Sit down."

Her nod indicated that the instruction was to all of them. Jeremy sat on the couch beside Beaver, but he didn't cuddle up to her like he normally would, looking awkward and uncomfortable.

"Joshua made his curfew?" Beaver asked lightly.

"We took him home first."

"Does Mary Lou know what happened?"

"Not unless Joshua decides to tell her."

"He didn't tell her he was in contact with Campbell while he was in the city; I don't think he would tell her about... this," Erin said.

"I'll touch base with him later. What exactly did Cam tell him?"

"It sounds like... pretty much everything where Brianna was concerned. Joshua had a list of places to look for her."

"And no luck?" Beaver asked, looking at each of them and meeting their eyes. "No sign of her?"

"No sign of her. I would guess... she got on a bus and kept going."

"Except she didn't have any money," Vic pointed out. "So how could she buy a bus ticket?"

"Turn a few tricks," Beaver said with a shrug. "Or she hitchhiked or took off with a friend. I hope that's what happened."

"What do *you* think happened?" Erin asked.

Beaver looked at her for a minute. "That would be for me to investigate, Miss Erin. Not you."

"Don't bust her chops," Jeremy said, rubbing his forehead. "She's the one who was trying to talk us out of looking for Brianna. And who got a whiff that something was wrong at Mickey's."

Beaver nodded slowly. "At least someone's got some sense. You should pay more attention to her."

Erin's cheeks got warm.

"There are a lot of heavy hitters involved here," Beaver said. "Wolf getting killed is not a good sign."

Erin was tired and shaky, coming down off of the adrenaline rush brought on by the danger they had faced at Mickey's.

Beaver chewed slowly, looking at them. "You were actually *at* Mickey's? He didn't just get word that you were asking questions?"

"We didn't know," Jeremy protested. "We thought... it was just somewhere a friend lived. She'd crashed there, like Cam was crashing with friends."

"Really. You thought she had a friend who could afford a place like that."

Jeremy looked at Vic and then at Erin. "I guess... yeah. I didn't think anything of it. I mean... Campbell was hanging out with this crowd, and he wasn't homeless. He could go back to Bald Eagle Falls anytime, and his mom's got a nice place. I mean, I know they lost their money, but they still live in a nice house. So maybe... Brianna's folks lived in a nice place. Or some other friend or relative that she hoped would help her out."

"And you?" Beaver looked at Erin.

"I didn't feel good about it. I didn't want to go in. The kind of people that operate out of a hotel, with young girls coming and going... she didn't go there looking for a handout or a couch to crash on."

"No, she didn't," Beaver agreed. "You should have listened to that warning voice."

Erin nodded. She had only been one of four, but she had been the oldest and most experienced and should have been more assertive about not going in. She should have put her foot down and told them no. But she didn't know if they would have listened. If they had gone in without her, would the results have been any different?

"We're really sorry," Jeremy repeated. "Are you going to be in trouble for this? I wasn't acting on anything you said, it was what Cam had told Joshua..."

"You know my head is already on the chopping block for Cam's part in this. If he's telling Joshua this stuff when he was clearly instructed to keep his mouth shut… who knows what else he might have said to other parties. Who he might have accidentally tipped off. I thought he was a good bet, but this is turning out to be a disaster."

"You couldn't have known that he would say something when he wasn't supposed to," Jeremy commiserated.

"It's my job to know. I'm supposed to be able to judge when someone is ready and when they're a bad risk. I should have known that he was too young and impulsive." Beaver's words clearly encompassed Jeremy and Vic as well, and they both looked shamefaced. Beaver had picked Jeremy to be her partner, even knowing that he was so much younger than she was, and had been involved at some level with the Jackson clan. Jeremy agreeing to go with Joshua to the city to help him find Brianna had clearly been a poor choice.

Erin wondered whether Beaver's words were true of her too. Was she any better than the teens, sure that they could just rush in and rescue Brianna?

"What's done is done," Beaver said briskly, and cracked her gum so loudly it made Erin jump. "No way to go back and change it now. But going forward… I'm going to have to see what can be done to salvage the situation."

They all sat around the living room, not sure what to do or say next. Beaver slapped her hands down on her thighs.

"I've got my car, so you don't need to wait for me," she told Jeremy. "I'll catch up with you."

Jeremy took the dismissal well, looking relieved. He had probably been wondering, as Erin had, whether that would be it for their relationship. "Okay." He stood up, giving Beaver a swift peck on the cheek on the way to his feet. "I'll see you tonight."

"If I get there," she said. "Don't know for sure what the night will bring."

"Okay. Then… whenever."

Vic decided it was time for her to go too. "Don't know if Willie's back yet or not. You'll be okay?" she asked Erin.

Erin nodded. "Yeah. Thanks. I'll be fine."

Beaver pretended to be gathering her things as Jeremy and Vic said goodbye and departed. She straightened and looked at Erin when they were alone.

"I'm sorry too," Erin told Beaver. "I should have been… more insistent."

"What did you think of Mikhail?"

It took Erin a minute to remember that Mickey had referred to himself once as Mikhail. A much more Russian version of the name.

"He scared me. We were all surprised to find out he was working with you. I'm worried… he might be involved in Brianna's disappearance and Wolf's murder."

Beaver nodded briefly. "What did he say?"

"Not very much… he wanted to know what had happened, why we were looking for her. He said she and Wolf were involved… I don't know any details, but I guess you know that already. He didn't say that much more to us than he did to you."

"You have good instincts. I think you read people well."

Erin thought about how many time she had been mistaken about who had committed a crime. Who had been guilty and who had been innocent. Who had been safe and who was dangerous. She couldn't agree with Beaver's assessment.

"Sometimes, maybe. I miss a lot."

"We all do. Hundreds of signals every day. What's really surprising is that any of us can get along and communicate with each other, considering how little we understand about human interaction."

Erin laughed. "Well, that's comforting."

"Why do you think he was involved with Wolf's death?"

"Were they rivals? Partners? Did they work together, or was Brianna playing two different sides against each other?"

"Probably all of the above. Alliances change. You've heard that there's no honor among thieves? It's true. And no honor among murderers, mobsters, pimps, or any other classification of criminal. Wolf and Mikhail are similar in a lot of ways—passionate, changeable, egotistical, greedy. They may look different, try to brand themselves as a different class of criminals, but they're still cousins. They're still very similar under the skin."

"They're cousins?"

"I didn't mean it literally, but these Russians all are, if you go back far enough. So… you didn't answer the question. Why do you think he was involved in Wolf's death? Just because they're the only two Russian mobsters you've run into lately? Because he was connected to Brianna?"

"No. It's silly. I shouldn't even mention it."

"Mention away."

"You're going to think it's nothing."

"So what? It takes hundreds of infinitesimally small clues to build a case. It's not like on TV where they know who did it, and all they have to do is go through his drawers or his car or run his DNA, and then they can prove it. Building a case is hundreds and hundreds of pieces of information that you fit together like a puzzle."

Said the treasure hunter. Erin could see why she enjoyed her job and her hobby so much. They were mirror images of each other. She loved to solve a mystery.

"Okay, but I warned you. When we opened the car door, Wolf's door… I caught just a whiff of a sweet smell. A cologne or deodorant."

"Yes…"

"And when Mickey came in to the room, he was reeking of the same scent."

Beaver raised an eyebrow. "So they use the same deodorant? That connects them?"

Erin shook her head. "Mickey was there. He was there with Wolf. He admitted as much when we were there."

Beaver chewed her gum slowly. "Okay," she agreed. "Mickey was there. He had contact with Wolf. Did he kill him?"

"I don't know."

"What motive would he have?"

"That's why I asked how they were connected. Whether they were friends or enemies. Because I don't know."

Beaver nodded. "It's one more puzzle piece. Don't worry. I'll put it to good use. And you… stay away from gangsters."

Chapter Twenty-Eight

ERIN LOOKED TOWARD THE bedrooms. She hadn't heard a sound from that end of the house since she had gotten home. She had thought at first that Terry had just gone to the bedroom to read when Beaver said that she wanted to talk to the rest of them in private. But Terry would have heard the others leave. And he hadn't as much as moved enough for the bedsprings to squeak. "Is Terry home?"

It was strange, not only to find Beaver sitting in the living room by herself, but also not to have heard from Terry and to find him absent once more. Had he let Beaver into the house? And then left? Had she let herself in?

"He went out," Beaver said vaguely. "I'm sure he'll probably be back before very long."

Erin opened her mouth to say something, and then wasn't sure what. Beaver wasn't in charge of Terry. She wasn't his mother or his wife. He had told her he was going out, and had gone out. Erin had no idea whether he knew that Erin and the others had run into problems, or if Beaver had been just as vague about Erin's whereabouts as she now was about Terry's. She had probably just told him they were on their way back from shopping and she wanted to catch Vic and Erin before she went home.

And Terry had gone... for a walk. Or to visit with a friend. To help Willie out with something. Or for a drive to clear his head.

"What's wrong?" Beaver asked.

"I'm worried about Terry. It's been so hard on him, having to be at home all day. Not being able to go back to work yet. It's not like the department is keeping him home when he feels like he's well enough to go back. He knows he's not ready to be back on duty again, and that's even more frustrating. You can't fight with your own body."

Beaver nodded. "I'm always restless and angry when I have had to wait for my body to heal. And that's without a head injury. Painkillers make you fuzzy enough; I would hate to have a concussion or other brain injury on top of that. The days are too long."

Erin nodded. "I'm like that too, when I'm off work. When we were between bakeries... I drove everyone around me crazy."

Beaver smiled widely. "I remember." She pulled on her jacket, with lots of pockets to store the equipment she liked to carry. Some of it lethal, some of it less so. "He's worried about you too, you know."

"I know. But I'm doing okay. And I'm working, so that I at least have a distraction during the day. If I wake up at night and can't get back to sleep, I can plan out my week. Work on the next advertising campaign. Whatever. There's always something to do, even if I'm not baking."

"Speaking of baking…" Beaver tilted her head toward the kitchen.

"You know you can help yourself to whatever is in the freezer. It's not like I'm going to run out."

Beaver ducked into the kitchen to go through the leftover baking that Erin kept on hand for dinner and treats. She put a few things in a bag and gnawed on a frozen chocolate chip cookie.

"You need to talk to each other," she advised. "You could probably help each other more if you weren't both trying to avoid upsetting the other."

"We talk…"

"About…?"

Erin thought about the last few weeks with Terry. How often had they had a real conversation? About something that mattered to one of them? Beaver was right; they were both tiptoeing around the real issues, anything that might trigger flashbacks or nightmares or an angry mood. They kept pretending there was nothing wrong, watching TV or cuddling, having meals together and, while that was nice, it wasn't helping.

"Maybe you're right," she sighed.

"Keep doing your tai chi."

Erin was surprised. "Really? No one else thinks it will help. They say it's just mumbo jumbo, or it's spiritualism, and I should pray to their god, or whatever."

"You're the one who knows your body and what the trauma is doing to you. You're the one who knows your brain and what fits in your belief system. It isn't up to anyone else to tell you what is the right or wrong thing to do."

"But you're telling me to do it?"

Beaver grinned. "That's because you chose it. You're doing what's right for you. And you should keep doing it, despite any flak you might be getting from anyone else."

"They think it's a religious thing. That alienates people, and I don't want to lose customers because they think I'm… worshiping the devil in my meditation."

"Where else are they going to go? Into the city? To the grocery store? They know your product. I don't think it matters that much what they think of your private life."

"I don't know." Erin shook her head, remembering what it had been like when rumors had gone around that she was a witch. Business had dried up very quickly. For a few days. She didn't know how long it would have gone on if she hadn't sorted things out with Adele so that people wouldn't see any sign of her rites in Erin's woods. Then, the trickle of customers had started up again and things had gone back to normal. "Maybe you're right. I mean, they were buying bread from Angela, and even if she was a Christian, a lot of them thought that she'd killed her husband."

"People get over ethical conflicts pretty quickly when they're hungry and just need a dozen buns for company dinner."

Erin smiled. "Thanks. That makes me feel better. I was going to skip it today, but maybe while I'm waiting for Terry, I'll spend a few minutes connecting with my body."

"Attagirl," Beaver agreed. "And you know, I can help you with some other martial arts too. Ones that can be useful during a physical confrontation, not just for meditation."

"Meditation is what I really want. I'm not that well-coordinated, so I like the slowness of tai chi."

"You can learn the others slowly as well. They can be very relaxing." Beaver's eyes closed slowly, almost all the way, like a cat having its back stroked. She opened them again and nodded. "Take care of yourself."

Chapter Twenty-Nine

ERIN HAD JUST FINISHED her tai chi and was walking back toward the house when Terry got home. Erin was relieved that Beaver had been right and he hadn't been too long. She hesitated whether to ask him where he had been or what he had been doing. She'd been trying to give him his own space. But maybe space wasn't what he needed.

"Hi. I was worried about you," she told him.

Terry held out his arms and hugged her close when she stepped in.

"I'm a little sweaty," Erin apologized. "You wouldn't think that moving that slowly could raise a sweat, but…"

"You're just fine." He buried his nose in her hair and breathed warm air into her scalp. Erin squirmed.

"That tickles."

"You smell good."

"I don't; I'm sweaty."

He bent closer, the short whiskers of his chin rubbing against her face as he leaned in to kiss her. Erin returned the kiss, then looked into his eyes.

"Are you okay?"

"Fine. Why? A man can't kiss a pretty lady without something being wrong?"

"No. I just wanted to make sure that everything is okay."

"Everything is fine."

They turned together and started walking back to the house, up onto the porch, in through the back door, into the kitchen.

"What did you do today?" Erin asked him.

"Not much, just puttered around the house. Fixed that sticky window in your attic room. Took K9 out for a walk."

"I just wondered, since you weren't here when I got home, but Beaver was."

"I told her you wouldn't mind her waiting here for you." He looked at her curiously. "Was I wrong?"

"No. Of course not. I don't mind any of our friends hanging around here. I like it that people feel comfortable here and like they can come over when they want to." When she had been young, she had envied the foster sisters who

131

had been more popular, who had friends who would come over to the house, and they would always have something interesting to do. Erin had rarely had friends who were close enough to invite over for no reason. She needed to have a birthday or a party, an event that she could invite people to. People didn't just want to be around her.

"Good. You... worked things out with her?"

Erin wondered how much he knew. Was Beaver able to tell him more because he was a law enforcement officer, even though he wasn't on active duty? Or did he have an intuition that something was wrong? Erin was sure Beaver hadn't told him that their lives had been in danger. Terry wouldn't be nearly so calm and relaxed if he knew that. He'd be lecturing her about staying safe and he'd want to go confront Mickey, which wouldn't be a good idea. It was better if he didn't know everything.

"Yeah, I think so," she said vaguely.

He studied her, eyes quick and calculating. Trying to decide if he was going to push for more details. Did he know that it was about Campbell's case or related to the murder? He had to know that was what Beaver was focused on.

"So, you had a good day?" she asked him.

"Sure. Just fine."

Erin ran her hand down his arm. "Are you doing okay? We should talk more."

"We're talking."

"Really talk."

He stared into her eyes. "You don't want to *really talk* about it."

"I know. But we should anyway."

They walked into the living room. Terry looked for a moment at the couch, where they had spent many hours lately watching TV and comfortably not communicating. He took her hand and pulled her toward the bedroom.

Erin's stomach clenched. He was right. She didn't want to talk about it. As soon as she thought about sitting down and discussing her feelings and the dreams, flashbacks, and other emotions she had been feeling, her body clenched up and all of the benefits of the tai chi disappeared.

They walked into the bedroom and, when Erin stopped, Terry bent down, swept her off her feet, and dumped her on the bed, falling down beside her.

Erin was on the wrong side of the bed, and she immediately felt anxious about being trapped, penned in by him lying on the side of the bed nearest the door. Terry leaned in close. He kissed her cheek and stroked her hair back.

"I'm here."

Erin nodded. Her throat was hot and her breathing labored, like all of the air had been sucked out of the room. Her eyes immediately filled with tears.

Terry put his arm around her and bumped his forehead against hers. For a few minutes, they both just lay there, breathing on each other and not saying anything.

"I was scared," Terry said softly.

Erin pressed closer to him. She closed her eyes and nodded. She hoped he understood that she wasn't trying to shut him out, but just needed to block out the extra sensory input. There was only so much she could handle at once, and she was at her limit.

"When Theresa hit you?"

He didn't answer at first. Erin could feel a slight tremor in his body as he held her. "When I realized... what was going to happen. Going in there, neither of us realized that she was the one. We just thought she could give us some background. Jack knew that Biggles had lived with her family for a while. But he didn't know about... the history between them."

Erin sniffled, struggling to keep her emotions under control. "I was scared for you. When we found your phone."

"Yeah."

"Before that, even... that was the worst moment because I knew for sure... she had done something. Before that, I only thought that... you had been there. That it was K9's dog tag on the floor. I didn't know for sure. And I thought that you had just come and gone. Or I hoped that you had just come and gone and that you were okay. You were on your way home or had stopped for a burger or a beer with Jack. But when I saw both of your phones there, there was no way for me to make up a story anymore... I knew that she had done something to you."

Terry cleared his throat. Erin opened her eyes briefly to see the tears shining in his eyes and starting to run down his cheek.

"She took us both off guard. We didn't know. We just... didn't have any idea. I don't know what happened... it's all a jumble in my mind. Not like a memory where you can walk through it sequentially and remember each of the steps. Instead... it's everything at once, like an avalanche. I can't tell you what order anything happened in, and if I told it to you ten times, it would be a different story each time, because different things come to the surface. But the fear..."

Erin nodded.

"I've never felt like that before. I've been in plenty of dangerous situations before in my life. Most of them, I didn't know I was in danger until it was over. Or I knew, but I didn't feel it at the time because of the adrenaline rush, or because I knew that I had a job to do and I just had to do it, and I didn't let myself feel it until it was all over. But she had me around the throat. I couldn't breathe. She cut off the carotid and my brain couldn't get enough oxygen. That's what happens. But what it feels like is... dying. I knew I was dying. All she had to do was to keep holding me in that position and I would be dead. I was terrified about leaving this life with things undone. Leaving you behind. Never having the chance to..."

He couldn't talk for a few moments, sobbing and trying to catch his breath. Erin stroked his short hair, wishing she could take it all away from him.

"Never have a chance to grow old together. To have a family. A home that belonged to both of us. It was just all wiped out in that one moment. She could erase it all forever."

"But she didn't," Erin whispered.

"I don't know what made her stop. I can't remember. Jack said that she let go and I hit my head on the table. You know that. You know as much as I do. I can't remember that part."

"And then she attacked Jack."

"I think… she must have attacked him first."

"But he saw her attack you."

"I saw… I saw her stab him. Not just once. That knife." He shuddered.

Erin remembered it. She hadn't seen the blade. Only the hilt, sticking out of Jack's back. While he talked to her like there was nothing wrong. Her stomach lurched, and she was worried about what would happen if she were sick and couldn't get out of the bed fast enough with Terry blocking her exit to the door. She managed to calm it again and stayed where she was.

"You saw? And then what happened?"

"There is no 'and then.' I told you, it's all at once. It's not in sequence. I was… I was trying to help him, to treat him and to find a way to get help… and she was there. I didn't see her coming. I don't know where I thought she was. Did I think she had run?" He shook his head, impatient with himself. "I don't know. I can't remember. Why would I turn my back on a crazy killer like that? I wouldn't do that!"

But he clearly had, somehow, assumed that Theresa was no longer there and that he could do something for Jack Ward. So he had done what any cop would do and stopped to help his fellow officer rather than pursuing the culprit. But she had not run away. She had circled around and caught him from behind.

Erin ran her fingers through Terry's hair, now damp with sweat, starting to stand up in little points when she touched it. She just kept stroking him, letting him know she was there.

"I'm so sorry," Terry said hoarsely.

"Sorry? Sorry for what? You didn't do anything wrong!"

"But… I did. I let down my guard. I did the wrong thing. And because of that, you almost lost me. We almost lost each other."

"No. No, it wasn't your fault. You can't always do the right thing. There isn't always a right choice. What else were you supposed to do? You had to take care of Jack. He could have died."

"We could have both died. I should have made sure that she was gone. Or gone after her. Or dragged Jack out of there. Something."

"You didn't do the wrong thing. You had to help Jack."

"I know."

Erin ran her hand down his rough cheek, his five o'clock shadow sharp against her fingers.

Chapter Thirty

"YOUR TURN," TERRY SAID.

"Hmm?"

Erin opened her eyes and looked at him. She had been starting to drift. She felt exhausted, as if she had been there beside him, fighting for his life and Jack Ward's. She felt physically and emotionally drained, and her body was ready to shut down and go to sleep.

"You need to talk too. Not just brush me off and tell me that you're okay. I need you to talk to me."

Erin swallowed. She rubbed her eyes with one fist. "Not tonight. I'm too tired."

"Don't keep putting this off. You said it. You said that you needed to really talk."

"You can't force me," Erin protested.

"I'm not forcing you. I'm not telling you that you have to go into therapy. I'm not giving you an ultimatum. I'm telling you it's time to talk. You said so."

Erin rested with both palms over her eyes, her body stretched out along his. She was still on the wrong side of the bed and desperately wanted to switch places with him to reassure herself that she wasn't trapped. She knew in her mind that she was safe with Terry and he wasn't going to do anything that would make her run. And he wouldn't force her to stay if she needed to get up. But she still felt anxious and trapped.

She cleared her throat and tried to figure out what to say to him. He already knew her problems. He knew what she dreamed and why she dreamed it. There was nothing left to tell; it would just be a repetition of what he had heard before.

"I don't know. When Mr. Inglethorpe died, it was different. Different than any of the others."

He was silent, waiting and listening, not asking questions and demanding that she explain herself better.

"The other deaths bothered me. I hated to think about them and I did dream about them sometimes, but it was different. When I saw Mr. Inglethorpe, I couldn't even take it in. I couldn't understand what I was seeing. My brain wouldn't accept it."

She stopped talking. She didn't think she could go on. She didn't think there was anything else she could say. He knew it all.

"When I came in, you were frozen," Terry said. "You were standing there, with the rolling pin in your hand, just frozen in the middle of the scene."

Erin nodded. She couldn't remember it all. It wasn't like he had described his experience, with everything happening at one time. It was like she was stuck in time, in another reality. It was too much for her brain to take it in, so she had removed herself from the situation. She had seen it all, but at the same time, she had refused to see anything.

"I dream about it every night," she admitted. "Not just the nights you wake me up. Sometimes... all night long, over and over again."

He cupped his hand around her cheek. Her eyes were closed again and she didn't open them to look into his. She let the warmth of his hand soak into her skin. He didn't tell her that if she was that broken, she needed to go to the hospital or had to see someone.

"I'm afraid if I talk about it, that it will get worse."

"It's not getting better by *not* talking about it," he pointed out.

Erin nodded. She wasn't saying that she wasn't going to talk about it anymore, but why it was so hard for her—one of the reasons.

"I think about it during the day too. I have flashbacks. I'm jumpy."

"I know," he murmured. His tone told Erin that he hadn't just noticed these things in her, but that he was struggling with them too. And why wouldn't he? What he had gone through had been horribly traumatic.

When she thought about him lying in that garage, bound, waiting for someone to find him, she remembered her own experiences. It wasn't only dealing with the crime scenes that she had seen. She had nearly died in that cave. And that hadn't been the only time her life had been in peril. She'd had some very close calls. And so had her friends.

"I'm scared of caves."

Terry's chuckle came out as a snort. He gave her a squeeze, brief but heartfelt. "Of course you are!"

"I never, ever want to ever go underground again."

"And I'll never force you to," he promised. "That isn't going to happen."

"Sometimes I dream of that, or of other things that have happened. Vic and the others getting caught in the mine collapse." She swallowed. Her mouth was as dry as a desert. "But mostly, it's Mr. Inglethorpe."

He rubbed her back in slow circles.

"That's all I can do right now." Erin sniffled. "Even though I don't want to dream... I just want to go to sleep now. I can't talk about it anymore."

"Okay. You go to sleep."

"Will you stay with me?"

"Yes. But I don't want to keep you awake with my tossing and turning."

"I just need you here."

137

"If I have to get up for a while, I'll come back."

Erin snuggled against him, but the anxiety was a yawning pit in her stomach.

"Terry…?"

"Mmm-hm?"

"I have to sleep on the other side."

He laughed. "You are a creature of habit."

"It's not just habit. I need… to be close to the door."

He didn't argue or demand an explanation. Wrapping his arms around her, he rolled over, flipping her from the side of the bed closest the wall back to her side, on the very edge, where she could get out the door in a heartbeat. Erin giggled at his maneuver. She was so tired, but it felt good to have something. Terry backed up to give her a little more space, and she cuddled against him once more, telling her brain it was time to be quiet and to let her get to sleep.

Chapter Thirty-One

THE AFTER-SCHOOL CROWD was starting to dwindle when Erin saw the Fosters approaching. She smiled, happy to see one of her favorite customers, young Peter Foster. He led the pack, his younger sisters and mother following close behind. Mrs. Foster was getting slower, her tummy larger. The girls went straight to the display case to look at the goodies and discuss what kind of cookie they wanted to get with their kid's club cards. Peter stood behind them supervising, looking very grown-up.

"We got lots of treats for Thanksgiving," he advised her.

"I remember. How did it go? Did you like them?"

He nodded. "Most of them. I remember when I could only have one kind of cookie, from the store, when we had treats. That was before you came here."

"That's right. It's a lot nicer to have some choices, isn't it?"

He nodded vigorously. "It's so much better!"

Vic returned from the kitchen and waved cheerfully at the Fosters. "Afternoon, y'all!"

"So what didn't you like?" Erin asked curiously, having noted Peter's 'most of them.'

"Oh…" Peter glanced over at his mother, probably having been told it would be rude to say he didn't like something. "Mom said lots of kids don't like pumpkin pie. Or gingerbread. Because they use strong spices."

"She's right. A lot of times we don't learn to like them until we've had them a few times. And as our taste buds get older things don't taste as bitter as they do to kids."

"Then maybe when I'm older, I'll like them."

"Maybe. I didn't like them when I was little, but I do now."

Peter nodded again. "Yeah." He looked at the little girls and edged around the display case to get closer to Erin. She leaned closer to see what he wanted. "I heard about what happened," he said in a whisper. For a moment, Erin didn't know what he meant. "About that guy," Peter clarified. "They were talking at school about how he died back there!" He motioned toward the parking lot.

Mrs. Foster swatted him. "Peter!"

He jumped and looked at her guiltily.

"I told you not to bring that up!"

"I was quiet," he protested. "They didn't hear." He indicated his sisters.

They were now looking at Peter and their mother, wide-eyed, trying to figure out what was going on.

"Did you decide what kind of cookie you wanted?" Vic asked, trying to distract them.

They were reluctant to be pulled away from the family drama, but Vic coaxed them until they were engaged once more in getting their cookies.

Mrs. Foster rolled her eyes at Erin and shook her head. "I'm sorry. It's so hard to teach boys social graces! He won't just obey me when I tell him something. He has to know why, and if I tell him why, then he thinks he can argue and get around it." She fixed her gaze on Peter. "If you aren't going to be polite, then I will not come here when school is out. I'll go while you're in class, and you won't get to see Miss Erin or get a cookie."

"Why isn't it polite to talk about it? Erin knows what happened." He widened his eyes at his mother. "She *saw* him."

"You don't talk about it because it's upsetting. You don't make people talk about upsetting things."

"She's not upset."

"She doesn't look upset," Mrs. Foster countered. She looked at Erin. "What did I tell you? Going to grow up to be a lawyer, that boy!"

"He's very bright. I'm sorry, Peter, but it is upsetting for me to talk about, and you wouldn't want me to cry on your cookies, would you? And you wouldn't want the girls to get nightmares."

"I wouldn't get nightmares."

"Maybe not. But I do."

"Oh." This seemed to bring his more sensitive side back out. "I'm sorry. I didn't know it would bother you."

Erin nodded. "Now, pick out a cookie, or the girls are going to get all of them."

While he joined the scrum, Mrs. Foster stepped forward, nodding at Erin. "Sorry about that. Mom can tell him a hundred times, but until he hears it from someone else, he just doesn't believe it."

"Yeah." Erin recalled how she had been much quicker to believe trusted school teachers than any of her foster parents, and could relate. "So, what else do you need?"

When the Fosters were gone, there was a lull. Erin wiped the fingerprints and nose-prints from the display case and tidied up. There would be one more influx of customers who needed things for supper or for breakfast the next day, and then it would be time to close up.

The doorbells tinkled. Erin was surprised to see Joshua. He slouched into the bakery, looking at his feet. He raised his eyes to look at Erin.

"I just wanted to say… that I'm sorry for everything yesterday. I didn't mean to put anyone else in danger."

Erin shrugged. "I know you didn't mean to. You were just trying to help find Brianna."

"Campbell and I both got in trouble with Beaver." He gave a low whistle. "Let me tell you; you do *not* want to get on her bad side."

Vic laughed. "I can imagine. Well, I don't have to work that hard to imagine it, since she was waiting for us after we dropped you off last night."

"Yeah, but it wasn't your fault. It was mine."

"And Campbell's. He wasn't supposed to be telling anyone about it."

"But I knew that. I should have gone to Beaver instead of looking for Brianna myself. I just thought… we'd have better luck."

Vic nodded. "Less threatening. I know. There was a chance it would work."

He was looking down at his feet again. "Not as good as I thought it would. I guess this Mickey… he's a real gangster. Not someone to mess around with. If he wasn't working for Beaver…"

Vic looked over at Erin, aware that she was the only one in the group who had seen him for what he was. Who had known before they even walked into his hotel room.

"It's over," Erin said. "Over and done. You can't change anything by going over it."

Of course, the same was true of the things that her brain insisted on hanging on to. Could she go back and stop Mr. Inglethorpe's murder? Would anything change what had happened in the past? By that logic, she should be able to leave it behind, but it still had a pull on her. It still affected everything she did.

"Well, thanks," Joshua acknowledged. "I just wanted to let you know how sorry I was."

After a couple more apologies, he was on his way. Erin watched him go. She noticed an unfamiliar car parked across the street and watched it for a minute, trying to figure out who it belonged to, but nobody got in or out. Someone who was visiting town or who had just purchased a new car. She turned her attention back to her work.

Chapter Thirty-Two

VIC AND ERIN WERE both glad to be heading home at the end of the day.

"I didn't get much sleep last night," Vic admitted. "I was so wired that even with my Ambien, I couldn't shut my brain down and get some sleep."

"Did you tell Willie what happened?"

Vic looked at her sideways. "Well, no. Not really. Said that we went into the city... did some shopping... ran into Jeremy... Did you tell Terry?"

"No. But we talked about some other stuff."

Vic raised her brows, waiting for more information.

"Stuff that we've been avoiding talking about," Erin explained. "About... when Terry got hurt, and emotional stuff..."

"Good. You needed to. I'm glad. Did it help?"

"I think it helped us... but it didn't help my sleep. I was exhausted, but I kept waking back up again, and I think I kept him awake too." Erin glanced at the clock on the dashboard. "I haven't heard from him all day. Hopefully, he got more sleep after I left. It makes me nervous when he doesn't call at all during the day. I worry that he's sitting at home depressed all day. He doesn't want to bother me at work or bring me down, but I'd rather know if he's having trouble."

"Did you tell him that, during your talk last night?"

Erin sighed. "No. I guess we've still got a lot of ground to cover."

"We all do. You know, I look at the relationships of some of the couples that I know that have been together twenty or thirty years, and they're still working out the bumps. I don't know if you can ever truly know someone else one hundred percent."

"Huh. I guess. But I wish I knew a little bit more... or that it wasn't so hard to tell him things or figure things out. It looks so much easier when it's someone else's relationship. You don't see all of the little things that don't quite match up, or how many different ways you grew up, or think about one thing or another. You think, when you're looking at it from the outside, that everything just goes smoothly."

"I lived with a bunch of different families growing up," Erin contributed, "It wasn't easy for any of them."

142

"Great." Vic rolled her eyes dramatically. "That means I'm going to have to keep working at this for the rest of my life. It doesn't just start getting easier after a year, or whatever the cutoff is."

Erin looked in her rearview mirror, frowning at the car behind her.

"What?" Vic asked.

"Nothing. I was looking at that car earlier this afternoon, trying to figure out who it belonged to, and now I see it again. Someone bought a new car."

"Could be." Vic looked at it in her wing mirror, then turned around in her seat to get a better look. The car turned at the intersection before she'd gotten a good look. "Gone now. I guess we'll find out sooner or later."

"Well…" Erin pulled up to the house. "Here we are. Time to practice getting along with our… guys again."

"What's wrong with boyfriends?"

"I don't know. It feels… juvenile. We're partners, not kids going out to the movies."

"We should go out to a movie," Vic said brightly, getting distracted from the point.

"Okay. You pick one, and we'll work it out. We'll make it a double date with our *boyfriends*."

"Well, when you say it in that tone of voice it sounds silly," Vic agreed. "But I mean it. It sounds fun. We'll go to a movie in the city when neither of us works early the next morning. Right?"

Erin nodded. "It's a date. Have a good night!"

Vic agreed and headed around back to her apartment. Erin turned her key in the lock and looked around once the door was open. "Terry? Are you home?"

Once again, the house was quiet. The animals greeted her, Orange Blossom meowing loudly about something important in his life. He must have been happy that K9 had been out during the day and he had his domain back. Erin petted the cat and the rabbit and followed Orange Blossom into the kitchen to give him one of the homemade kitty treats she was testing. He happily gobbled it up. Marshmallow ate his treat of apple and carrot more sedately.

Erin decided that since Terry was out, she would do her tai chi immediately, rather than waiting until later. Then they could spend what time they had once Terry got home with each other. She removed her shoes and socks at the door and went out into the grass in her bare feet to the spot that had quickly become her practice area.

She had barely started her tai chi when alarm bells started going off. Erin tried to calm her brain, reminding herself that she was in a safe place, she was working on her body-mind connection, and that occasionally that would mean something uncomfortable came to the surface.

But telling herself that she was safe and trying to focus on the forms didn't work. She heard her own voice again, telling Terry how jumpy she was all the time. That was perfectly normal. She had been through some traumatic experiences. It was normal for her to be affected by them.

She couldn't keep her eyes closed, so she opened them and tried to focus on the forms she was practicing.

An engine stopped nearby. An engine that didn't sound familiar to Erin. Everything she was hearing seemed out of place. Like she was standing in someone else's yard instead of her own. Or in a different time, her world out of sync. She shook her head, trying to shake off the feelings of alarm, and focused on her practice. She needed to start again, unable to remember what she had already done and where she had stopped.

A door slam, again in an unfamiliar pitch. Parked close to her house, but she wasn't expecting any visitors. But when had that stopped people from coming over? Erin turned around, looking at the gate to the yard. If she had company, she wasn't going to get her tai chi done.

There was silence. She couldn't hear a knock on her door or the doorbell ringing. Maybe it was someone visiting a neighbor rather than Erin. But she stood there frozen, still unmoving. Something was wrong.

The gate opened, and standing there was the Russian named Mickey.

Chapter Thirty-Three

ERIN'S HEART POUNDED SO hard in her chest that it hurt.

Mickey?

What was he doing there? How did he know where she lived and why had he come? To check her out and see if the story they had told him was true?

To return the two guns to her and tell her that she could give them back to Jeremy and Vic if she thought they had learned their lessons, but not to come around his territory again?

He had to be there looking for Beaver. He knew that they knew Beaver, so he stopped by to ask her where Beaver lived. She wasn't listed, after all, she just roomed with Jeremy when she was in town.

"Mickey?" Erin couldn't think of what to say to him.

"Miss Erin Price, specialty baker," the Russian said.

"Yes, that's me. I told you I had a bakery."

"I saw you there today. You do good business."

Erin nodded. "It's been a good location. We get pretty good business from Bald Eagle Falls. Sometimes even from other towns nearby."

All the time she was talking, she was wondering what to do. What an inane topic it was. He didn't care what she did. Whether her business did well or not. He was trying to keep her occupied while he walked closer, watching her carefully. He knew that she hadn't been carrying a gun when she had shown up at his hotel. He had spotted Jeremy's and Vic's weapons without a problem, so he knew that she wasn't armed, that she couldn't do anything to stop him from whatever he had in mind.

Mickey's eyes went to the stairs up the side of the garage to the loft apartment over it. Had he asked around? Did he know that Vic lived there? Maybe he'd even been watching them.

The unfamiliar black car. That was who it had been. Mickey staking out the bakery, watching them and then following them home. And of course, Terry wasn't home. Mickey had probably already checked out the house and knew there was no one else there. Maybe he knew that a policeman was living with Erin, and maybe not. But for the moment, it didn't make any difference. Terry might as well have been on the other side of the world.

She swallowed. "What are you doing here? Are you looking for Beaver?"

145

"No. Not looking for Beaver." His eyes flicked around the yard, looking for any dangers. "Why don't we go into the house, where it is more private?"

"I'm... not ready to go in yet. I was doing my tai chi."

He blinked at her, clearly not expecting that response. He reached under his jacket and pulled out a gun. He pointed it at her, making sure she understood that she was being threatened.

"You come in the house now," he suggested again.

"No, I don't think so." She stood her ground. Inside the house, no one would be able to see or hear what was happening. At least outside, there was some chance of someone noticing that something was wrong. Vic and maybe Willie in the loft apartment. Neighbors who might hear something. Walkers through the wood behind her house. Bald Eagle Falls was a small town and people weren't afraid to walk the streets. They were friendly and dropped in on each other. Maybe today would be the day that someone dropped in and saved her from a gangster with a gun.

If it were a movie on TV, then Erin would be able to put her recent tai chi training into action, kicking the gun out of his hand and gracefully punching him in the face, all with perfect tai chi form.

Only she hadn't learned any gunman-disarming moves, and she was still just as uncoordinated as she had been when she started.

Mickey stood looking at her, stymied. He didn't want to stay outside, but if he were going to force her inside, he was going to have to use physical force. Which might be witnessed by neighbors. Or he could shoot her right there and beat a hasty retreat. Either option had a reasonably high likelihood of being seen.

"Instead, why do you not tell me," Mickey said in a precise voice that didn't entirely wipe out his Russian accent, "where is Brianna?"

"I don't know where Brianna is! Why would we drive all the way into the city and spend the afternoon knocking on doors and facing... unhelpful people... if I knew where she was? If I knew where she was, I wouldn't be looking for her."

"Maybe you are not looking for her. Maybe you are only pretending to look for her."

Erin shook her head in exasperation. "Why?"

He kept the gun pointed at her. "Someone knows. Maybe you. Maybe Beaver. But someone knows the truth. She did not just disappear into the thin air."

"She ran away. I don't know where. I don't know who helped her. She probably hitchhiked or caught a bus. And she's hundreds of miles away from here where she is safe."

"Someone would know. Someone would still see. Would catch her on camera."

"Then where do *you* think she is?"

Mickey took a couple of steps closer to her. "I think Beaver has her. I think she has Brianna stashed somewhere."

Chapter Thirty-Four

NOT A BAD GUESS."

Erin knew the voice without even looking. How could she not know her boyfriend's voice? Terry stepped out of the house, K9 at his side, his gun trained on Mickey. The weapon could have been on a tripod, it was so straight and steady. Erin breathed through her mouth, feeling like she wasn't getting enough oxygen. Terry kept sighting Mickey down the barrel of his gun, taking a few steps out of the house and down off of the porch.

"How about you put the gun down, Mikhail?"

"Who are you?"

"I'm a friend of Erin's. And I don't like you pointing a gun at her. So why don't you drop it? Right there. And put your hands behind your head."

Mickey grinned and shook his head. "Oh, you talk big, cop, but if you shot me, Erin would get hurt. Maybe killed. You don't want to risk that."

K9 was bristling at Terry's side, eager to do his part in bringing down the villain. Erin breathed shallowly, hoping that neither of them would be hurt. Mickey's gun wasn't pointed at them, but that could change in half a second.

There was another whisper of sound at the gate, and Mickey whirled around, gun hand automatically moving to point at the figure at the gate. Erin was no longer at the wrong end of the barrel, but Officer Stayner was.

He stood there, grim-faced, and didn't back down. He also already had his sidearm out, so it was two against one. Mickey could see things starting to fall apart, and his head moved on a swivel, looking for an opportunity to escape. His gun stayed pointed steadily at Stayner, but he was nervous, no longer in the position of power he had hoped to be in.

"Drop it, Mickey," Stayner said. "You heard him."

"You don't know me. You don't call me Mickey."

"We haven't been formally introduced," Stayner said slowly, "but I've heard all about you. I feel like I already know you."

"You don't know anything about me. None of what you are hearing is even true."

"You killed Wolf, and now you're here to take out any witnesses. Brianna. Erin. Anyone you think might know too much. Maybe you've even got your eye on taking out Rohilda Beaven. But you're not going to do it."

Erin was a little surprised that he knew who Beaver was, and knew her legal name. Stayner hadn't been around town for that long and didn't work directly with Beaver.

"Are you trying to impress me? Make me think that you know Beaver? You don't know her. Maybe you met her once or twice, but it takes a lot more than that to know a person like Beaver, someone who has so many false faces, someone who always lies about who she really is."

Stayner was not distracted by Mickey's chatter and threatening manner. Mickey took a step toward Erin and the back of the property. Erin didn't know whether he intended to grab her and use her as a hostage or make a break for it through the woods. Maybe he thought he could do both, grab her and then hold her hostage while he worked his way through the woods to safety.

But he didn't know his way through the woods. He didn't realize how dense they were. Or who he might find there.

Terry and Stayner were still pointing their guns directly at Mickey, and he was moving more quickly, gliding across the grass toward Erin like he was on wheels. Erin took a couple of steps back. The last thing she wanted was for him to grab her and use her as a shield. She wanted to leave Terry's and Stayner's lines of sight unobstructed. Mickey still pointed his gun at Stayner, but he was getting farther away, and before long he would be choosing a new target.

"You don't want to come this way."

The woman's voice was quiet and firm. Erin thought for a moment that it was Beaver because they had been talking about her. But the voice was not Beaver's. It was Adele. Erin could barely see the shape hidden behind a tree, barely a shadow, but the shadow definitely had a long gun, and Mickey might not want to run directly into that.

"What is all this?" Mickey demanded. "Some kind of set-up? What is going on here?"

"You weren't set up," Terry told him, chuckling. "No one made you come out here. That was your own idea, your own choice. But we're not going to let you threaten citizens of Bald Eagle Falls."

Mickey's eyes were still on the woods, his best avenue of escape. He shuffled another step or two closer to it, trying to make out the shape behind the tree and to see if he had any chance of getting past her.

"Just try it," Adele said. "Let's see if I still have the skills."

Mickey's jaw clenched. He looked over at Erin, but to bring his gun around to point at her now, he would have to swivel around and bring it across his body. The three opposing gunmen would know in an instant what he was trying, and they would put a stop to it. With two handguns and a rifle pointed at him, he knew he wouldn't stand a chance.

Flushing with fury, Mickey bent slightly and reached as far away from himself as he could before dropping the gun.

"Hands behind your head," Terry prompted.

Mickey slowly obeyed. None of the three guns dropped; they all remained trained directly at him. Erin wondered whether she should pick up Mickey's gun so that he could not dive for it in one last escape attempt. But she figured if she wasn't prepared to use it, she shouldn't pick it up.

"Take two steps backward, toward me," Terry instructed.

Mickey obeyed, distancing himself from the gun.

"Now, down on your knees."

"No one does this to Mikhail," Mickey growled. "No one!"

"Then you shouldn't come hunting my family."

Mickey lowered himself to his knees. He was not a young man, and his knees appeared to give out as he got lower, ending up with him landing much harder than any of them expected. But he didn't manage to get close enough to his dropped gun to pick it up again and put it to use. Terry next had him lie down, then approached carefully. He stood there over Mickey and nodded to Stayner, who also approached. Then while Stayner kept his gun trained on Mickey, Terry pulled his hands behind his back to cuff them and patted him down for any other weapons. He pulled Mickey's jacket partway down his arms to hamper his movements further, and took his time checking all of Mickey's pockets and anywhere else he might have secreted a weapon.

Erin found herself breathing more easily once Mickey was in handcuffs. She could finish her tai chi now that he was in custody.

But she knew she wasn't going to. She found her legs were weak as jelly and, before she could get to the porch where her lawn chairs were, her knees gave out, and she ended up sitting on the ground. Terry twisted his head around to look at her. "Erin? Are you okay?"

"Yeah. Just... resting."

"Okay. You're not hurt? He didn't touch you, did he?"

"No."

"Good thing," Terry said, giving Mickey a shove. "It's a very good thing that we caught you before you could do anything you might regret later."

"You are lucky you got here when you did," Mickey retorted, pushing back against Terry. "Things might have turned out very differently."

"Put out the word to stay away from Bald Eagle Falls."

"How about I put out the word about your snitch? We see how long Cam Cox lasts when *that* gets around."

"That wouldn't be very good for your health. How are you going to fare in prison if people know you've been working for the feds?"

Mickey sneered. "You do not have anything on me. I get a walk. That's the deal. I don't go to prison while I'm working with Agent Beaven."

"Attempted murder is not one of the charges they will let slide. You overreached."

"Attempted murder? I just talked to Erin Price. I never try to kill her."

"We caught you here with a gun on her. You don't think a jury will interpret that for exactly what it was?"

"I was holding a gun." Mickey shrugged. "Minor weapons charge. I walk. I never said I was going to kill her. I never pulled the trigger. I did not even resist arrest." He smiled smugly. "You don't know how it works. You'll see."

"Erin is a personal friend of Beaver's. She's not going to let it slide."

"She has bosses. They will decide."

Terry pushed Mickey toward Stayner. "I'll let you take this scum in. It's your arrest."

Stayner brightened, clearly pleased that it would be his arrest rather than Terry's. As green as he was, he could probably benefit from the mobster's arrest being attributed to him. He took Mickey's arm.

"Check him one more time before you put him in the car, and don't let him talk you into anything," Terry advised. "Treat it like any other arrest."

Stayner nodded and escorted the Russian out of the yard, poor Mickey still complaining about how he was being mistreated and would be released once the authorities found out what was going on.

Terry offered his hand to Erin. "Can you get up?"

She grasped his strong hand and let him pull her to her feet. She stayed on her feet, breathing slowly. Her muscles were still quivering, but she wasn't quite as weak as she had been. Terry put his arm around her and held her close. Adele crossed the fence line and approached them.

"How did you know?" Erin asked, trying to grasp it. "How did you all know that he was here?"

"Stayner saw the car when he was on patrol, thought it looked suspicious. He ran the plates, which rang all kinds of alarm bells, and both Beaver and I got calls. The sheriff is out of town and Tom is down with the flu, so I agreed to help. Stayner was keeping an eye on the car, so he knew when Mickey followed you here."

"I saw the car, but I thought I was just being paranoid... it turned down another street, and I thought everything was okay..."

"He probably realized his car would stand out as not belonging in the neighborhood, so he fell back to give you a false sense of security."

Erin shuddered. "And you called Adele?"

Terry shook his head. "No, Adele showing up was a pleasant surprise."

Adele reached them. "I was going to stop by and say hello to you. Then... it seemed like you could use a little help."

Erin shook her head. "You deserve some kind of bonus. That's going above and beyond what a groundskeeper should have to do."

"Not at all," Adele said with a shrug. "I'm supposed to be watching and keeping intruders and unsavory characters away from your land."

"Well, thank you. You were there at just the right time. Three guns to one were just too many for Mickey."

"And Mickey is…?" Adele asked.

Erin looked at Terry, realizing that she hadn't told him the story, yet he wasn't asking her who Mickey was or why had had come after her. She cleared her throat.

"He's… uh… someone that might be involved in Campbell Cox's case. We ran into him in the city… and I guess he decided we might know something about someone he's looking for."

"You and Terry?" Adele asked. "Why would he come after a cop? And why would the two of you…"

Terry was shaking his head, and Adele stopped. She raised one eyebrow.

"You know Erin," Terry said simply.

Adele looked back at her. "But who is 'we'?"

"Uh…" Erin looked at Terry, wondering if he already knew the details. "Joshua Cox, and Jeremy, and Vic."

"And you were lucky enough that he picked you to go after first."

"I guess so. He knew I was a baker, so he followed me from Auntie Clem's." A thought occurred to her. "Joshua came by while the car was there… he didn't go after Joshua or Campbell, did he? Before he came here?"

"Stayner was following him," Terry reassured her. "He came here first. He probably already knew where to find the Coxes. Their address is listed. Or has been, in the past. It would only take a two-minute internet search to track them down."

"Maybe someone should go by there to make sure everything is okay."

"Mikhail came here."

"But he could have sent someone else to the Coxes. He could have sent someone to each house."

Terry considered this for a moment, then nodded. "Okay. Give me a minute and I'll make a couple of calls. That's easier than running all over the place." He let Erin go, his movements slow. "Will you be okay? I'm just going to go into the house."

"I'm fine," Erin told him, managing to keep her feet. "I'll be in in a few minutes."

She knew that Adele preferred to talk in private.

As she was about to thank Adele again for her serendipitous appearance, Vic's apartment door opened. Vic stepped out and looked down the stairs at them. "Hey, what's up? I heard voices."

"You missed the excitement," Erin told her, laughing.

"Excitement? What happened?"

Chapter Thirty-Five

ERIN HAD TOLD VIC the story, Adele had visited briefly and then gone on her way as darkness fell. Vic and Erin moved into the house and talked until Terry was finished his phone calls. He approached Erin from behind while she chatted with Vic and wrapped his arms around her in a hug. Erin leaned back into him.

"Beaver would like to see you," Terry said, leaning down close to her ear.

Erin looked over her shoulder at him. "Why would Beaver want to talk to me? We got Mickey; she can talk to him at the police department. Does she not believe that he was threatening me? She can't let him off."

"She's not going to let him off. She understands what happened, and the only one she is upset with is Mickey. But she would like your assistance."

"My assistance."

"Yes, ma'am."

Erin frowned, thinking about that. "I can't think of anything she would need my help for."

"Can't you? Well, why don't I take you over there, and we'll find out."

"Um… okay." Erin looked at the clock. "Does it have to be tonight? I should be getting ready for bed."

"Any way you could get someone to cover for you tomorrow?"

"I suppose. Vic, could you see who is available?"

Vic nodded. "Yeah. No problem. You didn't have anything special planned, did you?"

"No. Nothing out of the ordinary. All of the plans and recipes are in the binder for the week."

"We'll take care of it, then. Don't worry about anything. You and Terry can sleep in." She winked.

"Okay, I guess I'm free," Erin told Terry.

"Good. Get your handbag, and let's go."

Erin could have just grabbed it and put on her shoes, but she was still feeling off-balance from the events of the evening and was unsure why she had to talk to Beaver right away. She dragged her feet, feeling like Terry was rushing her.

He had been too remote lately, not telling her what he was up to, where he was going or when he would be back. She felt like he was holding back from the relationship. When they had talked the night before, she thought it had heralded a change, that they would both be able to be more open and vulnerable to each other, but Terry was still not keeping her apprised. At one time, it would have been unthinkable for him to disappear for a few hours without telling her what his plans were.

Of course, she hadn't told him about going to see Mickey, either, and Beaver had filled him in on at least part of the story. So he knew that she had still held something back. Why should he tell her everything?

"Erin? Are you ready?"

Erin focused on Terry, standing by the door with K9, waiting for her to get herself together.

"Yeah. I know. I just feel like... are you sure we couldn't do this tomorrow? I don't feel like going out. I just... want to cuddle and go to bed. Beaver can wait."

"Let's get it over with. You'll feel better once we're done."

Erin sighed and followed him out to his truck.

They didn't drive in the direction of Jeremy's apartment, which was where Erin had assumed they would be going. And it wasn't in the direction of the police department. Erin looked at Terry, confused.

"Where are we going?"

"Safehouse."

"A safe house? A safe house for who? Campbell?"

"Be there in a couple of minutes."

Erin didn't think that Bald Eagle Falls would be a very good place to have a safe house. Everybody knew everybody else's business. How could they hide someone there?

She watched out the window, intrigued. A couple of minutes later, they were out of the town limits, not yet at the safe house. A few more minutes down the highway, Terry turned off onto a gravel road, then took several other twisting turns in the dense trees, until she wasn't sure she'd be able to find her way out again if left to her own devices. She would have to leave a trail of breadcrumbs to find her way home.

It was dark when they reached the cabin in the trees. There was a light on inside, but no lights outside that would act as a beacon to anyone trying to negotiate the rabbit trails that twisted through the woods. Terry parked the car and opened his door. K9 jumped out after him. He leaned down and looked into the vehicle at Erin.

"We're here."

"This is a safe house?"

"Yep."

Holding her purse on her lap, Erin looked at it. She didn't want to get out of the car and walk through the dark into the isolated, unfriendly-looking shack.

"It doesn't *look* safe."

"I promise you, it is. Do you think anyone could find it without being given directions?"

"I don't know. Maybe a helicopter with one of those heat-sensing cameras."

"Exactly. And then all they would see is a couple of people in a cabin. Nothing to give away that it's any different than any of the other remote cabins around here. And it isn't the only one. There are plenty of people who don't want to live right in town." Terry stood with his thumbs in his pockets, staring up at the starry night sky. "Some people like to be out in the wild, at one with nature."

Erin had been trying to achieve some kind of Zen state with the world around her with her tai chi, but living in a place that was so isolated would be way too much for her.

"Come on. Beaver's inside. With her and me there, you couldn't be much safer."

"I want to see her first."

Erin didn't know why she was being so stubborn about it. It wasn't like she thought Terry was lying or was going to lead her into a dangerous situation. She was perfectly safe with him by her side. With Beaver there too, she was that much safer. But it wasn't her logical brain dictating her actions; it was the same primitive instinct that had been troubling her since finding Mr. Inglethorpe.

Terry said something under his breath that she couldn't make out and walked up to the cabin. He spoke at the door for a minute, and then the door opened wide and Beaver stepped out. She stood there on the doorstep where Erin could see her, and Erin finally relented. Beaver was there. With both of them insisting it was safe, she couldn't really argue.

She opened her door and walked reluctantly up to the cabin. Beaver nodded and went back inside. Terry stood on the doorstep and motioned Erin in ahead of him. He stood for a moment longer after she was inside, looking and listening for any sign of trouble.

Erin was sure that no one had followed them. It would be impossible for someone to know which turns they had taken without keeping them in sight, and there had been no one behind them.

Erin looked around the rustic cabin. It looked friendlier inside than it did out. There was a fire burning in the fireplace, old furniture covered with handmade blankets and quilts, and various boating and fishing equipment and memorabilia on the walls.

The girl sitting close to the fire looked up as Erin came in. Erin's jaw dropped.

"Brianna!"

Chapter Thirty-Six

RIANNA DIDN'T SAY ANYTHING in response, dropping her eyes and then turning her head to the side, as if there were something far more interesting to see in the dark corner beside her.

"Come on in and sit down," Beaver encouraged.

Erin followed Beaver's motion and sat down on the couch adjacent to Brianna's. She shifted, looking for a comfortable position. The couch itself was comfy enough; it was Brianna who made her restless and self-conscious. Erin looked at Beaver.

"Did you know where she was all along?" She couldn't quite make herself believe it. Maybe Brianna had run, and Beaver had followed her trail. Or someone else had brought Brianna out there.

Beaver chewed her gum. "Yep."

"You knew? Since when? Since she left the Coxes' house?"

Beaver pursed her lips. "Pretty much, yeah. Since Saturday night, or early Sunday morning."

"How?"

Beaver raised an eyebrow, not answering.

Erin looked at Brianna, trying to connect with her. Why had Beaver wanted Erin? Why hadn't she made the trip into town, if she wanted to talk to Erin? That would have been less risky than letting someone else know about the safe house. The more people who knew about it, the more dangerous it became.

Terry walked over from the door and sat down next to Erin. He put one arm around her shoulders and held her hand in her lap with the other. Much more intimate than she would expect him to be in front of strangers. K9 lay down at his feet with a sigh. Terry turned his body slightly to look at Erin, studying her face as if she were the only one in the room.

"I've been taking guard duty to allow Beaver time to deal with other parts of the investigation."

"This is where you've been?"

"Yes. I'm sorry I didn't give you any explanation. I didn't want to lie to you, but I didn't want to have to bring you in on the secret either. It was better if you didn't know anything."

Erin nodded. "Yeah. Okay. That makes sense." She hesitated for a moment before asking, "How has it been? Have you felt..."

"Back to normal? Not exactly. I can only take a few hours at a time, with the headaches and fatigue. It's better here than in town, where there are so many distractions pulling me so many different directions. Being... jumpy and anxious all the time. It's a bit easier out here to relax and just watch and wait."

Erin nodded.

"I was talking to Brianna about our talk yesterday." Terry's cheeks were a little red, but it might have just been the firelight. "Just about... how you have felt since Mr. Inglethorpe's... death. Like you were telling me."

Erin looked over at Brianna, who still wouldn't meet her eyes.

"I thought that maybe Brianna would like to hear about that from you. Maybe share something about her own experience."

Erin wasn't sure what to say. She looked at Terry and then at Beaver, who was standing back out of the way, clearly trying to stay in the background so that Brianna wouldn't feel like they were all ganging up on her.

Erin looked down at her hands. "I don't know how much Terry told you. I've had... some kind of awful experiences since I moved to Bald Eagle Falls. I mean, I love the town, and the people are great, mostly, but the things that have happened while I've been here are... challenging."

Brianna made a noise that could have been a sob or a grunt of disgust.

"When Mr. Inglethorpe got killed..." Erin looked at Terry, and he nodded, encouraging her to continue. "It was... very violent and... I was the one who found him."

Erin swallowed. She glanced toward the girl. Brianna was looking toward Erin, out the corner of her eye, without turning her head toward her. Like a trapped animal trying to figure out if she were a danger.

"When I saw him, I just froze up. I couldn't believe what I was seeing. My mind kept making up other explanations for what I saw. I couldn't function. I couldn't do anything. When Terry came, that's how he found me, in the middle of the scene, holding my rolling pin... just... paralyzed."

Erin stopped for a moment to swallow and try to slow her breathing. It had been one thing to talk about it to Terry. She had told him that she didn't want to talk to therapists about it, and telling it to Brianna with Terry and Beaver listening in was not easy either. It wasn't something she could talk about dispassionately.

Brianna nodded and looked in Erin's direction. Her face was still pointing down, but she raised her eyes in swift glances to look at Erin.

Something that Erin had said was getting through to Brianna and she wanted Erin to go on. She didn't say anything, but her body language was clear. Erin took a long breath in and let it out.

"I remember Terry telling me that I fainted, but I don't know... I don't remember that part. And I don't think I actually fell down, but I can't remember a lot about what happened. He took me out of there… they had to collect evidence. Get the blood and any evidence from my hands and clothes. I had to tell them what I had seen and done, but I don't know if I was very coherent."

Erin looked at Terry, expecting him to comment, but he didn't. He just nodded at her, encouraging her to go on. The fire snapped and crackled in the fireplace but, other than that, the room was silent, waiting for her to continue.

"That's all, really."

But it wasn't. That wasn't all that she had told Terry and, even if she hadn't told him anything else, he still knew that wasn't where the story ended. She had been different since finding Mr. Inglethorpe. It had affected her more deeply than any of the other deaths. Or maybe they had all built up over time, and Mr. Inglethorpe's was just the one that had pushed her over the edge.

"Since then… I've been really jumpy about everything. If someone moves too fast, or there's a loud noise… anything can scare me. Being in a room where there is someone else between me and the door so I can't get out quickly. I've been… emotional… crabby without any reason…"

Terry squeezed Erin's hand. She swallowed and nodded her appreciation for his support. It was silly for the next part to be so hard. How were her dreams a sign of weakness? It wasn't like anyone could be expected to control their dreams. It was just the way her brain was trying to deal with all of the stress. If she could just calm her body and brain down before bed, like she'd been trying to do with the tai chi, then maybe she could get some control over her sleep again.

"I have trouble sleeping. I'm too restless and anxious to get to sleep. And then when I do… I have nightmares. It isn't just now and then, like I tell people. It's every night. Sometimes all night long. It's… terrifying. I dream about people I know dying. I see them in that murder scene over and over again. I dream different people I know are the killer, or victim, or even trying to kill me. I don't know how many times I've dreamt about someone trying to kill me since it happened."

Erin wiped at the corner of her eyes, trying to stay in control. She looked at Brianna and saw the tear tracks down her cheeks.

She was just a kid. Sixteen or seventeen. Maybe she was eighteen but, even if she was, that didn't make her a grown-up, able to deal with grown-up problems. *Erin* couldn't deal with all of her grown-up issues, so how could she expect a teenager to? She went to Brianna. She sat down beside her and put her arms around Brianna, holding her tightly.

"It's okay, honey. It is. It's okay, Brianna."

Brianna shook her head. "I'm so scared," she whispered.

"I know. I would be too. I *am* scared too. Even when I'm not in any danger, I still feel it. Like someone is watching me, just waiting until I'm vulnerable and distracted. Waiting until it's my turn… you know."

Brianna clutched Erin's hand. She was sobbing openly. Erin stroked her braided hair. "Tell me about it."

Brianna scrubbed at her eyes with both fists, and attempted to get herself calm and under control once more. But the dam had burst and there was no stopping the flood.

"I was there," she blubbered. "I was there. I saw it all."

"You were where?"

"I was… I called Wolf. I wanted him to get me out of there. I told him I'd do whatever he wanted, I didn't care. I'd do whatever he wanted if he would just get me out of there. I was scared that they would be coming after me. The cops. Because they had taken Cam, and I know those weren't his drugs. He'd never leave them in the car like that. He didn't deal. He'd never have that much on him. I knew he was being set up and that… it wasn't going to stop. I didn't know for sure who was behind it, but… I had to protect myself. I had to go back."

"Go back where?" Erin held Brianna, rocking slightly, trying to give her some comfort. She was a stranger; what kind of comfort could she provide to the girl? But she did her best anyway.

"Back to the old life. It was too hard. Cam was so good to me. He was always so kind, and he'd talked me into getting out of the life, into trying to… do something else with my life. Get free. I knew it wouldn't work." She shook her head despondently. "I knew it wouldn't, but he kept saying… he could help. He could help me to get clean, to get my own place, an honest job, all of those things. But he wasn't that much older than I am. He didn't have any money or job himself. He couldn't get a place of his own, so how could he help me?"

Erin nodded, not sure what to say, just encouraging Brianna to keep talking, to get out all of the feelings that she had been holding in.

"I wanted to believe him, so I did. I told him that Wolf and the others weren't going to like it. I told him that. They wouldn't let me. They'd keep me there. They just… wouldn't let me leave. There are ways to keep girls from leaving. I didn't want them to hurt me, or Cam, or someone else I was friends with. And they would. Those Russians, they're nasty dudes. When they talked about stuff they saw in prison…" Brianna rolled her eyes upward and held both arms across her stomach. "It would make me sick, just hearing them talk about it."

"But Cam talked you into leaving."

"I wouldn't say yes. I said I would have Thanksgiving dinner with him. That's all. Just… go home with him for turkey day. I never told anyone I was leaving the life, that I wouldn't work for them anymore. But I guess… they knew."

"And you think that Wolf, or one of the others, set Campbell up. Planted drugs so that he would have to go to prison, and then if you didn't fall in line, they would get you too."

"They've got guys on the inside. There are plenty of Russians in the prison. I was so scared that they were going to kill Cam. I thought... he wouldn't ever get out. They'd kill him as soon as he was transferred."

"He's out on bail. He's on house arrest, but he's back home, and he's okay."

Brianna wiped at her eyes. "Beaver said that. But I didn't know if... that was true."

Of course not. How could she trust a cop to tell her the truth?

"So... then what happened?"

Chapter Thirty-Seven

RIANNA DIDN'T SOBBED ALOUD, COVERING her face. "It was… I can't tell you. I can't tell you."

Erin pulled Brianna's face to her shoulder, sheltering her protectively like a mother with a child afraid of monsters.

"It's okay. It's okay. Wolf is dead and Mickey has been arrested. You're safe. This is a safe place."

"It can't be. Nowhere is safe if I tell."

"It's okay," Erin repeated soothingly, rubbing Brianna's back. "You called Wolf," she recapped. "You told him that if he would come to get you, you'd do whatever he wanted."

Brianna nodded. She sniffled. "I begged him. He said he would come. But I was his. I would be his forever. I didn't care. I didn't want to go to prison. I didn't want to get killed."

She gulped and cried into Erin's shoulder.

"I told him to meet me at the bakery. I didn't want him going to Cam's mom's house. I know he could have found out where they lived anyway, but I thought if I didn't meet him there, he would leave them alone."

"Yeah. That was good. You were looking out for them."

Brianna was quiet. Erin rubbed her back. "And then what?"

She was afraid herself. She didn't want to hear what happened. She had seen the results, and she was doing everything she could to keep it from taking root in her brain, where it would keep coming back in her dreams like Mr. Inglethorpe's death. She didn't want to visualize what had happened.

And she was afraid that Brianna was going to say that she had done it. And what would happen to her then? Would Beaver put her in prison? It would be Erin's fault if she did. She was the one who was encouraging Brianna to talk because that was what Terry and Beaver wanted her to do. Not because it was best for Brianna.

They would tell her it was good for Brianna to talk about it and get it off of her chest, but that wasn't why they had brought Erin there.

"I was late getting there. I got cold feet and didn't want to meet him. I didn't want… my life to be over. I didn't want to give up on what Cam had tried to get me to do. But I was hungry and tired of hiding. I knew it was the only way. I had to."

Erin stroked Brianna's hair, her heart breaking for the girl and the choice she was faced with. It wasn't fair that her choice was between Cam being murdered in prison and giving herself over to the man who would continue to pimp her and feed her addiction and probably end up killing her anyway. Cam had tried to help her to find another way, and they had taken him out of the picture.

"I got myself out of there. Made myself go. I thought maybe if I went back, they'd leave Cam alone, at least. It didn't matter what happened to me."

Erin remembered Brianna's face after the Thanksgiving dinner and Cam's arrest. The mask of indifference. The hopelessness in her eyes.

"Wolf was still there, waiting in the bakery parking lot."

Erin saw his car again in her mind's eye. The unfamiliar vehicle parked in the back lot, waiting for Brianna. Forever waiting for Brianna, until Erin got there and called the police and Stayner opened the door so they could see what had happened.

"He didn't see me. He was talking to someone else in the passenger seat."

She swallowed.

"Mickey?" Erin asked. He had left his scent behind. She was sure it couldn't have been anyone else. And if Brianna had seen Mickey with him, then she wasn't the one who had killed Wolf.

Brianna didn't move or say anything for a long time. Then she finally nodded.

"Mickey's door was open so that I could see in. He and Wolf were arguing. I couldn't hear what they were saying. Mickey pulled a knife and he pounded it into Wolf's chest. Like he was trying to drive a stake into a vampire's heart. Really hard. And Wolf made this awful noise. But he didn't fight back... he just went still."

Chapter Thirty-Eight

ERIN COULD FEEL EVERYONE in the room relax. Once the words were out of her mouth, the tension went out of Brianna and she sagged in Erin's arms. She had fought herself so hard not to tell what she had seen, and now that she had told, a weight had been lifted from her shoulders. Her breathing changed from frantic, shallow breaths to longer, even respiration. Erin continued to rub her back.

"I was so scared," Brianna said softly. "I didn't know what to do. I just wanted to run away from there, all the way home, and never look back. But there wasn't anywhere to go. No way to get out of town. Wolf was my one way out. It's like you said... I couldn't believe what I had seen. After Mickey left, I kept watching Wolf, waiting for him to move, to be okay. I don't know how long I stayed there. Then I started walking. I don't know... where I went or how long I walked..."

"She was lucky I came across her," Beaver contributed, speaking for the first time. "She was in a state... shock, fugue, whatever you want to call it... it was before you found and reported Wolf's death. I didn't know what had happened, but I knew I couldn't leave her on the street like that."

Erin turned her head to look at Beaver. "So you brought her here and pretended you didn't know where she was."

Beaver chewed for a minute. "Well, it was a little more complicated than that. I didn't have this place yet, so I had to move her a couple of times without being seen, which is not easy in a place like Bald Eagle Falls."

Erin could imagine.

"What am I going to do?" Brianna sniffled. "I got nowhere to go now. No way to get anywhere."

"You're not going anywhere yet," Beaver told her. "We're going to need a signed statement and more details from you. Once everything is in place, we can talk about options. I'm sure we can help you get to where you want to go, make sure you have a starting point."

"What about the witness protection program?" Erin suggested. "You could give her a new name and everything."

"It doesn't work like it does in the movies," Beaver advised. "WITSEC is very rare. It's used for high-level targets. Someone like Brianna… she's low profile. She can get a new start anywhere. Use a new name if she wants. No one is going to put any amount of time and effort into looking for her. Mickey was a danger, but he's in custody. If he's the one who killed Wolf, Brianna isn't a danger to anyone else. As long as she doesn't go straight back to the same neighborhood, she'll be safe."

Erin looked at Brianna, stroking her hair. The girl seemed so vulnerable. But once she got her equilibrium back, the tough front would reappear. Erin had moved to avoid trouble more than once. Brianna was a little younger than Erin had been when she'd been forced to make it on her own, but she could do it too, if she had a few breaks and could stay away from drugs and the street life.

"The biggest thing is to get clean and stay clean," Beaver told Brianna, as if she had read Erin's mind. "If you want a new life, then you have to leave the old one behind. No one is going to give an addict a job. A real job, not turning tricks or couriering contraband."

"I'm not an addict," Brianna snapped. "You're just assuming that because I'm black and on the street. That doesn't mean I'm an addict."

Beaver gazed at her, expressionless, giving nothing away. "It's interesting that Wolf didn't have any drugs or money on him. He's a drug dealer, known to indulge himself, and he's picking you up, knowing he's going to have to give you something to calm you down and keep you on the string. It's surprising that there was nothing on him, don't you think?"

Brianna pulled out of Erin's grip. She sat back, a few inches away from Erin, the walls going up. Her tears had washed away all vestiges of makeup from around her eyes, and she looked both young and worn by experience at the same time. How long had she been on the street and how many people had used and betrayed her in that time?

"I don't know what you're talking about. He'd know better than to be caught with drugs on him. Someone like that makes sure other people are holding for him."

"But there was no one with him. And he knew you would be jonesing. You'd already talked to him on the phone, so he knew what kind of shape you were in."

"I'm not the one who killed him." Brianna wiped her nose with the back of her hand. "If he had something, then I guess Mickey took it."

"And if I search your bag and this cabin, I wouldn't find anything?"

Brianna stared at her; challenging and defiant.

"I could use the dog," Beaver said, with a nod toward K9. "He could find drugs no matter how well you think you've hidden them."

Brianna's mask slipped. She glanced uncertainly toward the dog, lying next to Terry's feet but watching her intently. "He's not a drug dog."

"You think he couldn't find them? Are you willing to stake your future on that?"

Brianna clenched her teeth, the muscles in her jaw and neck standing out. "Fine. He'd find drugs. Wolf hardly had anything on him. It wasn't hardly anything."

"But even in your state of shock, you weren't too scared to go through his pockets and car to relieve him of it. And it's been enough to get you through four days."

"Because I'm not an addict. I don't have to be high all the time."

"There are plenty of people with addiction issues who don't use every day. It's not a requirement. Are you the one who planted the drugs in Cam's car?"

Brianna stared at Beaver, her face tight. "Why would I do that? Cam was my friend. Maybe my only real friend. The only one who cared about me as a person."

"You would do it because Wolf told you to. Maybe he threatened you. Or maybe Mickey did. You put the drugs in Cam's car. You were there. No one else was. Wolf didn't show up until Saturday night."

A tear escaped Brianna's reddened eyes and ran down her cheek. Brianna didn't admit it, but Erin realized with a sinking feeling that Beaver was right. Brianna didn't offer any other explanation, didn't point to anyone else. It wasn't Stayner; he hadn't been working with the gangsters. One of the Russians could have sent someone to Bald Eagle Falls to plant the evidence, but why do that when they already had a puppet on the scene who they could control?

"And Cam knew it was you, but he didn't say anything," Beaver suggested. "He just let them arrest him."

"I couldn't let him go to prison."

"But you did."

Brianna shook her head. "I tried to stop Wolf. I told him he didn't need to do anything to Cam; I would go back to him. I'd do what he wanted."

"But that was *after* you'd already set Cam up for him."

"I tried to stop him," Brianna insisted, voice cracking.

"Did you?" Beaver took a couple of steps closer to Brianna. "Was it Mickey who killed Wolf or was it you?"

"It was Mickey! I couldn't. I was too scared of him. If I tried... he'd kill *me*."

Erin tried to picture Brianna meeting with Wolf. Erin hadn't known Volkov in life, but she'd met Mickey and didn't imagine that Wolf would be any less threatening. She pictured Brianna getting into the car with him, shaking, terrified, desperate.

Would Brianna's concern for Cam be enough to overcome her fear of Volkov, the man who had been controlling her with threats, violence, and her addiction? Erin thought Brianna was telling the truth. She wouldn't have had what it took to kill the Russian.

"Where's the phone you contacted Wolf on?" Beaver asked.

"I dumped it." Brianna snuffled loudly, gulping. "In some creek I walked past that night."

"And where is his phone?"

"That one too. Both of them."

"Together?"

Brianna nodded.

"And if I was to recover them, would I find Mickey's number on your phone?"

"What?" Brianna's eyes got wider.

"After you arranged for Wolf to pick you up, did you call Mickey?"

"Why would I do that?"

"To get Wolf out of your life. Because he wouldn't leave you alone. He made you set Cam up and just laughed at you when you told him that Cam was a nice guy and to leave him alone. You were mad at him, but you were too scared to do something yourself, so you called Mickey. What did you tell him?"

Brianna's jaw worked. She dragged her eyes away from Beaver to look at Terry and Erin. "I didn't tell him anything."

"There's no point in lying to me. We have Mickey in custody, and you didn't have a burner number for him. Your number is going to show up as an incoming call on his phone Saturday night."

Brianna sank back. "You can't open his phone."

"You wanna bet? Are you going to bet the next ten years on that? If you want to stay out of prison, you need to tell me the truth."

Brianna stared at her with hollow eyes. The seconds ticked by. Finally, Brianna leaned forward, elbows on knees, and covered her eyes. "Yes. I called Mickey."

Chapter Thirty-Nine

WHAT DID YOU TELL him?" Beaver asked. Her tone was flat and without inflection. No accusation. No disappointment or thrill that she had been right. Nonjudgmental, seeing what Brianna had to say about it.

"I told him…" Brianna swallowed. She looked sideways at Erin, then away again. Maybe regretting that she had opened up to Erin. Or that she had to disappoint Erin by admitting what she had done. "I just told him about Cam getting arrested."

"He didn't know yet?"

"No. It was the weekend and I was the only one there. The only one connected to Mickey."

"But Campbell wasn't working for Mickey," Erin said slowly. "So why would he care?"

Brianna gnawed on her lip.

"He didn't care about Cam," Beaver explained, working it out. "He cared about the drugs."

Brianna nodded.

"Why?" Erin was still lagging behind, not seeing what Beaver could. But Beaver had been involved with these people. She knew what they were like, what was likely to happen. She wasn't out in the cold like Erin was, trying to see her way in.

"Because she didn't set Campbell up with Wolf's drugs. She set him up with Mickey's."

Terry let out a whistle. "No… is that what you did?"

Brianna rubbed her eyes. "I did what Wolf told me to. He said to tell Mickey I had a line on a really good prospect in Bald Eagle Falls. That I could get him to buy from Mickey. Wolf told me that he was going to arrange it and Mickey would be real grateful when we got it all set up. I could get a share of the money."

"Why use Mickey's drugs? Why wouldn't Wolf use his own?" Terry asked.

"I don't know. He had his own chain all tied up. Mickey was bigger; he had more product free. He said Mickey would be happy when he found out what we had done."

"But there was no buyer," Beaver said.

Brianna shook her head. "No," she whispered. "There wasn't anyone. He tipped off the cops to search Cam's car, where he'd told me to leave the drugs. So the cops got it all."

"How did Wolf plan to explain that to Mickey?"

"He didn't. He was gonna leave me flappin' in the wind. Leave me to take all the heat. Maybe tell Mickey that I had planned it myself. Or me and Cam." Brianna dug her knuckles into her eyes so hard it made Erin wince. "He wanted to break me and Cam up. I thought if I just did this one more job for him, he'd leave me alone."

"But Wolf stabbed you in the back," Beaver summed up. "So you called Mickey and told him that it had been Wolf who had lost him the drugs. And Mickey got his revenge."

Brianna sniffled. Erin stared at Brianna, trying to reconcile the picture of the vulnerable, weeping girl in front of her with that of a person who had intentionally had the double-crossing gangster murdered.

"It wasn't fair," Brianna said. "He shouldn't have done that to me."

Beaver nodded. "He didn't realize he was putting a plan in motion that would result in his own death."

"I didn't want to go to prison. I wasn't going to let him put me there. Or let Mickey kill me."

"I assume you were supposed to meet Mickey, once the deed was done."

"Uh-huh. I was watching the whole time. He hung around, calling my name. Telling me it was safe to come out. But I knew better. I was the only one who knew what had happened, so he'd kill me too."

"So you waited until he was gone. You took whatever drugs and money Wolf had on him and the burner you had called him on. And then there was no one left for you to call."

"It was like she said," Brianna explained, nodding to Erin. "It seemed like it wasn't really real. None of it. From the time the cops came and arrested Cam. I was in shock. And seeing Mickey kill Wolf like that..." Brianna screwed her eyes shut, but Erin knew from experience that wouldn't shut the images out. "I never saw nothing like it. I didn't know what to do then."

"Other than rifling the body and covering your tracks."

"It wasn't like that," Brianna insisted. "I had to take care of myself. If you don't take care of yourself, no one else is going to."

Beaver let Brianna go to bed when she'd finished squeezing as much information from her as possible. She waited until she heard the bedroom door shut, then walked across to the bookshelves and pressed the button on a black box sitting on one of the shelves. A red light that Erin hadn't previously noticed winked out. Erin hadn't realized that the whole conversation was being recorded.

She looked at Terry. "So you used me to get information out of Brianna. So you can throw her in prison."

"You helped to get information vital to a murder investigation, yes." He hesitated for a moment. "But it was your choice to talk to her. I didn't force you."

"You kind of did."

Terry sat there for a minute, thinking about it. Then he nodded. "I'm sorry... I didn't tell you what was going on, and just expected you to do what I said."

"Is she going to prison?" Erin asked Beaver. "After you get me to convince her to spill her guts, are you going to send her to prison for drug trafficking or conspiracy to commit murder?"

"No. I don't think so. I'm not in charge of all of that, but my input will be considered. And I would like her to be protected. Get her into rehab and try to give her a second chance at life."

Erin looked toward the back of the cabin, where Brianna had retreated to go to bed.

"There are bars on the windows," Beaver said. "She can't get out."

"I was more worried about drugs. She could overdose. If she thinks she's going to prison..."

"I'll check on her in a minute. Managed to keep her alive until now."

"Yeah, but you hadn't wrung the truth out of her then. Forced her to incriminate herself."

"She wasn't forced. That will be clear in the recording."

"She's just a kid."

Beaver nodded, her expression softening. "Yes," she agreed, "a kid, an addict, and someone who essentially put out a hit on her pimp."

"And someone Campbell Cox cares about."

"I told you, I'll do my best to get her the help she needs."

Chapter Forty

ERIN WAS SIPPING A cup of hot chai tea and eating one of the leftover miniature pumpkin tarts from Thanksgiving on a quiet Sunday morning when she heard footsteps and voices outside. She peeked out the window to see who it was and saw Mary Lou and the boys coming up her sidewalk. She brushed crumbs from her lap and got up to open the door for them.

"Hi! How is everyone?" Neither she nor Mary Lou were normally huggers but, after all the family had been through, Erin didn't feel like a wave or a handshake would be enough. She gave Mary Lou a brief hug and cheek-touch as she entered, and gave Campbell and Joshua more vigorous hugs.

She put a plate of treats out on the coffee table and pointed out the tea kettle for anyone who wanted to help themselves.

"You're off of house arrest," she observed to Campbell.

He lifted his pants to show off his bare ankle before sitting down. "Yes. Thanks to you and everyone else who helped."

"It isn't anything I did," Erin said with a modest shrug. She hadn't been the one to make the arrest or to do any of the other paperwork required to ensure that Mickey would be going to prison for a long time and that Campbell would be able to go free.

"You were the one who talked Brianna into telling what happened," Campbell countered. "If she hadn't talked, I don't know whether I would have gotten off."

"You were innocent. We would have gotten you off somehow."

"Well, thank you anyway," Mary Lou said firmly. "I know who my friends are in this town."

"You have a lot of friends. So many people were concerned when Campbell was arrested. Everyone wanted to do something to help you."

"Most of them were just vultures. They wanted a good look at the carcass."

"No... a lot of people care, Mary Lou. But there wasn't a lot anyone could do. You said you had a lot of casseroles."

"Oh, heavens," Mary Lou rolled her eyes. "Fewer casseroles and more sincere prayers. That's what we needed."

Erin felt a little pang at Mary Lou's need for prayers. That was one thing that she hadn't done, and didn't think she would ever do. Hopefully, Mary Lou would understand that and accept a plate of cookies or whatever support Erin could actually offer.

"I'm sure people did what they could." Erin looked at the boys. "So... what are your plans now? I guess you've had a chance to think about what you want out of life."

Campbell shifted uncomfortably. "Lots of time to think," he agreed, "but I'm not sure I got any further on it than I ever did before. My life... just doesn't go the way that I plan."

"If you had better plans—" Mary Lou started, and then she stopped herself. "You can still set goals, and the rest of us will help you all we can."

Campbell nodded. "I just don't know. I get why Mom wants me to come back here, and to finish school, and I know that's the only way I'm going to be able to get a decent job. It's just... I don't want to do that right now. I want to have some fun while I'm still young enough to enjoy it. I can finish school later. And then get a good job. I've only got so much time to be a kid."

"You're lucky," Erin said. "I knew I had to finish high school before I turned eighteen because, after that, I'd be out on my own. I had to get a job lined up, figure out where I was going to live... there wasn't any safety net."

Campbell nodded. "We have it pretty good. I know that. I'm just... not ambitious that way. All of these years..." His eyes focused off in the distance. "We worked so hard for so many years. And Mom's worked really hard too. But I just... burned out. I can't do it anymore. I can't keep pretending that everything is okay and that I want to do well academically and get a job or go to college. I don't want any of that. I don't want any responsibility. I've done enough and I just need to be able to stop and think for a while."

Erin glanced over at Mary Lou, whose face was tired and worn, despite perfectly-applied makeup. Mary Lou would love a break too, she was sure. But she wasn't going to get one.

"I hope everything works out for you," she told him. "I know you've had a tough time."

He nodded.

"And... what about Brianna? I haven't heard much about how things worked out for her. Whenever I ask Beaver, she says that there are privacy issues and she can't tell me about it."

"I don't think Bree would mind. She's in detox. A twelve-week program and, hopefully, that's long enough for her to get clean and develop some new habits and ways to cope. They'll help her with job hunting too, but I don't know what she's going to find. Nothing that's going to bring in very much money. So how is she supposed to support herself? That's why I wanted us to... share resources. Maybe then, she can stay out of trouble."

"I sure hope so. I think she really cares about you."

"I care about her… but we'll see what she thinks when she's out of rehab. I don't know if she'll want anything to do with me then."

"Why wouldn't she?"

"I was trying to get her out. I talked her into Thanksgiving dinner, but that's about all I could manage and that didn't turn out real well. If she's clean and has a job… then I don't have much to offer her anymore."

Her company was gone by the time Terry's truck pulled back in front of the house. Erin was glad to see him and hoped he wouldn't be too worn out after spending so much time at the police department. When he stepped in the door with K9, Erin studied his face, looking for signs of fatigue and any other indicators of whether things had gone well or not.

Terry smiled. Tired, but he seemed to be satisfied.

"You had a good meeting?" Erin asked.

"It was good."

There were a few bits of desserts left on the tray on the coffee table, which Erin hadn't bothered to clean up yet, and he picked up a small gingerbread cookie and a chai apple tart and ate them without a plate to catch the crumbs as he settled on the couch beside her.

"They're going to keep Stayner on," Terry said. "He's done pretty well here, and they've managed to work his salary into the budget with me being off, so they said he might as well stay if he wants to."

"And does he?"

"I guess so. I figured he'd want to go into the city once he was finished his temporary assignment here. But the place grows on you." He smiled at Erin. "Or so I've been told."

"But does that mean… they can afford both of you? And Tom? No one is going to lose their job if he stays on…?"

"They've apparently worked it out. That's good enough for me. He's green, but he's trainable. He's already showing progress."

"He's the one who noticed Mickey was out of place and followed his car and took action on it."

Terry nodded. "Exactly. Good instincts, as long as we keep refining them. He's had a couple of blunders, but who hasn't? We all make mistakes. Some big, some not."

"It's just that his mistakes could cost lives. Or convictions. They're pretty vital."

"Which is why we're working on him. He's not going to replace me, and it will be nice to have one more person on the squad. We get spread pretty thin sometimes."

"It will be nice to have you home more."

"You're not tired of me yet? I'd think you would have had enough of me while I've been on leave."

"That's different. And I'm not here the whole day, so I don't really notice that. It has been nice having you here evenings and nights, when you aren't sneaking off to guard safehouses or buy emergency crankshafts for Willie."

"It was an auger."

"Whatever."

Terry used his finger to try to pick up the crumbs left on the platter. Erin watched him. "There's more in the freezer, you know. If you're still hungry…"

"I know. I have to watch the desserts, though. Don't want to put on weight."

"You're not putting on weight. You're dropping it."

"Because I'm being careful."

Erin knew that wasn't the reason he'd been losing weight, but she didn't pursue it. While they needed to share more with each other and to be open about their feelings, she didn't need to keep picking at sores that were starting to heal. If Terry was happy with the way things had gone at his meeting, then his stress level would be lower, and maybe he would eat more. She didn't want to raise his stress level by harping on him how he needed to eat more.

"You didn't get very much. I can get a few more out for you."

"No." Terry put his arm around Erin and pulled her closer. "Let's just cuddle."

Erin took long, deep breaths, staying still and focused for a long time, before releasing her last pose. With both feet flat on the ground and her arms hanging loosely at her sides, she breathed in a few last practice breaths through her nose.

She heard Vic's door open and the footsteps and low voices of two people trying to be quiet, but not doing a very good job of it.

"Don't interrupt her," Vic whispered. "She needs to stay focused."

"I'm done," Erin said.

"Shh," Willie advised. "We're supposed to be quiet."

Erin grinned at him. Vic smacked his arm lightly. "Are you making fun of me?"

"I'm laughing with you, not at you."

"But I'm not laughing."

"Maybe you should be."

Vic rolled her eyes at Erin. "Somebody's in a silly mood today."

"Enjoy it."

Vic wrapped an arm around Willie. "I am."

"Where are you guys going tonight? Out on a date?"

Vic made a show of examining her clothes. Not a dress or an outfit that showed off her slender figure. Baggy cargo pants like Beaver often wore. A rain jacket. A ball cap and her hair pulled back in a ponytail. Willie was dressed similarly grungy, but she never could make any judgments as to what he was planning from his clothing.

"Okay, not a date," Erin amended. "What are you doing?"

"We're going fishing tomorrow."

"Oh. Right. I remember that. But isn't it... cold? Don't the fish... I don't know... hibernate during the winter?"

Vic shook her head and ignored Erin's ignorant questions. "Tonight, we're out to get some bait."

"Who sells bait here in town?"

Another pronounced eye roll. "We're not buying it. We get our own," Vic told her patiently. "Earthworms, grubs," a shrug, "whatever."

"Ick. Not my idea of a fun date."

Willie chuckled and squeezed Vic. "Some people just don't know how to have fun. See you tomorrow, Erin. We'll bring you back some fish for supper."

"Just don't bring me back any bait."

Erin awoke slowly. It was light out, which meant that she'd slept much later than her usual baker's hours. She stretched, feeling warm and comfy and relaxed. She was feeling something elusive that she couldn't quite put her finger on. She rolled over and looked at Terry. He was awake, his face relaxed, watching her.

Erin smiled. "How long have you been looking at me? How late is it?"

"You're not working this morning, so it's not late."

Erin started to turn back toward her nightstand to check the time on her phone, but Terry caught her shoulder before she could. "It's not late," he repeated. "It's just right."

Erin relaxed and stayed facing him. She closed her eyes and opened them again in a long blink. "I feel..."

He traced a light finger down her arm, waiting for her to finish. He smiled, the dimple appearing in his cheek. "Did you have a good sleep? I didn't hear you wake up last night."

Erin thought about it. "I don't think I did. I think I slept through."

"That's good."

"So I guess I feel... rested."

He cupped her cheek. "Good. Hopefully, the first night of many."

"Don't jinx it."

"Sorry."

But Erin couldn't help hoping that he was right. If she could start sleeping again, she could go back to a normal life in Bald Eagle Falls. And there would be no more dead bodies or missing persons to investigate.

Did you enjoy this book? Reviews and recommendations are vital to making a book successful.
Please leave a review at your favorite book store or review site and share it with your friends.

Don't miss the following bonus material:
Sign up for mailing list to get a free ebook
Other books by P.D. Workman
Read a sneak preview chapter
Learn more about the author

Sign up for my mailing list at pdworkman.com and get Gluten-Free Murder for free!

Preview of Santa Shortbread

Chapter One

ERIN spoke to young Peter Foster as he bent close to the bakery display case, examining the newest gluten-free treats with his younger sisters.

"What are you going to make for Christmas?" he asked. "You made lots of really good cookies last year."

"We will again this year," Erin assured him. "I just met with Charley, my partner, on the weekend. We have a nice list of what we are going to have for you this year. We're going to do some of the little one-bite desserts like we had at Thanksgiving."

She saw the disappointment chase across his face.

"I know you didn't like the pumpkin tarts and gingerbread, but that won't be all that we have. And there will be lots of different kinds of cookies. I'm going to make some cut-out shortbread cookies. You'll like those, and we can do all kinds of fun shapes."

"Christmas shapes?"

"Yes, of course. Stars and trees and gingerbread men and snowmen. All kinds of things."

"Santa?" one of the little girls asked, bouncing up and down. Her sticky fingers were on the glass of the display case and Erin or her assistant Vic were going to have to clean it again after they left, but Erin didn't mind. She loved her littlest customers, the Fosters especially.

Erin looked at Vic and glanced at Mrs. Foster to see what they thought. Vic had warned her against using too many secular symbols of Christmas. Bald Eagle Falls was in the Bible belt, and they had to be careful not to offend the customers who didn't want to see pagan symbols or a lot of commercial crap around their religious holiday.

"I'm sure we can do some Santas," Vic agreed, and after a moment Mrs. Foster nodded too. The kids had won that round. They were so inundated through the media that they couldn't be expected to be completely blind to Santa and the other commercial offerings.

"And the Grinch?" Peter demanded. "You have to do the Grinch!"

Erin laughed. "Hmm. I'll have to see what I can find. We're going into the city to look for some new cookie cutters, and I'll have to see if I can find a Grinch. I haven't seen any around."

"That would be cool. We'd buy them."

"The Grinch is green," Karen contributed.

"Yes, I would have to make green cookies or frosting," Erin agreed.

"Green cookies! You can't make green cookies!"

"I certainly can."

"How?"

"Magic," Erin teased. Then, thinking better of the comment, changed her mind. "Just with green food coloring, Karen. It's really easy."

"I haven't had green cookies before."

"Then I'll have to make some for sure, won't I? What did you guys want today?"

They made their choices for the kids' cookie club and Vic handed them out. Mrs. Foster ordered the baked goods she would need for the week and stood with her hand on her slightly-protruding belly while she waited for it all to be wrapped up and totalled.

"I know I've said it before, but I can't thank you enough for all of the lovely gluten-free baking you do. I used to have to do so much extra baking to make something safe for Peter so that he could have something other than the packaged baking from the city. And half the time it didn't even turn out. I always felt bad that he didn't have any choices and just had the same kind of cookies and bread over and over again. Now... it's just so nice to come here and know that he can have anything in the bakery, and it's all so good!"

Erin flashed a look at Peter. "Even if he doesn't like pumpkin pie!"

"Mom says lots of kids don't like pumpkin pie."

"But I do," Mrs. Foster assured Erin. "And I much prefer yours to the ones at the grocery store!"

When the Fosters had gone, there was a lull. Vic went around the display case to wipe down fingerprints.

"I'll be right back," Erin told her. "I need to fix my hair."

Several dark strands had escaped her hairpins and baker's hat, so Erin ducked into the commode to look in the mirror while she took care of it all and then washed up again. Vic, with her long, blond hair, seemed to be able to manage to keep hers tidy and out of her face all day, but Erin frequently had to take a break at some point to get hers back in order. Maybe she should grow hers longer so that she could pull it into a ponytail or bun rather than trying to keep the shorter locks pinned back.

She returned to the front of the bakery, looking presentable again and smiled at the approaching customers. It was getting noticeably busier as Christmas approached and people were buying more baking for parties, presents, and preparing ahead for their Christmas meals.

Melissa was one of the latest customers. She gave Erin a broad smile and stepped up eagerly to look into the display case. While she lived alone, Erin knew that she would be hosting a dinner for some of the other single women in her church group, and later on Christmas day would be off to the penitentiary to see her friend, Davis Plaint. Melissa never referred to him as a boyfriend or in a romantic way, and wouldn't mention him in front of the other church ladies. Erin often found herself puzzling over their unusual relationship.

"What would you like today?" Erin asked. "Need anything for the department?"

"I think it would be nice if someone other than me sprang for muffins for the police department now and then," Melissa said with an irritated shake of her head that set her dark spiraling curls bouncing. "I only work there part-time, so my paycheck is lower than anyone else's. Maybe Clara or the sheriff could buy them some time."

Vic's eyebrows climbed. "I always thought you got reimbursed for those."

"No, it's just out of the kindness of my heart. Seems to me it's time for someone else to buy them this time."

Erin nodded uncomfortably. She had taken muffins over to the police department herself occasionally, but like Vic, she had always thought that Melissa's purchases were covered by her employer. She would mention it to Officer Terry Piper when she saw him later in the day. She was sure they didn't mean to take advantage of Melissa; probably no one had ever thought twice about it. "Something for you, then?"

"A person can only do so much," Melissa muttered. "With all that I do for the department, they could show some appreciation."

"Yes," Erin agreed. "Everyone like to be recognized for what they do. Anything interesting going on lately?"

Erin didn't usually encourage Melissa's gossip about the police department or crimes going on in Bald Eagle Falls, but she felt the situation called for a little distraction.

Melissa leaned forward. "Actually..." She looked dramatically left and right to see if anyone was listening in. There were customers behind her, but they were waiting patiently and didn't appear to be eavesdropping. Though Melissa put on a show of being discreet, she preferred an audience. "Have you heard of the Grinch?"

"We were just talking to the Fosters about the Grinch," Erin laughed. "They want me to make green Grinch cookies for Christmas."

"No, not the Dr. Seuss character. The *real* Grinch."

Vic leaned on the display case. "There is no real Grinch."

Melissa nodded vigorously. "There is. At first, we didn't think it was anything more than the usual holiday thefts. You know, there are always a few cars broken into, usually in the city. People leave newly purchased gifts in full view and then are surprised when someone breaks into their car in the parking lot. But Bald Eagle Falls has had an unusual rash of thefts the past couple of weeks."

"What counts as a rash of thefts?" Erin asked.

"I don't know for sure how many have been reported; I haven't filed all of the reports. But there have been house and car thefts, with some pricy items stolen."

"More than normal."

"There are always some. But there have been a couple of families…" Melissa frowned and shook her head. "They've lost all of their Christmas gifts. Folks in this part of Tennessee are not wealthy; some families really have to scrape to get a few things together for the little ones. And when someone like the Grinch comes along and takes everything away… there's nothing they can do. They can't afford to replace them."

"Oh… what about their homeowner's insurance, can't they make a claim?"

"Even if they can, if their deductible isn't too high and it's worthwhile to make a claim, they're not going to get the money in time for Christmas."

"That's so sad!" Vic exclaimed. "Who would do something like that?"

"The Grinch," Melissa said, giving a nod. "You see? Whoever it is, they're stealing Christmas from the children of Bald Eagle Falls."

Erin and Vic shook their heads. Bald Eagle Falls was a small community, close-knit, and it was hard to believe that anyone would want to hurt their neighbors that way. Especially little children.

"That's just terrible." Erin looked down at the products on display. She was mindful of the fact that there were other people lined up behind Melissa, so they couldn't gossip for long. "What do you think you would like today, then? We have chocolate chip muffins." She knew Melissa's weakness for anything with chocolate in it.

Melissa frowned, examining the various possibilities, and then returned to the chocolate chip muffins that Erin had pointed out and decided, "I do think it is a chocolate chip muffin kind of day."

Chapter Two

ERIN knew that Officer Terry Piper was working a modified afternoon shift, and watched to see if he would stop in at Auntie Clem's Bakery while he was on patrol. He and K9 were happy to be getting out of the house after Terry had been sidelined with a head injury and being choked out by an assailant. Neither one of them liked being cooped up all day with nothing to do. But Terry was still suffering from headaches and wasn't yet able to put in a full shift.

Under his old routine, Terry would stop in for water partway through the afternoon on a hot day, and for a cookie and doggie biscuit around closing time. The weather was chilly so close to Christmas, so they didn't need the extra water, but she was still hoping for a visit at the end of the workday, when they would be getting off work as well. But as she turned the sign on the door over to 'closed,' there was no sign of her boyfriend and his furry sidekick. Vic wiped down the display case.

"No visit from Officer Handsome today?" she teased.

"Doesn't look like it." Erin let out a sigh and left the door unlocked, just in case he came by before they were finished. "Hopefully, that means he went home and not that he's stuck at the office or dealing with a case."

"The sheriff said they'd make sure he didn't work too long."

"Hopefully," Erin repeated.

They fell into the usual rhythm closing out the till, cleaning up, and mixing up batters that would soak overnight for the next morning's muffins and breads.

"Grinch cookies," Vic recalled with a laugh. "I wonder if we'll be able to find some cookie cutters."

"Even if we can't find one that's specifically The Grinch, we could make Santa cookies and give him a green face. It wouldn't be perfect, but people would know what they were supposed to be."

183

"Perfect," Vic declared. "Great idea."

Erin drove herself and Vic home as usual. Vic lived in the loft apartment over Erin's garage, so when they were on the same shift, they almost always drove together. Vic didn't have a car of her own and was constantly getting after Erin to replace her old clunker. But Erin didn't like to spend more money than she had to, an attitude that had carried over from her lean years, even though she finally had money in the bank from cashing in on a crop of wild ginseng.

"One of these days, it's not going to make it," Vic commented, shaking her head at Erin's car. "It sounds worse than ever."

"I'll take it in for an oil change. That's all it needs."

"It needs a lot more than that," Vic said with authority. "Timing belt. New transmission. The electrical is all screwed up..." She had probably fixed up a lot of cars with her brothers on the farm before she had come out as transgender and been forced to leave home.

"It still runs."

"Until the day it doesn't."

"If I only use it for tooling around Bald Eagle Falls, I'll be safe. If we go out to the city, we can use Terry's or Willie's truck."

"Or you could get a new car."

"Not yet."

Vic shook her head. They walked up the sidewalk together. "Looks like Terry's home. Say 'hi' for me."

"I will. You and Willie going out, or are you going to come over for dinner?"

"We'll do something together. You can have Terry to yourself today."

"Okay. Have a good night, Vicky."

Vic walked around to the back and Erin let herself in the front door. Despite the fact that she had a perfectly good garage, it currently held Clementine's old Volkswagen, so she and the others always parked in front of the house instead.

She gave a mental shrug and walked up to the house. She opened the door and checked the burglar alarm and saw that it had already been disarmed.

"Terry?"

She heard the bathroom door open and Terry walked out of the hall. Orange Blossom darted past him with a yowl. Marshmallow hopped sedately out from behind the couch.

"Hi, guys." Erin bent down to scratch the rabbit's ears and Orange Blossom practically climbed into her arms, complaining loudly. Probably about the presence of K9, who he'd had plenty of time to get used to.

Erin made understanding noises to Orange Blossom, acknowledging his chatter, and looked at Terry with a smile, rolling her eyes.

Terry shook his head. "I think you might be thirty seconds late getting home; he's been pacing around here making a racket."

"Oh, is that the problem?" Erin pressed her cheek against Orange Blossom's head and squeezed him. "Well, I'm here now, so stop complaining."

He instead started with a rumbling purr. Erin scratched his ears. "That's better."

Erin studied Terry's face. "How are you doing?" There were lines around his eyes and he seemed pale. "Are you in pain? Do you want something for your head?"

"Mostly I'm just tired out." Terry thought about it. "Actually, I guess I might need a painkiller too. It's hard for me to tell, sometimes." He pressed his fingers to his temples. "I start feeling tired and foggy, and it takes a while to figure out I've got a headache."

"Let me get one of your pills."

"I can do it."

Erin shook her head. "No, sit down and relax, I'll get you one." She put Orange Blossom down and ignored his renewed complaints as she went into the bedroom and retrieved one of Terry's prescription pills. She got him a glass of water from the kitchen and returned to where he was sitting in the living room. Terry passed his hand over his face, looking slightly gray.

"I don't like to take too many of these," he said, taking it from her and swallowing it down with the water.

"You are allowed to take them when you need them. It doesn't help you to be in pain."

"But it doesn't help me to be dopey either. I don't want to spend the days in a haze."

"If they're too strong, then you can ask the doctor to prescribe a lower dose. But he won't know unless you tell him."

Terry nodded once. "Yes, you're right," he agreed. He went back to rubbing his temples. "I was going to have something ready for us to eat. Or at least to get started on supper."

"Don't worry about it. I can get something ready. You must be hungry."

"Not really. More nauseated than anything."

He had obviously waited too long after his headache had started. Once that nausea had set in, it tended to stay the rest of the evening. He had wanted to lose a few pounds after their cruise, but since the attack, he'd lost more than he should.

"What could you eat? Could I make you a smoothie? Some yogurt? What wouldn't bother your stomach?"

"I don't know. Give it a little while; maybe it will feel better after the pill kicks in."

Erin knew very well that it wouldn't. But he was a grown man and needed to be in control of his own body and life more than he needed her to mother him.

"Okay… but try to have something later. Don't just skip eating."

Terry grimaced, not looking at her. "I'll try. Later."

"And if you want me to go out and get something…" Erin offered. "If there is something you think you could eat…"

"No, you don't need to make a special trip for me."

Erin left him sitting on the couch. K9 was in the kitchen waiting for her, standing close to the cookie jar and looking her way with pleading eyes. He was very well-behaved, but he seemed put out that it had taken her so long to get there.

"Aren't you being patient," Erin crooned. "And such a gentleman. Unlike some animals around here…" She looked pointedly at Orange Blossom, who meowed loudly in exasperation that he hadn't yet received a treat.

Erin got all of the animals treats and checked the fridge for dinner inspiration. Her usual fallback was leftover bread or buns from Auntie Clem's with some locally-sourced jam. But she was making an effort to take care of her body better and eat something other than straight sugar and carbs, so she made herself look at the vegetables to see if she could put together a salad.

Vegetables were really not her thing, except for the ones that Vic had made at Thanksgiving, with lots of buttery sauces or nuts in caramelized sugar. Those had been really good. But she suspected that the benefits from the vitamins they contained would be counteracted by all of the fat and sugar, which would go straight to her hips, and with her small frame, every extra pound showed.

~ ~ ~

Santa Shortbread by P.D. Workman is available for order now!

About the Author

Award-winning and USA Today bestselling author P.D. (Pamela) Workman writes riveting mystery/suspense and young adult books dealing with mental illness, addiction, abuse, and other real-life issues. For as long as she can remember, the blank page has held an incredible allure and from a very young age she was trying to write her own books.

Workman wrote her first complete novel at the age of twelve and continued to write as a hobby for many years. She started publishing in 2013. She has won several literary awards from Library Services for Youth in Custody for her young adult fiction. She currently has over 50 published titles and can be found at pdworkman.com.

Born and raised in Alberta, Workman has been married for over 25 years and has one son.

~ ~ ~

Please visit P.D. Workman at pdworkman.com to see what else she is working on, to join her mailing list, and to link to her social networks.

~ ~ ~

If you enjoyed this book, please take the time to recommend it to other purchasers with a review or star rating and share it with your friends!